Slayer Player

Slayer Player

By

Daniel T. Sonnentag

Slayer Player

Slayer Player ISBN # 978-0-6151-4337-8

Slayer Player

Dedication

For Brian. There when I typed the first words to my first book. There for me now. Forever vigilant.

Sonnentag

Chapter 1

The black Mercedes rolled down highway 41. Still alive, three sixty-five, killer on the loose. Sometimes somebody's got to pay. Now was the time, or was it a few hours ago. Poppin knew there would be others. The party had just begun. Payback is a bitch, he smiled to himself. He was feeling really high, a little crazy, not really crazy, just ... a little unwell . He supposed that was the way it was supposed to be. He knew the first kill would be tough. Heart still pumpin', hands still shakin' on the wheel. A little oxy, that would do it. Slow it down. He could lean over a little, feel like pimpin'. Let the adrenaline slide. See a stripper, let the adrenaline ride. Up and down, back and forth, straight down the highway, takin' a ride. Wouldn't be long, he would be in Madison. Death behind him, death ahead. There would be others. Some mother's sons.

Poppin looked ahead and saw the capital building in the distance. The ten foot long American flag blew wildly in the wind. It wouldn't be long now. He'd be back in his element. Hips grinding on the stage. The women he knew. The women he loved. Some of his bros be in the house. He would tally on. Find a party. Chill out. The first kill was done. There would be others. The promises had been made many years ago. These men had to come down.

Poppin lit up a small, black and mild cigar. He was happy. A broad smile crossed his face, creasing down in a wide line beside his lips. He loved Madison, party town of the USA. Everything moved fast here. A white Mazeradi sped past him on the right with an attractive blonde woman hitting up on a bong in the passenger seat. Silver earrings flashed on the young, male driver. The Benz chewed up the pavement as he slipped the car into third gear and accelerated. Poppin reached into his pocket, pulled out a pill, popped the Oxy in his mouth and followed the pill with a slug of Bud Light. He needed to slow the car down, stay within the speed limit. Wouldn't do to get stopped for speeding. There was no hurry. Now it was party time.

Small sparkles of light flashed on the wet, black asphalt, but the sparkles barely shone in comparison to the sparkle emanating from the one hundred karats of diamonds imbedded in the silver cross that hung from a silver chain to lie upon the black T-shirt covering his chest. He pulled the 2006, jet-black Benz into a parking spot directly in front of the Sizzle. A six foot tall, red neon light flashed the silhouette of a buxom woman. The bouncer at the door smiled broadly and gave him props. They had rolled together many a time. Poppin blended into the darkness, the only giveaways were his shiny white teeth peering out, and the diamonds glittering from his necklace. His six foot-two inch lean frame shifted comfortably against a black, marble top, high-rise table. His heart twittered. Alyssa was on the stage, her beautiful body outlined in a sizzling silhouette. They'd been tight once, but Poppin had to move on. He had too many things to do. There was no time for a woman in his life. Maybe later.

With a cold, street stare, Poppin surveyed the surrounding clientele. Habits of a lifetime of street life never died. Half a dozen middle-aged men sat directly below the stage. Several older men, near seventy years of age, sat quietly at the bar, a little too shy to get up close for a good look, although occasionally one of the old men would walk up to the stage and give the dancer a dollar. The rest of the crowd was young men, some of them getting their first look at the live action between the women's legs. Poppin knew almost everyone present except for the assorted college students. They were no threat, indirectly; they were all probably customers of his.

He made eye contact with Rolly who was standing at the bar. Rolly and Poppin had been tight for years. It was a bond formed in their youth when they met at a foster home and had taken immediately to each other. Rolly was his main man, trust worthy, and ready to serve time for Poppin if he had to. In fact, he had done two years when a deal went bad. The snitching from the street had seeped all the way to him, but he had held firm, the last resort, protecting Poppin from what would have been his first bust. He was now pretty low profile with the police, had faded from their radar a couple of years after the bust. If he had only been more careful, hadn't gotten a little too loose and carefree, the bust would never have happened, but then again, some people had to learn the hard way. Poppin had schooled him since. Told him the way things had to be; the way things had to be done. Rolly now carried an almost military-like bearing.

Rolly saw Poppin in the bar mirror and flashed him an enormous smile. Rolly slammed his drink and headed out of the bar. Ten minutes later Poppin left. No contact need be made. The drop point was always made up in advance, carefully planned and rotated. They had worked together for years and each knew what the other would do.

Poppin rolled the Benz slowly down the street. He felt low now, in his element, in the element that he had built up for years. The money was so easy, the risk so low. He worked in a drug business where trust was paramount, and he had chosen well on both ends of the deals. Everything always went smooth, easy. Sometimes drug networks truly worked. No one at the top of the food chain was caught. Everyone was happy. Everyone got richer.

Poppin parked the car behind the white Cadillac that rested at the curb opposite the bus depot. Rolly exited the Cadillac and greeted him with a handshake and a smile. The two men proceeded to the back of the Benz where Poppin opened the trunk. He handed one suitcase to Rolly, and took hold of two by himself. One of the three suitcases was loaded with one hundred dollar bags of crack. The black Samsonite suitcases were identical. The two men moved forward and placed the suitcases in the back of the white Cadillac. The deal was done. Rolly would make the proper cash deposits from sales made on down the line, visit the different bank safety deposit boxes that had been set up. The money was always there; Poppin was never worried. Rolly was a trusted brother.

It was all so easy, so very easy.

Sonnentag

*****

Face down in a bed of roses.

Covered in white powder.

"I've never seen a body looked like this before," Grisky stated.

Deputy sheriff Melinda Holmes stepped forward. "Yeah, it is different. You don't suppose that white powder all over the body is cocaine?"

"Not likely, who would be crazy enough to waste that much cocaine. It's probably just flour."

Melinda bent over to get a closer look. Her taut, husky, five-foot six inch frame cast a small shadow upon the corpse. She brushed a long strand of red hair back over her head after leaning over and standing straight back up. Instinctively, she placed a black barrette into the hair on the right side of her head. She had forgotten to put it in that morning. "Pretty large dark spot surrounding the face down face. Looks like he, or she was shot in the back of the head."

"I think it's a he."

"How do you know?"

Grisky shuffled his feet on the ground in the direction of the man's feet. "Look at the shoes, those shoes look like the shoes of a man. Pretty short hair too."

"You never know though, now-a-days, you never know."

"We should get help on this one; this is too weird to not have very professional people look into it. Why don't you get on the line with the FBI down in Milwaukee, see if they're interested in this.

Melinda met Grisky's gaze. "Okay, I'll go to the squad and make the call."

Sheriff Grisky stepped back and surveyed the rose garden. He rested his right hand on his large, protruding beer-belly. The center button on his shirt was popped open as usual. The sun shone brightly off the front half of his balding head. A wisp of black hair from his comb-over shuddered sporadically in the slight breeze. The body lay directly in the center of a circle of grass about twelve feet in diameter. A small, two foot wide path led directly away from the center. One half the circle was covered in red roses, the other half covered in white ones. One would expect the usual smell of a dead body, but Grisky supposed the thick covering of white powder and the beautiful smell of the surrounding blooms was completely masking it. He took in a deep breath. How pleasant it was.

Melinda was soon in the center of the rose garden.

Grisky inhaled another deep breath of the beautiful rose fragrance. "What'd they say?"

"I got chased around a lot of extensions, but I finally got on with the Special Agent in Charge. They said they would like to see it, never heard of anything like it before. We're to secure the scene; somebody will be here in about two hours."

"That won't be hard. I'll put tape between those two trees at the entry path and stand guard. You go inside to question Mrs. Larsen, the house assistant, see if she's got herself under control."

Melinda nodded yes and walked away as Grisky headed toward the two small trees to cross them with yellow crime scene tape.

The massive twenty-four room, thirty thousand square foot colonial mansion called Harrison House sat on sixty acres of mostly marsh-land. Ancient oak trees dotted the land in places, small copses of willow and box elder trees dotted the land in others. A large field of wild-flowers adorned several acres to the left of the mansion. The tan brick of the mansion was old and dirty, the white window and door trim was yellow and faded. Massive growths of bright, green Ivy adorned the walls and rose to the rooftop. A large cupola sat directly in the center of the top of the house. The house was built in the late 1800's by a colonial land barren. In the nineteen thirties it was bought by Al Capone. Whiskey was produced on the farm, and at all times, a man with a machine gun could be seen nesting in the cupola.

In nineteen seventy, the mansion had been bought by William Harrison. It was in a great state of disrepair by then, having sat empty for twenty-five years. Harrison had gradually refurbished the place as he bought in more and more troubled, homeless youth. Now the building met all the modern state codes and was in pretty decent shape.

Melinda entered the back door and was greeted by the wide expanse of the empty dining hall. A large portrait of Harrison stood gazing sternly down upon an oaken table with thirty chairs seated around it. No one was in sight. She proceeded to a large set of doors to the left of the Harrison portrait and opened them slowly. A small, lushly furnished sitting room awaited her entrance. An elderly, white-haired woman sat on a white, plush couch at the back of the room. Melinda walked slowly forward and stood in front of the woman.

The woman's face was a flat, blank stare, not a thousand mile stare, but certainly a hundred.

Melinda moved forward to stand in front of the elderly woman. "Are you the woman who called the police?"

Nothing came in answer. The woman merely blinked her eyes.

"I need to talk to you. Are you able to talk?"

The woman blinked twice.

Melinda went to find the kitchen and returned with a glass of water. She handed it to the old woman and then gently rubbed the white tousle of hair on the woman's head. The aged woman took a long, steady drink, and then set the glass down.

The woman shook visibly as she stammered out the words, "I, I called."

"I need to ask you a few questions? Do you feel up to it?"

"Yes, I'll try," the old woman croaked a response.

"Was it you who found the body?"

"Yes, I was working on some laundry upstairs. I passed by a window that overlooks the rose garden and I looked out to see a large, white lump in the center of the garden. I didn't think too much of it at the time. I just thought someone had put a large pile of fertilizer there. It was several hours later before I actually went outside to investigate. I knew one of the children would have to be reprimanded for spilling the pile and leaving it there."

"Did you know it was Mr. Harrison right away?"

"Not right off, but then I saw the bright red stone on his signet ring on the ring finger of his right hand. There is no other ring

12

like it. He had it special made. I knew it was him when I saw his ring.”

The woman went stone silent as tears rolled down her heavily rouged cheeks creating a pink waterfall that fell upon her lacy white blouse. When Melinda tried to question her further, she was unable to get any response. Any further questioning was going to have to wait. She left the home and returned to Grisky who waited at the entrance of the rose garden.

Grisky had a pleasant smile on his face, “Get anything?”

“Not much, the woman is in a state of shock. It will take awhile before we can get anything out of her, that is, if there is even anything to get.”

“Okay, the FBI should be here in about ninety minutes. We’ll see what they have to say about all of this.”

*****

Joan Wendtworth rested comfortably behind the wheel of the silver 2004 L.T.D. The farmlands and pastures seemed endless, but in fact they had only to travel a total of about a hundred miles. Highway 41 North turned into Highway 21, which in turn turned into Highway 110. County trunk K was just three miles up the road. They were in rural Eureka now.

Paul Collins sat quietly in the passenger seat. He had enjoyed the smell of the 40 year old blond female that sat driving beside him. Now and again he would steal a side-ways glance at her. He didn’t know what to make of his new partner. She was stunningly attractive with her page-boy cut, blonde hair. Her deep blue eyes had penetrated his when they first met that morning. She was in one moment softly sensuous, and then in the next, cold steel hardness came over her. He was feeling the same way. Fresh out of the academy, at the top of his class, he didn’t know what to expect. Was this woman someone he could trust, someone he could put his life in the hands of?

Wendtworth pulled her small, five-foot six inch frame up and back against the seat. She reached back under her hair and

13

rubbed the back of her neck. He was so young, she thought. Handsome in an awkward kind of way, but then she would naturally see any young man as kind of awkward, especially a new partner. His short, black hair had been slicked back by some kind of cream. He seemed to have trouble with a long wisp of hair that kept falling over his forehead. He repeatedly brushed it back on top. She had noticed his athletic build right away. He looked stringy but strong as though he frequently worked out in the weight room. In his deep, brown eyes, she had seen nervousness, but strange comfortable warmth also. She also saw the slight sexual attraction. She wondered if she had briefly sent back the same message. It was only natural. The new FBI, what a hoot, she thought. The only thing that mattered was that they accept each other as partners, form that trust that she knew partners must have. She reasoned that the rest could easily be ignored, for weren't they twenty years apart in age.

Wendtworth turned the car onto the winding country road that was County K. They passed over a small creek, the Waukau nature preserve. Most of the preserve, including a large pond, was on the other side of Highway 116, from which they had already turned off. Only a small percentage of the actual preserve rested between 116 and County trunk K. This was the only part they could see from their vehicle. Wendtworth thought the preserve was so small that she let out a quick, staccato chuckle.

Collins shifted in his chair. "What's so funny?"

"This preserve, it's so small, we are definitely not in Kansas now Dorothy."

"Kansas, Dorothy, what do you mean?"

"Never mind, never mind," Wendtworth giggled.

Pastures were filled with Holstein milk cows. Soon they would be heralded once again into the barns for the evening milking. Wendtworth looked in the rear-view mirror and saw that the FBI Emergency Response Team was following them in the white Chevy cargo van. She shook her head. It wasn't much of a team this time. Only three people, but then again, what did it matter, this wasn't much of an assignment. She smiled and shook her head when she saw that both passengers in the van's

14

front seat were smoking a cigarette. Against the rules of course, but out here, in the middle of nowhere, who would ever know? She had the urge to light one up herself, but it had been six months since she quit smoking.

Rounding a curve, Wendtworth and Collins saw the mansion at the same time.

Collins pointed to the right side of the road. "Wow, that's quite a large building!"

Wendtworth glanced at the building. "Yeah, and out here in the middle of nowhere, must have been a lot of old money around here at one time."

Wendtworth pulled the auto into the gravel driveway. An old, heavy-set, black Labrador waddled up to the car and let out a weak gruff of a bark. He was missing some teeth, but it looked like he was smiling, as only dogs can smile, with a happy gleam in his eyes. He was definitely no threat. Wendtworth opened her door and the dog nuzzled his nose in, dripping drool on her black, patent shoes. She gave him a quick pat on the head and stepped outside the vehicle.

Wendtworth and Collins headed to the house with the ancient dog in tow. Halfway to the house they heard a loud rumble and the high-pitched squeal of brakes. They turned to see a shiny, yellow school bus pull to a complete stop at the head of the driveway. A large procession of kids began to get off the bus. The procession seemed endless. Boys and girls of all ages pushed and tousled as they grouped up in their walk towards the house. A few of the teenagers quickly lit up cigarettes, passing them around as they walked. The kids cackled excitedly when they saw the FBI Emergency Response van parked behind the silver LTD.

Wendtworth made eye contact with a tall boy of about seventeen who had black hair. His steely gaze held her own for several seconds, but that was all it took for her to realize he was a leader. The children would have to be questioned, but they probably knew nothing for they were in school when the murder happened.

Wendtworth and Collins watched the children enter the building and then proceeded to the rear of the house and up to the yellow crime scene tape. From a nearby bench, Captain Grisky got up and approached them with a bewildered look on his face. Without saying a word he removed the yellow tape, turned and walked toward the inner center of the rose garden circle.

Collins shook his head, "I thought these rural folks were supposed to be friendly."

Wendtworth followed, her gaze fixed on the roses ahead of her. "Yeah, well, he's probably a little bewildered right now, that, and a little bored from sitting here the last couple of hours."

The small group proceeded towards the center of the rose garden, and surveyed the dead body.

Grisky pointed at the body. "This is exactly how we found him."

"Looks like the makings of a giant biscuit," Collins stated to break the tension.

Grisky laughed, "Yeah, ain't that the truth."

The three man forensics team now joined the circle. The small area was becoming quite crowded. The lead forensics expert leaned over to within a few inches of the body. He took a small pinch of the white powder between his fingers, rolled it around, and then put it up to his nose. After a brief pause he rose back to his feet.

The lead forensics man rubbed the white powder on his jeans, "Fertilizer, probably some type of bone meal."

Grisky grunted in disgust, "Bone meal, what the hell."

"It appears our killer has a sick sense of humor," Wendtworth answered.

Wendtworth, Collins and Grisky left the circle in order to give the forensics team space to work.

"I don't think they are going to get much in the way of clues from that area. It looks pretty clean, even the grass is thick and plush. It must have been well fertilized. I don't think there will be any footprints," Wendtworth stated.

Collins had a sheepish look on his face. "Maybe the forensics team will be able to get some clues from the body. At least they will get the type of weapon used to kill the man."

Wendtworth sighed and put her hands on her hips. "Yeah, but this is going to be a tough one to solve, I can already see that."

The three huddled in a small group on the stone terrace and introductions were finally made.

Grisky buttoned the center button of his shirt. "We've already questioned Mrs. Larsen, the house matron. She wasn't able to tell us anything. She was still in a bit of a shock."

Collins stepped forward to present an air of authority, "We'll question her later, but right now, I want to get the children together in a group and ask them a few questions. It's obvious none of them were here, but they might have an idea as to why someone would do this."

*****

A loud murmur of voices joined the squeaks of chair legs as the children took their places around the large, dining room table. They jostled with each other and all in all seemed very impartial to the new circumstances. In fact, Collins and Wendtworth noticed that most of the children were smiling and seemed quite happy.

Wendtworth motioned for Collins to sit at the head of the table. This seemed to have a quieting and disorienting effect upon the children. They began to stare at the young man at the head of the table. Collins walked slowly around the table. She made eye contact with the young man she had done so with outside. The thin, darkly tanned, adolescent smirked and looked away. Wendtworth knew he was turned on by her, but that smirk, maybe it meant something.

Wendtworth smiled at the faces of the surrounding children. "You all know what happened here."

There was stone silence in the room.

Grisky pulled his trousers up and let out a small grunt to break the silence. Some of the children looked at him, and then put

17

their faces down. Many of the children had run-ins with Grisky before, and they knew the man had the propensity to be mean.

"Did any of you see anything; was anyone here when this took place?" Wendtworth stated firmly.

The room remained silent except for a couple of coughs. A small, blonde girl of about seven years of age rubbed her runny nose on the sleeve of her shirt.

"Does anyone know any reason why this would happen to Mr. Harris?" Wendtworth continued.

A couple of the children snickered, but angry, ashen stares overtook most of the young faces. The room quieted again as Grisky stepped forward to the table.

After a few seconds, a soft, yet strong voiced statement broke the silence.

"He was an asshole, he got what he deserved."

Wendtworth was not surprised to see that the youth behind the statement was the young man she had made eye contact with before. Wendtworth remained calm and engaged the man's deep brown eyes, "And why was this?"

The young man locked her in a stare but said nothing.

Wendtworth looked around the table at all of the young faces. They remained sober and cold. Clearly no more would be said in this group situation. Wendtworth walked over to Grisky, and asked him who the young man was.

"That's Shawn Jones," Grisky replied. Grisky had spent a lot of time with the boy when he had been picked up on a couple of drug busts. He was a hard case. An obvious leader of the kids because it was clear that he provided the young people with the drugs they wanted. He was a tough kid, having grown up in a series of foster homes; it seemed he had no allegiance to anyone but himself. Grisky told Wendtworth that it seemed no one could relate to him or get through to him. I will, Wendtworth thought to herself.

Wendtworth shrugged and turned back to the assembled youth. "All right, if anyone does think of anything they can tell us, there will be a stack of our cards on the entrance table to the foyer. Everyone is dismissed, that is, except Jones."

The children noisily bustled out of the room. Shawn Jones sat frozen in his seat. He was used to being grilled by the authorities. He liked it, and that is why he engaged Wendtworth in the first place, and he liked the look of her ample breasts. There really wasn't much entertainment out in the middle of nowhere, might as well have some fun.

Grisky led Collins, Wendtworth and Jones into Harrison's office. Grisky took a position at the rear of the room by the door and crossed his arms over his protruding stomach in an air of authority. Wendtworth took a seat in the massive leather office chair behind the beautiful, shiny, teak-wood desk. She noticed the desk was clear, orderly, and completely empty. Even the computer rested on an orderly workstation off to the right. Collins sat in a chair next to Jones in front of the desk.

Wendtworth made eye contact with Jones and held his stare. She softened her eyes and pursed her lips into a sexy pout. She knew she could melt the young man to get any information from him easier than she could threaten it out. She could see the young man desperately needed to be loved by someone. She gave him her best bedroom smile, and it had the desired effect. The young man slouched in his chair, and his eyes softened. Collins felt a slight pang of jealousy.

Wendtworth relaxed her posture and put her hands on her lap. "Shawn, why don't you tell us about yourself?"

Shawn shifted in his seat and tensed slightly. The sexual attraction between him and Wendtworth seemed to intensify.

"There isn't much to tell. I've been bounced around my whole life. My story's the usual. An alcoholic father, a drug addicted mother, neither one wanted me around, so what's to tell. I'm the result of that, just like thousands of other kids. No big deal. Life is life," Shawn tried and failed to sound wise.

Wendtworth could see the pain hidden behind the soft brown eyes and tough demeanor. She sat back in the chair and put her hands behind her head. Her ample bosom rose to the occasion. She watched Shawn's eyes as they fixated upon her chest. She let out a soft moan, almost sensuous in its tone. Shawn was definitely paying attention. He looked into her sensuous blue eyes and felt himself melt. It was easy, Wendtworth thought, for Shawn was such a virile young man. She leaned forward again and put her right arm on the desk, almost reaching out to him, her silver bracelet tinkling quietly on the teak desk.

At that moment, Shawn almost reached forward to touch her hand, and she knew he was hers for the taking.

"Shawn, you don't have to be tough with me. I like you. Just tell me anything that might help our investigation. Anything you know that might tell us why someone wanted Mr. Harrison dead.

"He was an asshole." Shawn blared.

"Define asshole if you will," Wendtworth stated.

Shawn laughed and then let out a long, deep sigh. It was true he wanted this woman, wanted her respect, and maybe even wanted to be her lover. He began to blush. This was fun, he thought. Hell, why not, he could tell her something helpful, couldn't he. Still it was hard. He froze, composed himself, and then let out the words in a quiet mumble, "Harrison liked young people in a sick way. He was no saint. I'm sure he made a lot of enemies over the years. Created someone who wanted payback."

Wendtworth was a little bewildered. What exactly was sick, she thought. She shifted anxiously in her chair, crossing her legs to bring her bare ankle up into Shawn's sight. The action had the desired effect. Shawn seemed to visibly relax. Wendtworth spoke softly, "Tell me what you mean by in a sick way."

Shawn froze yet again, his eyes softened, then turned steely. He shifted and leaned forward in his chair. He opened his mouth but no words seemed to want to come out. He garbled something unintelligible.

"I couldn't understand you," Wendtworth said.

Shawn's eyes filled with tears. "He abused children."

Wendtworth put her foot back on the floor, her eyes softened, and she felt herself tear up along with Shawn. She wondered if this young man sitting in front of her had been abused, but then anxiety overtook her and she realized he could be making it all up to get even with Harrison for something. No, she looked into his eyes and saw more tears there. She was taken aback. She

20

thought Shawn was tougher. She smiled inwardly to herself for she knew she had melted him.

Wendtworth broke the long silence, "How do you know this? Were you abused by him?"

"No, no way, I'm too old for him. He liked the young, defenseless ones. Some of them have confided in me. I'm like a father to some of these kids."

Collins raised his right hand. "We'll check it out."

Shawn threw his arms out in frustration. "You won't find anything out. They won't talk to you. They won't trust you, but take a good look around. Look at their rooms and behaviors. You'll be able to figure it out, all the signs are there. What I'm telling you is the truth."

"I believe you Shawn. We will check with some of the other kids. Thank you for your help, you can go now," Wendtworth finished.

Shawn got up from the chair and turned to walk to the door. He paused and turned back. Cautiously, he met Wendtworth's eyes. "Is there someplace I could write to you?"

Wendtworth knew she had made quite an impression on the young man, but the question caught her off guard. She was even more bewildered when she found herself taking out one of her cards and scribbling her personal address on the back. She didn't know what it was about this young man, but her heart went out to him. She reached out and Shawn came back to take the card from her hand, lightly brushing the tips of her fingers. He smiled at her, turned, and was quickly out of the room.

Collins shifted uneasily in his chair. "That was different."

"Yeah, it certainly was," Wendtworth responded softly.

Sonnentag

Chapter 2

The left breast of the red neon woman in the front window had gone out. Poppin smiled. The one-breasted woman looked funny, but somehow erotically attractive. Maybe he was losing it after all. A downhill slide on the way. No, he knew he could stop it. He just had to take his mind off of killing. He didn't seem able to. The thoughts lingered. What about the people this man would have left behind. He tried not to think of it, but the thought kept pounding at his brain.

Once inside the Sizzle, his eyes adjusted to the dim, red lighting. The red light bulbs that adorned the stage every three inches seemed to be brighter than usual. It felt like they almost burned his eyes. He had no interest in the young, buxom blonde who danced on the stage. He didn't know why, couldn't examine his own motives, but for some reason he had to see Alyssa. He felt the need to love her, and he became aghast at himself. Was this really what he wanted? Death and life, so intertwined, so confusing; what was he to do except follow his instincts.

He saw Alyssa sitting at the end of the bar alone. He approached her slowly. His heart pounding. He knew her beauty. He had tasted of it before, savored the love. After death, it was love he sought. He needed to be filled again, but could he do it. His brain whirled. Death, love, hate. So mixed up. Killing had not been as easy as he thought it would be. He became nauseous and for a moment thought he would have to go to the bathroom to throw up. He walked over to lean on the bar next to Alyssa. The smell of her sweat and sea breeze perfume brought him back to a stable consciousness. He made another decision. It would be love tonight if she would have him.

Alyssa turned, whipping back her long, red hair, and flashing her coal black eyes. Her black skin glistened lightly with perspiration. She must have recently finished a dance set.

Poppin saw the sparkle in her eyes. It had always been there, even from the first time he had met her. He knew she loved him, but he wondered if he had alienated her once too often. Would she sleep with him? Is that what he really wanted? His eyes smiled at her. He put his arms around her shoulders to give her a warm hug.

Alyssa held him tightly. "Poppin, you all right, you don't look so good."

Poppin forced a broad smile, his sparkling, white teeth drawing Alyssa's attention. He had beautiful teeth. Poppin sat on the next stool and leaned into Alyssa, suppressing the urge to put his head on her chest. He was surprised that he had to force back tears. He raised his eyes to meet Alyssa's. She was startled when she saw the dampness there.

"What's the matter baby?" Alyssa said softly as she reached out and gently brushed the back of his head.

Poppin let out a diminutive whimper, "I, I don't know."

"Yes, I think you do, you have to tell me. You know I still love you. I always will. I'll help you if I can."

Poppin's entire body trembled, "Come with me. I have to get out of here."

The couple climbed into the black Benz and drove slowly down the boulevard. Alyssa put her hand on Poppin's right knee. A slight shiver went through his body. He ignored her and kept his eyes straight ahead. Alyssa sighed. Poppin was such a hard man to reach. If only he would talk to her. He seemed to be shutting her out more than ever, but here she was, riding in the car with him. She wondered about herself. What was wrong with her that she always seemed to give in to this man? She guessed she was just a sucker for the needy.

Alyssa shifted lightly in her seat and sighed, "What do you want from me tonight?" She hoped the answer would be love.

Poppin kept his eyes ahead and straight on the road. "I don't know, I don't really know."

Alyssa had irritation in her voice, "Are you playing with me? What do you want? Is it pity, because you told me time and time again that you don't want love."

"Well, maybe things have changed. Maybe tonight I do want love."

"What's all this maybe business man? Are you putting me on? Either you want love or you don't. I'm tired of all this put-on, put-off shit."

"Please, I need you tonight."

"Need me, just what does that mean. Need me," Alyssa pouted.

Poppin's hands shook on the wheel. There was sweat forming on his forehead. He had to get it together. He thought Alyssa would be a help, but she was forcing him to think too much. Love, how the hell was he supposed to give her that? More than anything right now he just wanted comfort. He wanted to hold and be held.

Poppin took a left turn onto Beaker Street. "I just want to lay down with you. I want to hold you."

Alyssa paused and looked out the passenger side window. She didn't know whether to be happy or sad. She was so tired of trying to reach this man, but she couldn't help herself. Whenever she looked into his eyes it was if they were the same person. Was she the only one seeing this, or was Poppin seeing the same thing. He had to be. That look could not exist if coming from one alone. The hell with love for now, she finally thought. Comfort wouldn't be so bad tonight. It was cold and chilly outside, and her body was giving up on her. She was getting old for a dancer. Comfort, yes, comfort would be all right for tonight.

Alyssa put her left hand on Poppin's right knee again. "I will lay with you tonight. It would be nice to just hold each other."

Poppin smiled and loosened his grip on the wheel. They passed the stone edifice that was at the entrance to the heights. Poppin pulled the Benz into the spotless, white garage of the twenty- room, white, colonial style house, and parked it next to his gold, Ford Taurus. The rest of the garage was empty and spotlessly clean.

Once inside the house, Alyssa dropped all of her clothing off on the way to the shower.

Poppin felt a stirring in his groin. He didn't know if he wanted love, but at the moment he sure wanted sex. He walked into the bathroom and watched the water flow over Alyssa's body as she stood exposed in the octagonal shower. He watched the soap smears form on her butt cheeks and the large, full globes that were her breasts. He became mesmerized by her and began to forget all of his confusion. He had always marveled at how un-inhibited Alyssa was with her body, but then she had been a stripper for years.

Alyssa smiled at Poppin and raised her hand for him to join her. He dropped his clothes off and joined in a soap up. Alyssa lowered her head to his waist and made love to him. Alyssa stepped from the shower and led Poppin to his large, circular bed. He seemed comfortable now. He began to breathe softly in sleep. She wrapped her arms around him. Men, she thought, they were always so easy. There was always that one thing that would take their mind off everything, that one thing that would make them relax. She had sworn to herself that she would never give it to Poppin again unless he told her he loved her. She had broken that promise. She gave him a tender hug, and he sighed deeply. She fell off to sleep in love.

When Alyssa awoke the next morning, Poppin was gone. He got what he wanted, she thought sourly to herself. She made herself some breakfast and went back to bed. Maybe he would return later, and she would give him a piece of her mind. She really was tired of all the rejection and abandonment.

*****

Poppin sat at the curb in the gold Ford Taurus. He was dressed in a black T-shirt and black slacks. He had put away the one hundred caret diamond necklace in the need to be inconspicuous. As he knew would happen, the secretary of the counseling group of Stevens, Johnson, and Jensen had not shown up for work on time this morning. He knew she would be exasperated to find a long nail driven into the center of her radial tires. There would be no one at the reception desk when he entered the suite to the group of offices.

He crossed the street slowly, taking in a deep breath of fresh air. This seemed to relax him, but a thought still lingered in his mind. It had only been a month since the last kill. Maybe it was too soon to strike again, but the urge to act drove him bitterly on. He entered the lobby and proceeded to the elevator. He noticed the half-dead fiscus trees in various sizes that dotted the lobby by the long sofa couch. He walked to the elevator, entered and hit the button for the fifth floor. He was alone with his thoughts.

His mind seemed to be a whirlwind of hazy fuzz. In a matter of moments he knew the door would open and a rage would swirl up in his guts; he would act on this rage and get the job done. Weeks of preparation and tracking had come to an end. When he entered the office suite, he knew he had the right place, and he knew a person's life was about to come to a violent end.

Poppin stopped at the desk and looked at the open appointment book. He was in luck. Johnson did not have an appointment for another hour. There would be no collateral damage, and no witnesses, which was something he definitely didn't want. He turned and walked directly into the office, startling the middle-aged, gray-haired man who sat at his desk poring over an open file.

"Can I help you?" Stan Johnson finally managed to blurt out.

Poppin stepped forward to stand directly in front of the desk. "Yes, I saw there was no receptionist at the desk, so I came right in. I'm sorry if I'm disturbing you."

"Our receptionist had a flat tire this morning. She will be in later. Anyway, as long as you're here, what can I do for you?"

"I'm an investigator, my name is Paul Stanton, and I would like to know if you ever had a client by the name of Michael Turner. He would have been about thirteen years old when you counseled him."

"That name doesn't ring a bell, when was he in for counseling?"

"It would have been about ten years ago."

"Let me check the computer files and see if I have him on file."

Poppin noticed that Johnson quickly took on an ashen look about his face. His fingers were shaking as he punched on the computer keyboard. Poppin stared blankly at the man before him and waited for an answer.

Johnson's voice shook as he spoke. "Yes, he is in my records. I did counsel him about ten years ago."

"I thought so, do you remember him now?"

"No, not really, I've had so many clients over the years, there have been hundreds, and they all seem to run together after a number of years."

"Well, he remembers you," Poppin said as he pulled the silenced thirty-eight from his waistband where he had tucked it under his black T-shirt.

"What the hell," was all that Johnson was able to say before the silenced bullet struck him in the center of the forehead. Johnson slumped down and rolled out of the chair to fall dead on the floor. Blood oozed from the hole in the center of his forehead to fall and form a small, crimson puddle.

Poppin walked over to the body and took the paper sack from under his arm. He spread the white powder liberally over the body and made his way back to the elevator just as the other office door opened. Poppin hopped in the elevator and the doors closed behind him. He had narrowly made his escape.

Back behind the wheel of the Taurus, he had to still his nerves so as not to pull away too rapidly from the curb. He was calmer this time. He wondered, was he getting used to killing? He smiled to himself as he drove down the street. Killer on the loose. Another payment sealed. Yes, it was indeed getting easier to kill. Only five more to go. He would take some time off now. Shadow his next victim. Set everything right. Kill again.

*****

Wendtworth sat down at her desk and drew forth a deep sigh. Stacks of files littered the metal desk. Yellow Post-It notes seemed to be everywhere. She looked over at Collins who sat at his nearly empty desk and arranged three pencils in a small row. She laughed to herself and knew she would have to change that quickly. Grabbing a stack of files, she rose to walk over and throw them on his desk. "You can familiarize yourself with these."

Collins looked up glumly at her with his deep, blue eyes, questioning.

"They're files of cases I've been assigned. All of them unsolved. Unfortunately some of them are quite cold. Sometimes it takes years to get our man," Wendtworth sighed.

Collins pushed the three pencils to the right side of his desk. "Years, I thought a homicide needed to be solved quickly."

"Well, it's not always as easy as they make it out to be on television. This is real life. While many cases are solved quickly because the killer is usually someone close to the victim, there are those where the answer is not so readily apparent."

Collins grabbed the top file and began to read slowly through it. This was going to take some time.

An inter-office mail courier arrived to stand between the two desks. Her thin frame, fetching blue eyes, and long blonde hair immediately caught Collins attention. He gave her a small wisp of a smile. The female courier turned her attentions to Wendtworth.

The perky courier handed the file to Wendtworth. "Here is the autopsy report from the murder in rural Eureka."

Wendtworth sat down slowly at her desk. She sifted through the brief report, quickly finding the only pertinent information it held. "Shot with a thirty-eight, they recovered the slug in his skull. Nothing else interesting except this. The white powder the body was covered in was confirmed to be bone meal fertilizer," Wendtworth shook her head in disbelief.

Collins thought for a moment, "Looks like we got ourselves a gardener."

"Yeah, plug em and plant em," Wendtworth laughed.

Collins somewhat reluctantly joined in. He figured you had to have humor to survive this kind of job.

Wendtworth continued to sift through the file. "A gardener, yeah, that's strange. Why and the hell would a killer want to cover a body in bone meal."

"He's probably trying to hide any evidence we might find, fingerprints maybe."

"I doubt there would even be any fingerprints on the body in a quick kill situation like this. No, I think it goes much deeper than that. Some kind of psychosis is driving him. What we need to do is figure out what that psychosis is and where it came from."

"That's not going to be easy," Collins let out his inexperience.

"A profiler will give us all kinds of reasons, but it usually comes down to some kind of abuse the killer suffered as a child."

"Why would a killer leave such a hint when we really have nothing else to go on?"

"It's the nature of psychosis. The killer, for some reason, doesn't believe the job is done until he fertilizes his victim."

"But why fertilize them. What does it mean?"

"We'll have to go back to Eureka and question the young kids. If what that Johnson boy says is true, if Harrison was sexually abusing some of the kids, then he may have sexual abused our killer. We may have a motive here."

"Yeah, I think you're right, but how are we ever going to find out who the killer is. Dozens, maybe even hundreds of kids have passed through that place over the years. How are we going to find a person that was abused over a decade ago?"

"That's detective work. It always starts that way. We look and dig and question until we get a break. If it's there, we'll find it."

Collins just shook his head. He was having trouble adjusting to the reality of his job, but he did like puzzles, and this case promised to be a big one.

"What are we going to call this case then?" Collins asked. He paused for a moment. "The Gardener would be a good name."

Even though Joan was a middle-aged white woman, she loved rap music and it showed sometimes when she talked. "For shizzle my nizzle, the names been taken, we got us a Slayer Player here, doin' games on us."

"Okay, rap girl, I like that, then Slayer Player it is."

Collins rose from his desk. "Let's get going then, back to Eureka."

The pastures and cornfields blurred by and this time they all seemed familiar. It felt like they arrived at Harrison House more quickly, but it always seemed quicker once you had already been to a place. Wendtworth pulled the silver LTD into the drive and was greeted once again by the semi-toothless old dog. The old, black lab snuggled up against her leg when she got out of the car.

"Hello, my old friend," Wendtworth said as she patted the dogs head.

Tongue drooling spittle, the old dog followed her all the way to the entrance of the house. Several young kids were kicking a ball around the front yard.

"Should we question these kids?" Collins asked.

"Not right now, let's go inside and look over the rooms first."

Mrs. Larsen answered the knock at the door and reflexively stepped back. She didn't like any of this murder business. A blank stare came over her eyes. She motioned the two detectives to step inside the foyer.

Wendtworth spoke calmly, "Have you thought of anything else that might help us in our investigation?"

Mrs. Larsen froze with a bleary expression on her face. "No, I don't know anything, there is nothing to know."

Wendtworth was taken aback by the answer. Larsen seemed quite agitated. She wondered if the woman was upset about the murder, or was there something else the woman was hiding. If there was abuse in the house, did Larsen know, and was she hiding that.

"We want to take a look at some of the children's rooms," Wendtworth said firmly.

"Be my guest," Mrs. Larsen said as she turned and walked quickly away.

Collins let out a small chuckle, "Not very helpful, is she?"

"She's hiding something. She's hiding the abuse, but why?" Wendtworth answered.

The pair of detectives walked slowly down the well-lit narrow hallway, peering in a couple of rooms as they went by. The third room on the right caught the attention of Wendtworth. She entered and saw a small doll on the bedspread. She drew up closer to a picture that was crudely taped on the wall with masking tape above a small desk. It was a crayon drawing of a devil. A green body, a head with red horns, and the freaky eyes of a goat adorned the picture. Wendtworth walked over and pulled the picture off the wall. It was only then that she noticed the light pencil mark x that crisscrossed the head of the devil.

Wendtworth handed the colored drawing to Collins. "I think we know who this devil is."

Collins shook his head yes.

Wendtworth turned to walk out of the room. "It's time to question this child. Go out and find her, and bring her to her room."

Ten minutes later, Collins returned to the room with a small girl in a pair of dirty blue-jeans. The white blouse the girl was wearing was spotted with brown spots of dirt, and large, green, grass stains. She had been one of the kids playing kickball in the front yard. The girl had shoulder length, soft, brown hair, the kind of softness that only a young child can have. Her brown eyes were questioning, yet somehow showed a line of fear. Collins held her hands gently as he led her over to sit down on the bed.

Collins sat down on the bed beside the young girl. "This is Molly."

"Hello Molly, you may remember me. I was here last week. My name is Joan."

Molly nodded yes as Wendtworth reached out and softly shook the diminutive hand of the young girl. Molly awarded Wendtworth with a modest smile and a gleam in her eyes. From what little the girl remembered of her mother, she remembered her mother had blonde hair and blue eyes.

Wendtworth knelt down in front of the young girl. "Molly, are you happy here at the house?"

Molly drew back on the bed. It appeared that she wasn't going to speak. Wendtworth was surprised when Collins softly put his hand on the young girls head. At first she seemed taken aback, but then she began to warm to his touch.

"You can answer Joan, it's all right," Collins said.

It took a few more moments for Molly to become comfortable. "Yes, I'm happy here most of the time, but not always."

Wendtworth produced a motherly smile. "When are the times you're not happy?"

"I don't know, just sometimes I'm not happy," Molly responded.

Wendtworth held the devil picture down in front of Molly for her to see. Molly froze and drew back on her bed.

Wendtworth bent forward and gently touched the petite girl's knee in order to bring her back to some sense of reality. "Can you tell me about this picture?"

"It's the devil. He's the devil," Molly blurted out almost in tears.

Wendtworth had to fight to suppress her excitement. "Who, who's the devil?"

"He's dead now. Dead. Throw that away, just throw that away," Molly cried as tears began to roll down her face.

Collins tried to smooth the young girl's hair again but she would have none of it and wouldn't calm down. Wendtworth decided not to pursue the issue any further. She knew who was dead. She knew who the devil was. She would leave Molly alone for now. Let her go back outside and play. She knew that Shawn Jones had been telling her the truth. She was certain Harrison had abused some of the children. There was little doubt Molly had been abused.

33

Captain Grisky rushed forward to greet Wendtworth and Collins as they came out of the front door of Harrison House. In spite of the sixty degree temperature, his face was red and wet with perspiration. His chest heaved as he tried to calm himself. He looked down and tucked his T-shirt back into his pants before buttoning the ever-troublesome middle button that lay open across the wide expanse of his beer-belly. He slowly brought his breathing under control.

Wendtworth and Collins stared at him.

Grisky broke into a wide grin, his long jowls outlined by the deep creases at the side of his mouth. "I've got our man, arrested him last night."

Wendtworth brushed a long blonde strand of hair back over her scalp.

"Really, that was fast, how did you find him, and how do you know he is our man?"

Grisky swelled with pride as he took out a white handkerchief and wiped the sweat from his brow. "Shawn Jones, I picked him up on a search of a friend's truck when I was searching them for drugs during a traffic stop last night. There was a thirty-eight under the passenger seat where he sat. I knew the little shit would turn out bad."

Collins brushed by Grisky. "Finding a thirty-eight underneath the car seat doesn't mean he killed anyone."

Grisky gave Collins a wide berth as he passed. "Looks like he did. I arrested him, and I'm holding him down at the station. I'm going to question him later and get a confession out of him. I figured you two would want to be there."

Wendtworth stepped up briskly and followed Collins to the cars. "Yes, we want to be there, actually, I'd like to be the one who questions him."

Grisky spoke to the backs of the two FBI agents. "Well, I guess it really is your case. I don't mind, as long as I get the credit for the bust after he confesses."

"If he did it, that's fine. We don't care. We just want the killer. Now, let's get down to the station."

34

Grisky headed back to the squad-car. Wendtworth and Collins headed for the silver LTD and were soon following him down the winding country roads toward the Winnebago County Courthouse and Jail in Oshkosh. As they approached the city, Wendtworth was surprised to see how much the city had grown in the previous ten years since she had been there on another case. Numerous, expensive suburbanite houses dotted the landscape outside the city limits. A large, modern church was added to the area, and as they approached the inside of the city limits, she saw rows and rows of apartment buildings and condos. Urban sprawl had definitely had its effect here.

Collins glanced at a pasture full of milk cows that remained wedged between apartment complexes. "What do you think?"

Wendtworth gazed at the pasture and saw a female Heifer trying to mount another female. "I think Grisky is full of shit. I doubt if Shawn Jones killed Harrison. The kid may have some problems, but I didn't see the cold, dead look of a killer in his eyes when last we talked to him."

Collins shifted in the passenger seat. "I think you're right. I don't know what Shawn Jones is, but I don't think he's stupid. I doubt he would kill someone right under everyone's noses."

The silver LTD crossed the main street bridge that crossed the Fox River. On the right side of the road was the Oshkosh Convention Center. An old plaque of Chief Oshkosh had been affixed to the front wall. The greatest claim to fame of the Indian chief was that he had become the logo for a city beer brewed in the nineteen forties. The travelers took a left, then a right, and turned onto Wisconsin street. A mile up the road they pulled into the public parking lot of the jail. Once inside the jail, the trio of policemen regrouped in front of the interrogation room.

Grisky had called ahead, and deputy-sheriff Melinda Holmes had already placed Jones in the interrogation room.

Jones sat immobile, staring straight ahead, as the two FBI agents entered the room. Wendtworth took the chair opposite the empty table and in front of Jones. Collins stood loosely on her left.

Wendtworth leaned back in the hard, wooden chair. "Good morning Shawn."

Shawn simply smiled and answered back, "Good Morning."

Wendtworth detected no scent of fear or loathing in the bland greeting.

Wendtworth looked into the soft, brown eyes of the young man who sat before her. He seemed younger now, even younger than the eighteen years of age he had just turned. She smiled at him, and he smiled back in a smirk of resignation.

Before she could say another word, Shawn spoke, "I didn't kill the dumb bastard. He deserved to be killed, but I didn't do it."

Wendtworth leaned forward, a sharp edge in her voice. "Why am I supposed to believe you? How do I know you didn't do it? Grisky says he found a thirty-eight under the car seat. We'll have ballistics done on it. Do you know what we will find?"

"Yeah, you're going to find that the gun isn't a match for the killing. It isn't even my gun. I didn't know it was under the seat. It wasn't my truck we were in. I've never had enough money to own a vehicle of my own, and if I did own a vehicle, I would be the one driving. "

"The gun belonged to your friend then?"

"I guess so. I don't know. Like I said, I didn't even know the weapon was there."

Wendtworth settled back in her chair and let out a deep sigh, "I'm not going to question you any further right now."

Collins let out a short huff of disappointment.

Shawn looked gruffly at Collins, and then looked back at Joan. "You're not going to grill me?"

"What would be the point? First we'll wait and see if the gun was the murder weapon. If it's not, I don't see how there is any way to hold you," Joan stated matter-a-fact.

"What if it is? I mean it isn't my gun, but what if it is my friends and it really is the murder weapon. What then?"

"Then, you're in a heap of trouble," Collins said briskly.

"Let's not jump to conclusions. Let's wait and see what we find out," Wendtworth said calmly.

A lull of silence filled the room. Wendtworth looked once again into Shawn's tender eyes. She saw that familiar hint of sexual allure that she had cultivated with the young man earlier. She was puzzled. She couldn't explain the deep sexual allure she felt for this young man. She had never felt anything like it before with a man as young as this. She wondered why it was happening now. Maybe it was a way of distancing herself from the young age of her partner. Maybe that was all it was, but it unnerved her how he held her gaze. Shawn's eyes smiled with enticement, and she had no doubt her eyes were smiling back.

Wendtworth rose to leave, "Well, Shawn, stay cool, we'll have the ballistic results back within forty-eight hours. If there is no match, you're out of here."

Shawn sighed, "Thank you."

Grisky rushed out of the observation room in a huff, "What the hell was that? You were awful gentle with him. Hell, seems like you two are lovers. I thought for a moment you were going to give him a kiss."

Wendtworth's face glared with anger. "What do you expect? You haven't really got anything on this young man, and I don't appreciate your comment. You better back off and let us handle this. Leave Shawn alone. I don't believe he is a killer, but we'll find out soon enough."

Collins touched his partner on the shoulder and turned her toward the door to leave. "Let's just get out of here."

The clear, crisp air felt good on Wendtworth's face as the partners stood on the front steps leading down away from the jail.

Collins had a look of red-flanged jealousy on his face. "What was going on in there? Are you attracted to that boy?"

"What do you care, are you jealous? I just like him. I think there is an inherent kindness in him. A kindness that could never allow him to be a killer. And don't worry; you and I will never have an attraction for each other. You can count on that. So, if you are jealous, put it away now and forever. We're partners, and we'll cover each other's backs, probably become friends, but that's it. Any feelings I have about anyone else are all mine, and they're something you will never have to worry about."

"Fine, I didn't mean anything by it. Ease up. I think you're right about Shawn. This would be way too easy if it were true he was the murderer. Our murderer is a sick bastard, and I'm sure Shawn isn't that kind of sick."

Wendtworth was happy to have the confirmation. She took a deep breath of the crisp morning air and relaxed. Collins was surprised to see her in the passenger seat.

Collins took his seat behind the wheel. "Where are we going?"

"Home my young driver. Home."

Back in Madison, the two detectives sat silently at their desks. The room was eerily empty of other detectives.

Collins finally broke the silence, "What do we do now?"

"I don't know. We haven't got much to go on. Little to no evidence, no witnesses, a possible motive, but then again maybe not. Just because there was abuse in the house recently, doesn't mean there was years ago," Wendtworth answered.

"Yes, but I think that is the motive. A child grew up and is taking revenge. That is a strong possibility. It is probably our motive."

"But how do we find this now grown-up child. Hundreds of children had to have gone through that house over the years. What do we do? Investigate all of them, and even if we were able to find them all, what is to guarantee that any of them will tell the truth. Sexual abuse is something that adults usually keep pretty well hidden."

"How true, even in this day and age, it is such a secretive business, but what else can we do except delve into the past and try to find someone."

"It's going to be a long, tedious business," Wendtworth sighed.

"Yes, it is, we can get started Monday. This is Friday afternoon; would you care to join me for a drink?"

Wendtworth paused, frozen in place. She didn't know if this was such a good idea. Maybe she was making too much out of it. What could a little drink hurt? "Yeah, sure, why not?" She finally responded.

Collins grinned, he was quite happy with himself. "Great!"

The two detectives rose from their desks and grabbed their coats. As they turned and moved toward the door, they were met by the inter-office mail courier.

The young, blonde woman, much to his surprise, positioned herself in front of Collins.

"I have something that the Section Chief says will be important to you, they wanted me to deliver it right away." She handed the envelope over with a broad smile on her face.

Collins smiled back as he took the envelope. She almost curt-sied when she turned and walked away. He watched the sway of her behind, and became somewhat impervious to his partner who stood glaring beside him.

"Hey, earth to John, earth to John, give me that envelope."

"No, no, I'll open it," Collins stammered back.

Collins opened the envelope and scanned it quickly. Wendtworth buttoned her coat.

"Says here research has discovered a murder case that may be similar to ours. The murder occurred last night at a psychiatric counseling firm in Milwaukee. No clues at the scene except for the unusual covering of the body with a white powder, just like our murder case."

Wendtworth stood silently by Collin's side.

"Let's go, let's get to Milwaukee," Collins said excitedly.

"No, the scene will have been completely secured and analyzed by now. Probably released. There is no point in going there. If this happened on Friday during normal business hours, it will do us more good to go over there on Monday. Other businesses will be open and normal activity will be going on. We can can-vas the area and maybe come up with some kind of witness. Let's get that drink you promised me."

"Me, promised you a drink," Collins hadn't realized Wendtworth had taken the invitation was for him to buy. "Yeah, sure, let's go down to the Wisconsin Sports Bar on main."

"Sure, sounds good."

The Wisconsin Sports Bar was on Washington street two blocks east of the Capitol building. In such near proximity, the

Capitol building loomed like the giant that it was. Bright spot-lights broke the dusk and illuminated the large American flag at the top of the dome. One could not help but feel an experience of awe whenever they were anywhere near the building.

The sports bar was dedicated to the Wisconsin Badgers sports team. Bucky Badger seemed to be everywhere. The bar was liberally dedicated to the football team, the most successful and popular of all the Sports. Football Coach Barry Alvarez previously led the team to win back to back Rose Bowls and several other bowl appearances. It was too bad he resigned as coach at the end of the 2005 season. The fans had come to expect excellence from their teams, and there was great hope among the public that they would continue to see the same success in the future. Red and white permeated the bar everywhere right down to the "Go Bucky" drink coasters. Large, two by three foot photographs of glorious moments froze time forever. This was truly a sports-mad town.

Wendtworth and Collins took a table near the back of the bar. Wendtworth felt most comfortable with her back to the wall. Wendtworth surveyed the surroundings for trouble or danger. She was ashamed of herself for this habit. Maybe it was time to get off the streets and get a desk job. She couldn't shake the feeling lately that someone she had once put away would be out to get her. It was funny how perceptions change after twenty years on the job. She needed a drink. It was a feeling she seldom had. Maybe an agency counselor was the answer. Maybe she was just seeing too much of her naive former self in the young man who was with her this evening. She needed to relax.

Collins leaned in close to Wendtworth's ear, smelling the seductive female scent of the woman. "There's a game tomorrow afternoon at the stadium. There's quite a camaraderie going on in here tonight."

"Yeah, it does seem pretty rowdy for this time of the day. I feel kind of funny about being here. I think I'm too old for this."

"No, you're not old, just relax and enjoy yourself. There are a lot of people here your age, sure, they're mostly all men or the men's wives, but what the hell, you shouldn't feel out of place."

"You're right; I'll have a whiskey and water."

"Wow, whiskey and water, going right to the hard stuff."

"I don't have a drinking problem if that's what you think; it's just that I'm dealing with some strange feelings lately."

"Strange feelings about what?"

"Oh, it's nothing I can talk to you about. I can't even identity the feelings myself right now. I just need to relax."

Wendtworth took a sip of her drink and the strong alcohol content bit her tongue hard. "So you grew up right here in Madison did you?"

"Funny you should bring that up now after we've already been together for two weeks."

"I didn't know what else to say."

"And you, you grew up in Milwaukee," Collins stated flatly.

"No, not really, I grew up in Waukesha, a suburb of Milwaukee. I had a pretty easy life, a typical suburbia life. My father is a lawyer, and my mother is a nurse. We were never hurting for money. I'm an only child and they spoiled me rotten."

"Why did you go into police work?"

"It seemed like it was in the middle. I heard stories of shootings and such from my mother who was an emergency room nurse, and I heard legal goings on of such things from my father who was a prosecuting attorney. I was always mesmerized by what happened in the middle. That seemed to be where the real action was. I was bored with my upper-middle class life. I wanted to live on the wild side a little and this was my way of doing it."

"It must have been hard at first."

"Probably no harder than it is going to be for you. It's tough to break into the real thing, to see the real violence, hate, and insanity that can really go on in our society."

"I'm lucky to have a partner like you. I trust you to guide me along."

"I will," Wendtworth smiled back. She was growing to like her new partner. He was innocent and young, but he did seem sincere.

"How come there is no husband?" Collins asked bluntly.

41

"Where did that come from?" Wendtworth shot back.

"I don't know, I just want to know. You're an attractive, intelligent woman. I find it hard to believe that you're not married. Have you ever been?"

"No, I've always been involved in work, probably too involved. I've had dalliances now and then, but nothing seemed to last. Maybe I am just a little too spoiled. I've never cared to give that much of myself to anybody."

"That's too bad; you would probably make some man very happy."

"Why, because I got big teats," Wendtworth laughed. "No, no, that's just not a goal in my life right now."

Collins sat back, took a sip of his drink and thought. Married to her job, this was probably not a good thing. Maybe she was wound too tightly. He would have to keep this in mind. Perhaps he could be a comfort to her in some way. She was probably in some type of mid-life crisis. He would go easy with her, be her friend, but most of all be a good, trustworthy partner. He could see that she deserved that.

"Another drink?" Collins asked as he began to rise from the table.

"No, that's okay. I just want to go home and relax for the weekend."

"I'll take you home."

"No, I'll take a cab. You just stay here and relax. Maybe you'll run into some of your hometown friends."

"Truthfully, I do expect to see some of them here and there is a young lady I hope will be here too."

"Good for you," Wendtworth smiled. She put on her coat and headed out the door without looking back. She hailed a cab and was soon on her way home. Her head hurt. It wasn't the drink, it was something else, but what the hell was it. Just old age, she reasoned, she was just getting too old for this kind of job. Damn, she hated that thought.

Wendtworth walked into her spotless apartment and threw her mail on the kitchen counter. The top letter caught her eye when she noticed the word Eureka written on the return address.

That's strange, she thought, was it from who she thought it was from. She was anxious to see what was inside and nearly tore the letter in two trying to get it open. The signature at the bottom said simply Shawn. She needed another drink.

*****

Gettin' low, gettin' low, lights down low. Poppin sat back in his favorite black, leather recliner and put his feet up. He puffed on a Corona cigar. Alyssa sat on the black leather couch opposite him. Soft lighting drifted from two small lamps on matching glass end tables. The black carpeting picked up the shimmering light. Poppin let out a vast cloud of cigar smoke, "Let's get this party started."

Poppin picked up his cell phone and called Rolly. Rolly hadn't been to the house in a couple of months, but when Poppin called Rolly was quick to answer the call. He would be over in half an hour. Poppin breathed softly through the phone, "Do you know where Dan K is?"

Rolly laughed, "Don't I always know where he is?"

"Bring him along then," Poppin laughed and punched the cell phone off.

Alyssa sat uncomfortably on the couch. She caught Poppin's eyes. There was something there she had never seen before, but she couldn't place what that something was. She quickly shifted her gaze away from Poppin and spoke in a shy whisper, "Who is Dan K? I've never heard of him before."

"Dan K, yeah, he's a good friend of mine. He gets me super high and feelin' good all the time. We go way back. Smoke em up Johnny, smoke em up!"

Alyssa remained dumbfounded.

"Oh, Alyssa, you don't get it do you? Dan K is an airways name, code for dank pot, dank meaning great pot of course."

Alyssa laughed somewhat in embarrassment.

"Alyssa, I've got a special surprise for you tonight."

43

Propping herself up on the couch, she caught Poppin's gaze and this time she saw a warm twinkle in his eyes. Any fear of him she had previously registered disappeared in a blink. Alyssa squealed like a young child, "Tell me, tell me, I can't wait."

The doorbell rang with a deep base, rap background of a song. Poppin got up and opened the door. A large hulk of a black man stood in the doorway with a wide smile on his face. The two men embraced in a hefty bear hug. Poppin turned and headed back to the living room with the large man in tow.

Alyssa almost leapt out of her seat. "Is this who I think it is?" She smiled at the big man.

The large man stretched out his right hand toward her. "Big Pork Dog, here, my beautiful lady. At your disposal."

Poppin' laughed. What a star BPD was. What a ladies' man.

Big Pork Dog took a seat on the couch next to Alyssa. He was indeed a star. He was the first big hit for Breaking Out Productions, Poppin's production company. With the next rap songs done right, he might even for that brief moment, be the biggest rap star in the industry. Poppin had planned it all and worked for it endlessly. He had spent many hours on the phone, made appointments and interviews with sound and video people, worked distribution channels. He had the time, and he had the money, and he had the front he needed most of all.

Big Pork Dog shifted his large bulk. The couch creaked from his weight. He was a big man. Six foot six, and three hundred sixty pounds. His enormous cheeks flowed down his face and hung limply around his mouth. It wasn't bad now, but one could see he would be a man with a flabby jowl when he was old. His black eyes sparkled with light. It was easy to see this was a very happy and thankful man. A good man. Pork Dog's hair was cut short making his head look even larger than it was. Alyssa looked down at his wrists. Several gold bracelets hung from each one. His wrists were huge, twice the size of Alyssa's. His body was taut and in shape. He was large, but he was built like a brick. Alyssa thought briefly what it would be like to sleep with the strong, young bulk of a man.

Poppin let out a gigantic puff of smoke. The smoke was caught in the soft lighting and formed magical clouds of swirling mist. Everyone stared at the smoke designs until they dissipated.

Another rap song played out its thumping beat from the doorbell. Poppin nodded at Alyssa, and she got up to answer the door. He knew Rolly and Dan K had arrived.

Rolly strolled into the room, one foot meeting the other as his hand moved forward and down in rhythmic motion.

Poppin rose quickly and moved toward Rolly giving him private hand props.
"Yo my nigga."

Rolly smiled, "Bout time we party down and forget about the rest of the world."

Poppin turned back to his chair and sat down. "Ah, the rest of the world, there ain't no forgettin' that. It's always in here," Poppin pointed his index finger at his right temple.

Rolly laughed, "Yeah, well my niggah, maybe tonight we can get you so fucked up you ain't got no choice but to forget about it."

Poppin picked up his cigar again. "That would be down, real down."

Big Pork Dog blocked Alyssa's view of Rolly as he stepped in front of him. "Lean low my man, lean low."

Rolly broke into a wide grin, "Always do man, always do. Nice to finally meet you. I've been watching your progress closely, you're good."

Big Pork Dog looked down sheepishly at the floor and let out a boyish grin that made him look ten years younger than his actual age of twenty-five. "Thank you." Big Pork Dog moved to sit down.

Everyone rested comfortably in their seats. Rolly pulled out the bag of dank along with an exquisitely beautiful glass pipe covered in bright, multi-colored flowers. He knew everyone admired the artistry that had gone into the hand-blown glass. With the first hits taken the swirling colors grew brighter. They would only grow brighter as the night went on. Dan K was one hitter quitter, but of course one hit was never enough. By the end of the first bowl everyone was intensely happy and full of smiles.

Poppin went to the kitchen and brought back a tray of bottled, chilled mocha frapiccinos. He waited until everyone had taken the caps off and taken a swill to cool their throats.

"How's the new song coming Pork Dog?"

Rolly shifted in his seat, "Business, business, always business."

Poppin chattered back gaily, "Business is my pleasure. Business is my life."

Big Pork Dog blurted out a rap line, "Business priznezz, shizzle my dickness."

Everyone nodded and laughed.

Big Pork Dog jumped excitedly to his feet. "Wanna hear the new one?" His voice showed the excitement of the obvious love for his craft.

Everyone nodded affably as Rolly filled another bowl of Dan K.

Poppin got up, walked over to the wall and flipped on a row of strip light spot lights. He sat back down and lifted his cappuccino to his lips. Big Pork Dog got up and stood under the spot lights. He began to shake his enormous bulk to a rhythm that built slowly inside of his head. Soon that rhythm would spill out. The anticipation sent a chill through the small, private audience. Big Pork Dog was going to perform a new song for the very first time for them alone.

Big Pork Dog stopped his movements in a freeze frame. He threw out his hands and began to rhythmically pump them up and down. He held an invisible microphone in his right hand. He had done it thousands of times before. It felt natural as the words began to flow out of his mouth and soul.

> Hand on my Glock
> Cocked in my pocket.
> Try your luck
> You gonna say fuck-it.

Slayer Player

Act like a clown
I'm gonna lay you down
Put you in the ground
Then look around.

Killin' in my blood
Hit you like a flood.
Shoot the wabbit
Like Elmer Fudd.

Any holes I'll plug
Cause I'm a thug
Squish you like a bug
Then give my bitch a hug.

Done with my bizz
Gonna sip some kriszz
Go take a piss
Grit my teeth and hiss.

Make you dead with a kiss
Then hit on some sizz
Wait for the cops
Come to give me their quizz.

They get no answers
Gonna skirt their skit.
Like a break-down dancer
On your grave
I'm gonna dance to this hit.

Big Pork Dog broke into a wide grin and dropped the imaginary mike to the floor. The small group clapped and yelled shouts of enthusiasm.

BPD smiled, "I'm working on more verses, but I think this is really a good song."

The small crowd clapped in agreement.

BPD took a seat on the black, leather couch. "There's this great line though that I didn't fit into the song. Maybe I'll use it in another song some day."

Alyssa beamed with excitement. "What is it; tell me, what is the line?"

A gigantic smile crossed BPD's face. "When you get this message, eat the wrapper."

Everyone laughed. Alyssa jumped up and down in front of the couch and shouted. "That's a great line; you could use it at the end of everything and anything."

BPD laughed. "You're right, maybe I'll make it my catch phrase mantra, or sign off with it at the end of everything," BPD sat back comfortably on the couch and relaxed his hands over his large belly.

Poppin rose to shake BPD's hand. He would make the song a hit. The material was definitely there. Everything else was in place. He was already imagining the video in his head. A couple of puffs of dank later, and he could see the whole scenario. He was a happy man. The darkness in his soul temporarily gone. He smiled as he sipped on the mocha and let the sugar fill his veins. The night was a roaring success. Friendships growing stronger. Poppin growing stronger still.

Chapter 3

Joan Wendtworth sat on the plush, burgundy couch and looked over the letter again. It was the fourth time she had read it. She kept reading the same lines over repeatedly. "I can't wait to see you. I know there is something special between us. I can't wait to see what that something special is."

She didn't know what to make of it. She was excited and yet somehow taken aback by the words. It seemed she did want this young man, lusted after him. She imagined herself in bed caressing his strong, young body. This is ridiculous, she thought. She was twenty-two years older than him. Was this some kind of mid-life crisis? It didn't matter. The erotic thoughts seemed to take on a life of their own.

Joan put the letter on the end table and went to take a shower. There was work to be done today.

Joan had dressed quickly when the apartment door buzzer rang. Her heart leapt in her throat. Could this be Shawn? She pressed the intercom button.

"Who is it?" She was surprised at the thick tension in her voice.

"It's Collins, let's get going," Collins answered.

Joan calmed her nerves, "I'm coming right down."

Collins stood shuffling his feet at the door, "You look kind of flustered this morning, what's going on?"

Joan shook her head. "Nothing, I'm just feeling a little under the weather."

Collins turned and walked away. Joan was surprised at how she stared at his behind as it moved away ahead of her. She definitely had young men on her mind. She smiled to herself. So what? It was alright. She was single. It felt good to feel some lust in her heart again. It had been a long time. Maybe there was something to be said for a female mid-life crisis.

Collins headed the LTD down the highway.

"Did your young woman show up last night," Wendtworth ventured.

Collins couldn't help bragging. "Yes, we had a real good time. She came to my house and spent the night."

"Well, at least someone is some love."

"Joan, Joan, don't worry, your time will come again. You're a very attractive woman."

"Thank you, but I don't seem to be able to find anyone to let into my life, though; there might be someone on the horizon."

"Oh, really, who is it?"

Joan paused and then said softly. "I don't think I better say anything more. I think I'm just fantasizing about it anyway."

"Okay, it's your business."

Joan flipped a CD in the car CD player.

"Rap music. Joan, you still surprise me," Collins said.

"Yeah, I'm into this new CD by Big Pork Dog. I don't know why I like this stuff so much. I guess I like the poetry of the words. I like the real life tension of it. I can relate to the tension."

Collins sighed. "I think you've been working crime too long."

"You're probably right."

The car traveled down Highway 90/94 and passed by the Milwaukee County Stadium, home of the Milwaukee Brewers.

Collins gawked. "That's an amazing structure. That's got to be one of the biggest roofs in the world."

"Yeah, and it cost a fortune. I heard it cost a life too."

"Construction is a dangerous business, almost as bad as ours, maybe even worse," Collins sighed.

Joan turned the car to the right and took the Main Street exit. By the time the CD had finished Collins was pulling the car to the curb in front of the Counseling offices of Stevens, Johnson, and Jensen in downtown Milwaukee. The pair of detectives got out and surveyed their surroundings.

Wendtworth took charge. "Let's check out that deli over there next to the office building. Maybe someone saw something that will help us."

The hearty smell of cheese and sausages blasted the detectives' nostrils as they entered the door. Both knew that lunchtime was going to come early today. A young, black woman in her early twenties stood behind the counter. She had an electric smile on her face.

At the back counter stood a large, black man who easily weighed over three hundred pounds. His face was sweaty with perspiration as he sliced sausage on the automatic slicing machine.

Joan thrust her hand forward with her credentials. "Hi, we're with the FBI, we're here to ask you if you might have seen anything last Friday when the murder occurred next door."

The young, black girls face saddened and a tear came to her eyes. "I liked Mr. Johnson, he was always very friendly, and he always left me a large tip. I'm going to miss him."

The detectives gave the young woman a moment to compose herself.

"We're sure he was a good man and that he did a lot of good in the community. We're going to try our hardest to solve this murder. That's why we thought we would talk to you. Maybe you saw something that could help us," Joan stated.

The young woman looked down sheepishly. "I don't think I know anything that might help you."

Collins reached out and put his hand on the glass counter. "Anything might help. The smallest detail. You never know. Was there anything different about that day?"

The young woman gave an exasperated smile. "Well, yes, last Friday, I was about a half an hour late for work. I missed the first bus. I don't think this means anything, but when I entered the shop I saw a black man entering the building next door."

Collins spoke up. "About what time was it?"

"It was about eight-thirty."

"Anything else?" Collins asked.

"No, there was nothing unusual going on. I got really busy so I could catch up on my work. I was too busy to see anything else."

Wendtworth shrugged. "Okay, thanks for your help."

The pair of detectives ordered two Milwaukee Clubs, the submarine special sandwich of the house, and returned to their vehicle.

In between a bite of their sandwiches Collins said, "What do you think?"

Wendtworth swallowed. "This sandwich is good."

"No, about the black man, what do you think?"

"I think it's pretty weak, but our man may be black. Who knows, it might help."

Collins took another bite, and with his mouth full mumbled. "What next?"

"Let's go down to the precinct and talk to the local detectives, see what they've got."

Collins swung the car over two blocks and stopped in front of the police station at Twentieth and State Street. The station was a bustle of activity, but the agents knew that in a city like Milwaukee there would always be crime business going on.

They took the elevator to the third floor and entered the detective squad room. Once inside the room, they were greeted by an elderly, black woman who was the receptionist.

Wendtworth thrust her hand forward. "We're with the FBI. We want to talk to the detectives that have drawn the Johnson murder case that happened last week."

The black woman examined their identification and turned to her computer. "That would be Hansen and Beller. Hansen is out right now, but Beller is in. He's back at the corner desk. I'll buzz him."

A moment later the receptionist spoke. "You can go back there now. He'll see you."

Beller rose from his desk to shake hands. The man did not match his name. He was in his mid-fifties, gray and balding, and when he spoke his voice came out in an almost silent creak. "Nice to meet you, I've been expecting you."

"What do you mean?" Collins ventured.

Beller let out a small chuckle. "I saw that the FBI had accessed the case on our data base, and considering that the man was powdered with something after he was killed, I knew there was something weird going on here. I figured maybe you had others."

Wendtworth sat down. "Yes, there was another body found in similar condition. We think we have the beginnings of a serial killer. Do you have anything that can help us?"

Beller sat back in his chair. "There isn't much to go on, but there is one thing that may help you. When we checked Johnson's computer it was shut off, but when we analyzed the drive, we saw that the last entry was to check out a patient that Johnson hadn't seen in ten years. The patients name was Michael Turner; last known address is out in Wauwatosa." Beller scribbled the name and address on a piece of paper and handed it to Collins.

"Thanks, we'll check it out," Wendtworth turned to leave, and Collins followed.

Collins sighed. "Off to Wauwatosa?"

Wendtworth laughed. "Yes, you seem frustrated, what's the matter, detective work not as exciting as you thought it would be?"

"So far it's boring."

"It'll heat up. This Turner fellow is probably an important link."

Collins punched up the roadmap on the onboard computer. "It's only about fifty blocks, straight out on State Street. Sixty-eighth and State to be exact."

Wendtworth sat back and stretched in her seat. "Good, it won't take long to get there."

Wendtworth pulled the car into the driveway off of Sixty-eighth Street and began going up the hill towards a row of three apartment buildings. Dusk had fallen, and the agents could see a black light shining out of one of the apartment's in the center building.

Collins snickered, "How much do you want to bet that our man is in that apartment."

"Naw, you don't think so do you, what are the odds?"

"Remember, he's been in counseling, he might be a little different."

Collins stared at the eerie apartment. "Counseling, that doesn't mean anything. Everyone's been in counseling at one time or another. Hell, I have."

"You have. What did you go to counseling for if you don't mind me asking?"

Collins shrugged, "It's a long story, I'll tell you some other time."

Wendtworth thought it best not to press. She stopped the car in front of the apartment and was not surprised to see the numbers matched.

"This is it. I'm telling you, that's our boy," Wendtworth laughed.

The agents walked up to the door and looked at the voice call register. Turner lived in apartment four. Collins buzzed him on the intercom.

A gravelly voice answered. "Who is it?"

"This is agent Wendtworth and Collins, we're with the FBI. We'd like to talk to you a minute," Collins stated.

"Oh shit!" The croaked response came.

The blacklight flipped off in the apartment and a regular light came on. The stereo music that had been blasting disappeared.

The voice gave a nervous bark into the intercom. "I can't talk to you right now. I have company."

Wendtworth pushed the button again. "We really need to talk to you. Look, we don't care what you're doing up there. We can get a subpoena and make you talk to us, but it will go easier on you if you just let us in. We're not here to bust you. We just need some information that might help us on a case we're working on."

Turner's timid voice answered. "Can I trust you?"

Wendtworth laughed. "Hey, we're FBI agents, if you can't trust us, who can you trust?"

There was a long pause. The agents could hear quiet stereo music in the background.

Turner smiled and spoke, "Okay, what the hell, come on up."

The smell of the marijuana greeted the agents before they opened up the door. Once inside, they noticed the bright light had been doused and the blacklight had been relit. Turner walked over to the kitchen table and motioned for the detectives to join him.

Turner's hands trembled as he lifted his coffee cup. "Want some coffee?"

"No, No thanks," the agents answered in unison.

Wendtworth clasped her hands together on the table in front of her. "Look, you don't have to be nervous. We're not here to bust you for pot or anything like that. We just want to talk to you about something in your past."

"Like what?" Turner responded.

Collins could smell the strong smell of whiskey coming off the man. It was only seven-thirty at night and the man was well into a good drunk. Collins brushed his thoughts about the drinking aside. "We want to talk to you about the counseling you had about ten years ago with Dr. Johnson downtown."

Subtle, real subtle, Wendtworth thought. Turner froze, set down his coffee cup and nearly knocked it over. Wendtworth could smell the odor of booze coming from the cup.

She met Turner's eyes. "I know this may be hard for you, but we really need your help."

Collins continued bluntly. "We know from your file that we've already subpoenaed and have had access to that you were in counseling for sexual abuse. Want to tell us about it."

Turner sat stone-faced for a moment, and then his face reddened and his breath quickened. "I don't know why I should tell you anything about it. I don't see where it has anything to do with you. It's a private thing, let's leave it alone."

"Michael, we would leave it alone, but for some reason, right before Johnson was killed, he had accessed your old file. We want to know why."

"Killed, what do you mean killed? I don't know anything about that. I haven't seen him in ten years. I don't have any idea why now all of a sudden he would have been interested in me," Turner answered with a tension-filled voice.

Joan met his eyes again. "We don't know either, but there had to be a reason. I know the past may still be hard to talk about,

55

but his report on you says you were seeing him for adolescent behavioral problems. Just what were those problems?"

"Are you investigating me here, or him? I just had some typical teenage problems, nothing big. I saw him a few times and that was it. My parents thought it would help, but they were the ones who needed counseling. They broke up a few months after that. Abandoned me, and took off to their little separate worlds."

Joan sympathized, "That must have been tough for you."

"Yeah, they were really fucked up."

"What did you do then, where did you live?"

Turner shook his head. "My social worker thought it would be best if I left the city and went to someplace quiet and rural where I could have more personal care, make easier friendships. I was sent to a place called Harrison House up North."

Wendtworth and Collins jerked to attention. Harrison House, what was the link? The thought crossed their minds simultaneously. Maybe their killer was sitting right in front of them. A long silence filled the room. No one knew what to say next.

Turner coldly broke the silence. "I'm glad he's dead."

"What? Why would that be?" Collins interjected.

Turner's face went crimson, his breathing became labored, and beads of sweat began to form on his forehead. He mumbled. "The son-of-a-bitch abused me."

The agents let the tension ebb. Wendtworth spoke up softly. "What do you mean by abused me?"

"Sexually, all right, he sexually abused me. Why do you suppose I'm drunk and stoned all the time," Turner shot back as he began to cry.

The agents gave him a moment to gather himself.

Collins got right to the point. "Did you kill Johnson?"

"Hell no, I'm too busy killing myself, don't you see, but don't get me wrong, I'm glad he's dead. He deserves to be dead. Justice came to him at last," Turner snickered.

"Justice, you think murder is justice?" Collins said incredulously.

"Yeah, in this case. The universe has a funny way of righting itself, doesn't it?"

Wendtworth leaned forward. "If you didn't kill Johnson, maybe you know who did?"

"If I did know, I wouldn't tell you. I told you, he got what he deserved."

Wendtworth leaned forward. "When were you at Harrison House?"

Turner sighed. "I don't know, I guess it was about seven years ago. I'm twenty-two now. I was there from the time I was thirteen until I was eighteen. I would have been there from 1992 until sometime in 1997. Now, leave me alone so I can go on killing myself."

Collins brushed his hair back. "Before we leave, I should tell you, you need to get some professional help."

Turner laughed. "Thanks, I'll take it under consideration."

"Okay, we have nothing further for you now. We may be in touch," Wendtworth stated.

Wendtworth was saddened as she walked down the sidewalk to the car. So much pain in that young man. He definitely had the motive to kill Johnson, but there was no proof. She crossed her arms and shook her head once she sat down in the passenger seat of the car. She spoke softly. "I wonder what Harrison House has to do with this?"

"Yeah, that does seem to be a connection that can't be ignored. It is weird that it would come up. Maybe something happened there years ago, but what?"

Collins started the car. "Do you think he is our killer?"

Wendtworth sighed, "I don't think so. He's too busy killing himself to want to kill someone else."

"Yeah, but if that hatred turned outward, he could be the one."

"You're right. We'll put a surveillance team on him."

"Anything else we can do?"

Wendtworth leaned back in her seat, "I don't know. I'm so tired I can't think straight right now. Let's go back to the motel and get some rest."

"I agree, I'm all for that."

Sonnentag

Wendtworth lay in bed that night thinking of Shawn. It was a pleasant distraction as she fell off to sleep.

Chapter 4

Alyssa walked into her apartment and set the stack of books on the floor on the white, shag carpet in front of the white, velour couch. She looked at all of the whiteness that surrounded her. Everything in the living room was white from the table right down to the ashtrays. A long row of ceiling to floor mirrors covered one wall and reflected the whiteness upon itself. She couldn't help herself, but she always wanted to be naked in this room. She wanted to see her blackness reflected back at her through the mirrored whiteness. She stepped out of her clothes and admired herself.

It wasn't going to be as easy as she thought; this forgetting about being a dancer. She was so used to her naked body. She supposed she would spend a lot of time naked in her apartment. She was so used to it, the smell and the look of her body. She plopped down on the couch and picked the top book off of a ten inch stack of books on the end table. She read the title, an Intro-duction to Psychology, and smiled to herself. She could do this, she really could. It seemed she knew a lot about people. When people are sexual they expose a lot more of themselves than just their bodies. She had seen plenty of action, known plenty of men and women. She thought she knew how people ticked. Now she just had to learn everything in clinical terms. It would be fun; it would be easy; she told herself. She sat back and read the first two chapters of the book before falling asleep on the couch.

Alyssa awoke the next morning at five A.M., a full three hours before her first class was to start. She was nervous and had spent a restless night tossing and turning. For the first time in a long time she was about to step into a new world, it was a world she had forgotten mostly about. It was a world she never felt she belonged to. She'd always felt isolated growing up. She had been sexually abused by her father and an uncle at the age of twelve. Since then, it seemed like she always lived in a fog. Mary Ridle, her guidance counselor at the college had been a great help. She had even convinced her to see a counselor and talk about the new changes she was making in her life. It had helped a great deal. She felt she was ready. Ready or not, here I come new world, she thought.

The campus of Marian college was built on the rural outskirts of Fon du Lac Wisconsin. There was no shortage of real estate room. It was a small, private campus, only eight buildings in all. All of the campus buildings were surrounded by beautifully landscaped large yards. Each had a meticulously cared for flower bed or two. A small fountain rested in the center of the main courtyard. It was the end of summer now, and most of the flowers were in full bloom. Alyssa couldn't help but think how this mirrored the blooming of her own world. She stopped and smelled some of the beautiful fragrances. It was so different from the world she had just left. She looked up at the twelve foot tall, golden oak doors that were the entrance to the main building of classrooms. Here I go, she thought, changing my world forever.

She walked through the tall doors and stepped into the shiny hallway. The walls were decorated by numerous paintings done by students. The place reeked of creativity. Alyssa's mind flashed back to the gaudy blacklight pictures that adorned the walls of the strip club where she had worked, and she smiled. It was so different; she had such a feeling of freedom. She had enough money now to live on and pay for her education. She said a small prayer of thankfulness that she had never gotten highly involved in alcohol or drugs. She was thankful she had formed an intimate contact with God with the help of her grandmother when she was six years old. It had served her well. It would serve her well now in her new life.

Alyssa had studied hard as a child and gotten an A-minus aver-age in school. She had made a great escape from her problems. She loved learning and she loved her teachers. Her only regret was that she had waited until she was thirty to attend school again, but at least this way she could concentrate only on her schooling. The time span worked on her psyche as she walked into the classroom.

A brief glance was all she needed to see that all of the students were about ten years younger than her. It didn't matter; she had built up the fortitude. She walked forward and took a seat at the head of the class. She was all business. She was here to learn, and learn she would do.

*****

Poppin lay in bed and thought back to a day long ago at Harrison House.

The image was always the same, never lame, pounding on his brain. Faces in braces, faces ashamed. They looked up at him pleadingly, hoping for relief, hoping tonight they would be able to get some sleep. He must do something for them, make them a promise, put justice in his brain, justice in their hearts.

A small group of two young girls and four boys sat quietly before him in the dank basement. The locked room vibrated with evil. Spider webs crowded the dark surroundings to the far side of the basement. The children couldn't take their eyes off the golden oak door. Poppin knew what had happened to him in there, and he thought for a moment that maybe this was not the best place to meet, but he knew Harrison was out of town, and that Mrs. Larsen would never come down to the basement.

Poppin sat in front of the young children sitting in a semi-circle before him. "I've been reading the Bible, and I've had a revelation. God has inspired me, and he has asked me to be his warrior for you. He has asked me to be a sword of justice, and I am ready for it. I will help all of you get even for what has been done to you."

The frail, youngest girl was only eight, shiny gold braces on her teeth. Sky blue eyes peered through tears. Her blonde hair was in pony tails. Her face already showed signs of the beautiful young woman she would one day be. Heartache shown on her face, dark circles underneath her eyes. She had been moved to Harrison House, and she was now far away from her abuser, but the memories, the shame, lingered.

Poppin walked forward and put his hands gently around her face. "You are not to blame for anything that went on, it's as simple as that. You must believe me."

The youngest girl sobbed before finally bringing herself under control. "If I believe that what he did was wrong, how is he going to have to pay for it? Who is going to make him pay? I feel bad all the time. I feel dirty all of the time. I didn't want to do any of those things he made me do."

Poppin's heart went out to her. "I promise you justice someday. I promise you."

The young girl wiped the wet tears from her cheeks. "I wish he were dead."

Poppin stepped back and smiled. He felt he had to do something to ease the pain in these young children and make them feel safer. In his head and heart he made a decision that would change his life. In a voice deep with fear and rage, he spoke. "I will kill him for you, someday, when I am older, I will avenge what he has done to you."

The young girl smiled. The other girl was two years older than the first one. Her dark brown eyes rested pleadingly on Poppin's, but she said nothing. He stepped forward and stroked her soft, long, brown hair. "I will take care of your abuser as well." The girl smiled.

Poppin looked at the four young boys sitting silently in the semi-circle. He wondered what was going through their minds, when the oldest of the boys, who was twelve, broke the silence. "Killing is wrong."

Poppin stepped back and eyed each of the boys individually. They each met his gaze in turn, their eyes a mixture of fear and acceptance. They hated their abusers, one and all.

Poppin knelt down before the small group. "We have to all be together on this. We have to all agree. I know you all think that murder is wrong, but these men can't get away with what

they've done to all of your lives. I hate them for it, and I promise all of you, they will all pay for what they've done. We can
make a pact now, a secret pact, and I will carry it out. I promise
all of you. There will be justice. Justice by their deaths. You
will always know that they never got away with it."

The children all looked into Poppin's eyes. He expected them
all to look away, but none of them did. The uneven events of
their early lives left room for experimentation. It left room for
them to make decisions based on their own fear and hatred.

After a long silence, the oldest boy of twelve years of age
spoke up. "I agree, we all agree, the men should die." The oldest boy looked sideways at each of his male partners. The girls
he knew had already agreed.

Poppin's smiled at the group. He pulled a small writing tablet
out of his back pocket.

"You need to all write down the names of your abusers and
where the abuse happened, where the abuser lives, and what they
do for a living."

Poppin scribbled on the tablet for a few minutes and then
handed the tablet to the younger girl at the left end of the group.
One by one the children wrote down all of the details and signed
the paper below their information.

When they were done, Poppin held the tablet out in front of
them. "This is our pact then. You must never tell anyone.
When the time comes, when I am old enough, I promise myself,
and I promise all of you that each of these men will die for what
they have done to you. When it is all done, I will send word to
each of you that it is done."

The oldest boy spoke up. "When, when will it be done?"

Poppin sighed. "It will be a long time. It will be many years
from now."

Poppin stood, stepped back and reached his arms out to both
sides with the palms of his hands spread out and facing up.
"Join me now in this vow of vengeance."

The children stood up and joined hands with Poppin in a circle.

Poppin bowed his head. "God, we vow that we will seek vengeance from these men who have abused each and every one of

of us. I will be your tool of destruction as you have commanded me to be. We vow a pledge of silence. All of us in this group will never tell anyone about what has happened here tonight. We will now live our lives in peace and tranquility, knowing that one day your vengeance will be served upon these men. Each of you must promise to honor this vow."

One by one, the children answered. "I promise."

Poppin smiled. "Vengeance is mine sayeth the Lord. Go now and live your lives in peace."

The group, hands still joined felt a great presence of peace. It seemed God had truly joined their little circle, but they knew so little of God that it didn't matter. In any regards, they felt a burden lifted. They would be avenged. They believed Poppin, and a great pressure seemed to be lifted from their lives. There would be some peace now. Someday, they knew, they would be avenged.

But what about now, the children wondered. What about Harrison.

"I'm still scared," the youngest girl stammered. "I'm still afraid of Harrison."

Poppin laughed. "I will stop him. I will confront him and make him leave each and every one of you alone."

"How will you do it?" The oldest boy said.

"Don't worry, I will do it."

Poppin was true to his word. He protected the children like a guard dog. He confronted Harrison, and Harrison was afraid the truth would get out. He left the six children alone. After all, Harrison had thought, there were plenty of children passing through the home. Poppin and the children would soon be sent somewhere else and there would be so many other children, so many others.

Poppin shook his head and stared at the highway to bring himself back to reality. Harrison was gone now, and one of the other abusive men. He was happy about this. He was carrying out the promise he had made so many years ago.

But today, today was a day for happiness. He would visit the neighborhood where he grew up until he was eight years old and his life, his parent's lives, had fallen apart. He would find some of his old neighbors and make them happy. Today, he had decided, today would be a day for happiness.

An hour long drive from Madison and Poppin was taking the Thirty-Fifth street exit. He drove to Seventh and Cherry Street. Getting out of the Benz, his new hair corn-rows shone and twisted half-way across his head. The shiny hair gel made them gleam like lightning bolts in the bright evening sun.

Poppin walked up to the front of the old, high-rise apartment building. The sidewalk in front of the building was loaded with litter. A small mouse scurried beneath a McDonald's hamburger wrapper. It seemed little had changed since Poppin grew up here as a small boy. He opened the front door and entered the dimly lit hallway. Gang signs flooded the walls in every direction. He felt right at home. He gingerly walked up the stairs, touching the walls and feeling the remembrance of being home, the only real home he had ever known.

He wondered if some of the old neighbors would still be there. He decided to visit them first. He would save the visit to his old apartment until last. He walked down to the end of the hall and knocked at the last door. He hoped Mrs. Benson was still there. How old would she be now, probably in her early seventies? He heard a shuffling noise inside. Behind the closed door he heard, "Who the hell could be bothering me now. I never get guests."

The door opened slowly and the plump face of a white-haired, old, black woman looked out under the chain. The woman was barely over five feet tall and must have weighed nearly three hundred pounds.

The old woman grunted. "Who the hell are you, and what do you want?"

Poppin smiled. "Remember me?"

The old woman squinted her eyes. "I don't know, I don't see very good. Bring your face closer."

Poppin leaned forward, his face nearly touching the chain. The decrepit woman leaned forward until it seemed she would be face to face with her visitor. A wide smile slowly crossed her face when she began to see the face of the boy in the man. "Poppin, my beloved Poppin, is that you?"

"Yes, Mrs. Benson, it is me."

The old woman removed the chain and swung the door wide. She laughed in gleeful mirth. "Come in boy, it's nice to see you. I've missed you so."

Memories flooded into Poppin as he watched the woman waddle slowly away and into the living room. The room bore tattered furniture of an era long gone by. It was the same furniture that had never been new when the woman first owned it. Patches of cotton filling showed here and there on the arms of the furniture. Poppin remembered sitting in the overstuffed, soft couch and being comforted even more by the woman's overstuffed arms when he was young. He had come here to hide out when his mother and father had fought. It was always safe and cozy here, a direct opposite to the violence and hatred that always erupted when his parents had fought.

The woman's paunchy face smiled, her eyes radiated the same loving warmth he had known as a child. She wore a flowery smock dress, and she smelled of flower and grease. Poppin realized that she had been baking. He had always loved her fresh cookies and sweet rolls.

"I've just baked some cookies, would you like some with a glass of milk?" Mrs. Benson beamed.

"That would be wonderful," Poppin answered happily.

He watched the woman's behind as she shuffled towards the kitchen. She still walked with surprising briskness for a woman of her size and age. When she returned she set a glass of milk on the coffee table and handed Poppin a tray of freshly baked chocolate chip cookies. The sweet smell of the cookies quickly permeated the air. Poppin looked in the old woman's face and saw a white, chalky glaze in the woman's left eye. Her right eye gleamed with a sunny happiness. He took the tray from her, and she went to sit down in the plush lavender easy chair opposite him.

Poppin took a bite of a cookie, and it melted in his mouth. He was flooded with one of the happier memories from his childhood. "How have you been?"

"I'm been pretty good, I'm pretty healthy except for this damn eye. I've got cataracts in it, and I don't see so good out of it anymore, but what about you? I've seen you in the newspapers and on television a few times. You're a big-shot now, a record producer, huh."

"Yes, I'm doing alright, getting bigger all of the time. Anyway, I'm here to thank you, to thank you for being there for me when I was young. For showing me some of the only love I have ever known. I remember you that way, as someone who loved me."

"Oh, Poppin yes, dear boy, I always loved you. I tried to be there for you and do the best I could by you, but your parents, they were always so messed up and so hard to work around. I did the best I could to let you know you could still be loved," the old woman sighed.

"You did fine; you did a great job of it. I still remember your love, and now, I want to help you."

"What could you do young man? I'm old now. Nothing much can be done for me."

"I don't see it that way. Plenty can be done for you. I want to help you see better. We've got to get that left eye fixed."

"I can't afford it Poppin, and it don't matter much now. I'm old. I'll be gone soon."

"No, you're going to see the world clearly again. I'm going to see to that. I'll call and get you in to see an eye specialist. You don't have to worry. Before you die, you're going to see the world clearly again. I'll pay for it. You deserve it."

"Oh Poppin, I love you dear boy."

"I love you too Mrs. Benson. I'll make an appointment for you next week. Have you ferried back and forth, have you visited by a nurse, everything. I want to give you this gift. I want to make your life better as you made mine better when I was young."

"You're a good boy Poppin, a good boy."

Poppin and Mrs. Benson talked for an hour before Poppin excused himself with the promise to visit again. There was another tenant in his old apartment building that he wanted to see before the night got too old.

From the sound of the footsteps in the hallway Poppin could tell that whoever was moving along was moving at a brisk pace. The door opened freely, and the thin, skeletal looking frame of a wrinkled, old, white man stood in the opening. Bright, shiny, blue eyes peered out through a mass of long wrinkles on his face. His thin, wiry body showed no trace of withdrawal or fear.

"You're not afraid to open the door to a stranger?" Poppin asked.

"I don't care, I don't live with fear, besides, ain't never no strangers knock at this door. Come on in."

Poppin followed the man into the kitchen.

The skeleton that was Mr. Thomas turned to the refrigerator. "Want a beer?"

"Yes, a beer would be fine," Poppin answered. "Do you know who I am?"

"Yes, oh yes, you're Poppin. I could never forget that smile of yours. I always loved your little smile."

Poppin wondered how the old man had instantly known who he was. He was becoming used to hiding his identity, to living in a shadow, but there was no doubt here, the old man had identified him immediately. The old man handed Poppin a beer and sat at the kitchen chair opposite him.

"I hear you're getting quite famous."

"Yes, I guess I am," Poppin flushed.

"It's nice to see you're not all stuck up. It's nice to see you take time to visit an old friend, and let me tell you man, I am old."

"How old are you now?"

"I'm eighty-three," the old man said as he took a camel straight out of a cigarette package.

"I see you still smoke, and I guess you drink plenty too."

"Yeah, always have. After you helped me get off crack, and man you were little, but you sure had guts. Anyway, after you

helped me get off crack so many years ago, I never quit smokin'
or drinkin'. I guess I'm just a weak man."

Poppin took a sip of his beer. "I'm here to thank you."

"You, thank me, it's me who should be thanking you."

"I know what you mean, but the bond that formed between us
when you quit crack, when you believed in me for what I said it
could mean to your life. That meant a lot to me. I never forgot
that you believed enough in me to do that. It's more than my
parents ever did for me."

"It was a good thing. It seems we both benefited from that,
didn't we?"

"Well, I'm here to thank you, is there anything I can do for
you?"

"No, nothin' really, I don't need nothin'."

"Here's the deal, this is for you," Poppin said as he pulled ten
one hundred dollar bills out of his pocket. I want you to have a
good time, an easy time for awhile."

"Poppin', this is bad, I'll just spend it on beer and cigarettes."

"That's okay, whatever you like, just enjoy yourself and don't
overdo all at once."

"You the man Poppin, you the man," the old man laughed.

"Something else I'm going to do for you. I saw that old console television in the living room as we passed through. That
thing must be forty years old. The picture looks like hell. I'm
going to have a new plasma screen television sent up to you."

"What's a plasma screen television?"

"You'll see when you get it, you'll love it, they're the newest
thing and they're wonderful."

Mr. Thomas looked down at the table and brushed the bald top
of his head. "Why are you being so kind?"

Poppin paused and took another sip of beer. "Let's just say I'm
trying to do a little cosmic equalizing. I haven't always done
good things, but these things I'm doing today, let's just say, I've
been evening a lot of scores lately."

"That's a good thing, a life must have balance."

"Yeah, balance it is. Enjoy your money, your beer and smokes,
and your new television. Enjoy the rest of your life."

Poppin finished his beer, hugged Mr. Thomas goodbye, and headed back out into the hallway. He walked along and stopped in front of the door to his old apartment. He wondered what lie behind the door. Who lived there now? What memories would surface when he went inside? He knew there would be bad memories, but would there be, could there be, any good ones.

Poppin looked at the door to the apartment. It had been freshly varnished when he was a child, but now the varnish had yellowed and was peeling badly. Numerous scratch marks ran haphazard patterns all across the wood. Poppin knocked gently on the door, stepped back, and held his breath.

No answer came from within.

Poppin knocked harder and was surprised he was saying a little prayer that he would be let in. He hadn't realized how badly he wanted to see the apartment. After a few moments, he heard a shuffling of footsteps coming towards the door.

A timid female voice spoke out. "Who's there?"

Poppin spoke calmly. "My name is Poppin. I used to live here. I was wondering if you would be so kind as to let me in to see the place again."

A short silence pursued before the timid voice responded. "How do I know I can trust you?"

"Surely you must have heard of me. I'm a record producer. I don't mean any harm; I just have a real need right now to see the place where I grew up."

The sound of metal on metal penetrated the air as the latch was slid back. The door opened to the sight of a thin, five-foot-two black girl who looked to be about twenty years of age. A broad smile crossed her face. Two ponytails bounced when she shifted her head to get a better look at the man who stood before her. The young woman sighed. "I've got nothing to lose. I've already lost everything. Come on in."

The young woman turned and walked down the hall with Poppin following her. They entered a large living room that was scattered with rag-tag mismatched furniture. The young girl plopped down on the couch and looked at Poppin. "Have a seat."

70

Poppin sat in a large, green recliner opposite the couch. Though the room was a large sixteen by twenty-two feet, it seemed smaller to him now that he was a full grown man. The room had seemed monstrous when he was a boy. He looked forward and over the couch where the girl sat and saw the faded green curtains over the two double-hung windows. They were the same curtains that had hung there when he was a boy. Between the windows, he saw a water-color painting. He was astonished to see that it was the same painting that his father had hung there many years ago.

Poppin got up and walked over to take a closer look at the art-work that his father had created. The painting had a large oak tree in the center that was bright orange in its full fall foliage. The painting contained little else but a few almost indefinable brushstrokes of curvy hill and fence. He smiled to himself when he remembered how much comfort the painting had always brought him. He had often wondered how a mean drunk like his father could have created something he saw as beautiful.

The memories flooded back in a tidal wave of confusion and misery. It was in this very room in front of that very painting that Poppin's father had taken a gun to Poppin's head. He was so small then, only six years of age. The crime was leaving his socks on the floor. His father was raging drunk, staggering around the room and slurring his words. Poppin had the habit of pulling his socks off inside out. When the old man had to do the wash, he had built up a great resentment at having to spend ten or fifteen minutes picking up the socks and turning them all right side out so they could be washed. This time the drunken rage had swelled out of control. He put the gun to Poppin's head, and told him to never leave a sock on the floor again. Poppin remembered the fear and how the tears had poured from his eyes to cover his face. He could almost feel them now. He remembered the feel of the cold steal against his temple, the click of the gun. The sound of the empty chamber. He still imagined the sound of a gun going off when he had flashbacks. He remembered the feeling that he was dead, and the evil, sardonic laugh

71

that came from his father when he declared that damn, he had forgotten to load the gun.

Poppin had moved back over to the couch and sat very still the rest of the night as he watched his father drink until he passed out. He went over to the rust-colored overstuffed chair his father sat in and picked up the gun from the floor. He knew the gun was empty, but he picked it up anyway and put the gun to his father's temple. He heard the loud click of the empty chamber, and imagined his father's brains being splattered all over the chair and floor. Next time you son of a bitch, he thought, this ever happens again, the next time, I'll find the bullets and load the gun. Next time, the gun will be loaded, the gun will kill. Poppin calmed himself and breathed deeply as he turned around and went back to sit on the green recliner opposite the young woman.

The young woman smiled. "That painting was always there. It was there when we moved in. I like it. I left it be."

"My father painted that painting. I always liked it too."

"Oh, you're father was an artist."

"No, not really, well yes, he dabbled a little, but mostly he was a drunk."

The young girl smiled weakly. "My dad was a drunk too. A very abusive drunk. I married young to get out of the home. Too young, I guess, because my man took off and left me and my child here."

"You have a child?"

"Yes, Latisha. She is sleeping right now."

"And what is your name?"

"My name is LaToya. My father named me after LaToya Jackson. He always loved the Jackson Five."

A small whimper of a cry began to emanate from the other room.

"That's my baby. She's waking up. It looks like nap time is over. I'll have to go and get her."

"Can I come with you? I'd like to see the bedroom."

"Sure, follow me."

Poppin walked into the bedroom and his eyes widened when he saw the nursery. It was obvious the young girl hadn't had much money to decorate, but the room was covered with colorful ribbons and bows. She had painted stars on the ceiling and one wall was covered with numerous painted animals. The paintings looked like something out of a child's book.

Poppin watched the girl pick up a baby dressed in a pink nightshirt. "This room is very well done. It looks like you have some of the artist in you."

"Yes, I have always liked to draw. I wanted my baby to have a nice room. I think it is."

"Yes, it's very nice," Poppin agreed.

Poppin watched as the young girl took the child to the changing table and began to change her diapers. He looked around the room, the room that had once been his. A bad memory of his cowering in the corner trying to get away from his father tried to crowd in, but as soon as he looked at the wild animals on the wall, the memory was nudged out.

LaToya turned and smiled at Poppin. "Would you like to hold the baby?"

"Yes, yes, I would," Poppin was surprised to find himself saying.

As he stood in the center of his old room, it seemed that all the bad memories that had existed were banished. He looked down at the smiling, drooling infant in his hands and all he could think of was life. Life and death, so intertwined. So important in the grand scheme of things. He handed the child back to the young girl before the battle raged out of control within him. He had not expected to find innocent happiness in his old room, yet here it was.

Poppin followed the young girl back to the living room, and they both took their seats again. A sudden look of fear came over LaToya's face.

Poppin leaned forward and spoke gently. "What's the matter; you aren't afraid of me, are you?"

"No, it's not you; it's just that I'm worried about what I'm going to do. My boyfriend is gone. Just vanished. He's been gone two months now and there's no money left. I'm going to be evicted and I need food. I don't know what I'm going to do. I've been trying to get a job, but I can't find one. I just don't know what I'm going to do." LaToya began sobbing.

Poppin got up and went over to sit beside LaToya and the baby on the couch. Gently, he brought up his right hand and rubbed the back of her shoulder. "I will help you. I will help you right now, and I will give you a job working in my production company."

LaToya brought herself under control. "Why, why would you want to help me?"

"Let's just say that I'm really happy with what you have done with the place. I like the feeling of love and life that you have given to it. I want to help you."

Poppin pulled ten one hundred dollar bills out of his pocket and laid them on the couch next to Latoya.

LaToya's eyes grew wide. "I don't know how I can ever thank you."

"You just raise that child right, just like you have been. Teach her to be a good woman. Here's my card with my office number on it. Call my secretary at the office on Monday. I will tell her ahead of time that you will be calling. You can train as her assistant."

"Thank you, thank you so much, but who is going to watch my baby," LaToya said as she began crying again.

"There's an old man across the hall, and an old woman down the hall, I'm sure they would be more than happy to help you out. Just tell them Poppin sent you. Now dry your eyes, go talk to them, go out and get some food. Rest and relax. You're going to be okay."

"How can I thank you for this?" LaToya said after she brought herself under control.

"Just raise your young lady there with love and kindness. Teach her to be a good woman. That will be thanks enough for me."

LaToya rose as Poppin got up to leave. She was still holding the child in her arms when she gave Poppin a big hug. He hugged back softly, and a small tear came to his eyes. He left and closed the door behind him. Tears flowed freely now. Life and death, so intertwined. This time it was life.

Chapter 5

Collins walked up to the short, thin, sexy blonde at the water cooler and grabbed a paper cup from the rack. The young woman stepped aside and took a long drink of the cool water in her cup. Her eyes twinkled with delight. Collins smiled back and turned to draw his cup of water.

He found himself at a loss for words as he stepped back and looked deeply into the sparkling hazel eyes of the young woman. An intense sexual bond sparked between the young couple. The intensity of the feelings surprised both of them.

The young woman reached out and touched Collins gently on the shoulder. "How are you this morning?"

"I'm fine, couldn't be better. I think I'm finally adjusting to this job. I'm getting the feeling that every day is normal, though, of course, in this business I guess there will never be a normal day," Collins replied.

The young woman continued to smile broadly. "Yes, but that will mean the job is never boring, though at times it will feel like it is all consuming."

"And what about you, secretarial stuff, don't you find that boring?"

"Oh no, maybe in a regular business job I would, but around this place, there is always something happening. So many things to get ready, so many things to pore over, so much access to confidential information about ongoing cases. In a way it's like I'm writing or living inside of a detective television show. I love it."

"What is your name?" Collins asked.

"Mary, Mary Foxmore."

Collins laughed. "I must say, that is a very fitting name."

Even though the young woman had heard the come-on many times in her life, she remained polite. "Well, that is very nice of you to say, and oh, I already know your name of course."

Collins stood frozen for a moment, not knowing what to say. He stared into the bright, twinkling, loving eyes of the young woman and after a long pause filled with lust, he broke the silence. "I'll be spending the day in the office today, would you like to come over to my apartment for dinner tonight?"

The young woman didn't hesitate a second. "Yes, that would be fine."

"Okay, I'll meet you back here at the water cooler around five o'clock. Do you have your own car?"

"No, I ride the bus every day."

"Great, then I'll just drive us over to my place in the bureau vehicle."

The young woman beamed as she shook Collin's hand. "It's a deal then, see you back here at five."

Collins beamed with pride. What a cliché, he thought, a date made at the water cooler. He wondered if he should be doing this. He already had a girlfriend he was quite fond of, but as he watched the shapely blonde walk away from him down the hallway he knew he had made the right choice. There was something very electrical between them. Something he knew he had to explore more fully. It would be a long day of trying to keep his mind on his work.

Collins spent the day studying crime scene evidence and reports. At the end of the day, he was surprised to find that the young woman hadn't crossed his mind for several hours. The grizzly photos had indeed been very distracting. As five o'clock approached he found his heartbeat quickening and his hands becoming sweaty. He felt like a young teenager who was nervous about asking a girl out on a first date. He wondered what it was about this young woman that triggered such emotions in him. He guessed it was that she was so very attractive, and those eyes, he could not stop remembering the shining brightness of love that dwelled so deeply inside those eyes. He chided himself for thinking that this woman might be the one. The one we all search for and hope will someday enter our lives to fulfill that missing half of ourselves.

After a pleasant dinner date with Mary, Collins walked into his apartment and took a seat in the large, gray, plush recliner. He put his feet up and relaxed almost immediately. Even from the distance of ten feet, he could see the thick dust that had gathered on the shelves of the entertainment center on the opposite side of the room. He could see the dust gathering on the Nina, the Pinta, and the Santa Maria, the three ships that were the pride and joy of his fleet of twenty model ships that lined all the shelves on the entertainment center and six shelves lining the wall next to it. He had been building these ships since the age of nine. These were his first, and they would always be his favorite. Over the years it was getting harder to find ready-made model kits, so his half a dozen most recent ships were made entirely from diagrams that he obtained on the internet. Now it was getting more difficult to find a ship that he hadn't already built, and he had begun work on a new ship that was entirely of his own creation. This he knew was going to be his new pride and joy. When he finished with it he would buy a special glass case for it and display it under lights, directly to the right of the entertainment center.

Collins looked around at the Maritime accompaniments that filled the rest of the apartment, the heavy sea rope and anchor, the paintings of old ships and rough seas. He wondered sometimes what it would be like to live as a sailor in the days of old. It was this sense of adventure that had brought him to the FBI. It hadn't hurt that he had spent six years in the Navy, but the modern Navy wasn't what he wanted. He longed for the days of old and so he got out. He decided he would change his work life and stay buried as much as possible in his hobby. He had done well on all of his tests, reviews, and even risen quickly in rank while in the Navy, so he was readily taken into the FBI training school at Quantico.

Sadness overcame Collins as he looked at the dust gathering on the pieces of wood that were being worked for the new ship. He hadn't thought the FBI work would be so overwhelmingly time consuming. He had thought he'd have more time off, and more time to himself. But this, his first case was grueling in the hours that it demanded of him. Maybe after it was solved there would be some time to get back to his hobby, but then he remembered the large stack of unsolved cases he had looked through and wondered if there really would be time in the future.

Getting a cold beer from the refrigerator, he sat down in the easy chair, and began to think about the young blonde at work. Was this really what he wanted? Was there any way he could fit a woman into his life on top of everything else. He looked forlornly at the unfinished wood that lay on the table. He had the unnerving feeling that it would be laying there unfinished for a very long time.

*****

Wendtworth and Collins drove north through heavy traffic. Collins turned slowly onto the city of Berlin's main street, and his eyes opened with wonder at the beauty of the Christmas decorations that lay before him. Every block, all down the length of Main Street there crossed a decoration of holly with intermittent lights. Hanging from each light pole and at the center of each crossing band was a large Christmas tree type ornament of four feet in length. The decorations across the main street made the town look as though it itself were a Christmas tree.

Collins gasped. "This is absolutely beautiful!"

Wendtworth let out a small whistle. "I'll say, these decorations must be brand new. I have never seen them before. They look so shiny and bright."

Shifting slightly in his seat, Collins sighed. "I don't like to see Christmas at Thanksgiving, but this really doesn't bother me a bit, it's just so beautiful, it's wonderful to see it."

Joan laughed. "Well don't worry, you're mind will get back to Thanksgiving quickly when we enter my sister's house and smell the wonderful smells of the holiday. My sister and mother are excellent cooks."

The silver LTD cruised down a simple suburban street, a street like millions of others across the United States. The homes were like so many others in small suburban America. Homes formed from a lifetime of work and steady, simple upkeep. It was a place where people were always proud of where they lived. Joan's sister's house was no exception. The two story home on East Berlin Street was well kept up. Some of the Christmas decorations were already up. A couple of elves played happily in the front yard with a large Santa in the middle, and there was a bright white mini-light tree strung on wire to look like a tree off to the side. Joan smiled. She knew that in a week or so the decorations would quadruple in size. Her sister's husband was just getting started.

Wendtworth and Collins entered the house through the door by the side of the garage and found themselves directly in the kitchen. The smell of Turkey blasted their nostrils. The underlying smell of freshly baked pumpkin and chocolate pie made Collins' stomach grumble. How he loved desert, loved pie, with lots of whip cream on top of it. He felt sad for a moment that he couldn't be with his own parents who had gone out of the country for a holiday trip this Thanksgiving, but he realized that this was going to be a great place to be, a great place to make up for his loneliness.

Joan's brother Allen sat at the far end of the kitchen table, his voice rising above everything. He was talking about how little some plant supervisor knew about the work he had done on the previous nightshift. Allen was five-foot ten inches tall and was a stocky two hundred and fifty pounds. His arms were huge and strong. He had bleary looking hazel eyes that were full of happiness and rage all at the same time. He had once gotten his hair caught in the gears of a machine at the age of nineteen and ripped a four by six inch swatch of hair out of the center of his forehead, but one would never know, for his dishwater-blonde hair was still full and thick. Only now, at the age of fifty-two, the blondeness was beginning to give way to gray highlights. Allen worked night-time maintenance in a local factory, and he

81

was very proud of how he had done next to nothing on a ten hour shift. He was also obviously quite drunk.

Joan had warned Collins about this on the drive down so he was expecting it. Wendtworth and Collins took their seat at the table to the left of Joan's brother. Things quieted down for awhile but it wasn't long before Joan's brother was back on the same subject. He would cover this subject a dozen times in the next hour, repeating himself with almost the same words over and over as only a very drunk person will do. Joan just looked at Collins, gave him a small smile, and shrugged.

Allen took a turkey gizzard into his mouth and began to talk again. He leaned forward on the table and a large blast of watery fluid and food flew from his mouth directly onto the table in front of Wendtworth. Joan pushed herself slightly back from the table and forced herself to swallow the mouthful of food she had been chewing. Allen leaned forward and let forth another blast of fluids. Joan had to force herself not to throw-up right along with him. Collins and Wendtworth looked at each other and chuckled, but then noticed that Allen was turning severely red and couldn't breathe.

Allen pushed himself up from the table and croaked out the words. "I can't breathe."

Joan was unable to calm herself. She sat frozen at the table. Collins did the same. It was Joan's sister Christine who had quick wits about her. Christine rushed up from her chair and around the table. She quickly grabbed Allen in the Heimlich maneuver and forced the turkey gizzard out of his throat. In a matter of only a few minutes Allen had gotten his breath back and his normal color was returning.

After a half an hour everyone settled down and dinner was finished. Joan did not go back for seconds, but she noticed that Collins had no trouble filling his plate a second and third time. She laughed to herself, bachelors; it wasn't often a spread like this one was laid before them. Collins was going to eat no matter what.

It was a quiet ride back to Madison, the tryptophan in the turkey was doing its job. Collins slept like a baby that night. Joan tossed and turned in her bed. There was still a serial killer on the loose, and there had to be some way she could find out who it was.

There was also a sexy young man sleeping on the couch in the living room, and what, she wondered, was she going to do about that.

Sonnentag

Chapter 6

Goin' down, goin' down, another man goin' down. Justice was comin' for him, Poppin's justice. Cold, hard-blooded killer on the loose. It was time for another perpetrator to go down. There was no room for innocence or denial in his world. Justice would be served at the end of a gun barrel.

Poppin stood in the back of the church and craned his neck to get a good view of Father Iman.

"Our Father, who art in heaven.........," the priest spoke with hands outstretched facing towards the small gathering in front of him. The weekday morning mass was always so poorly attended. In a congregation of nine hundred people there were only about twenty regulars in attendance at the morning mass.

Poppin slunk back into the shadows as an old woman passed him by. She gave him a brief glance on her way to the restroom. She was seldom able to control her bladder for long now that she was eighty years old. The old woman's eyes widened when she saw the black man standing in the back of the church. She didn't know of any black people in the congregation.

Poppin cowered down and tried to hide, but it was impossible. What did it matter? The woman could never know what he was there for. Poppin made sure of his identification of the priest and quickly turned to leave. It was easy to make the identification. In the current day, with shortages of priests, this priest was the only one that served the parish.

From previous surveillances, Poppin knew what the priest would do next. A half an hour after services, the priest would be walking through the alleyway between the tan, stone church and the old school that had been abandoned for use many years ago.

He would be walking slowly and reading from his Bible, eyes fixed downward. The day was a perfect, sunny, seventy degrees. It was a perfect day for a meditation stroll.

Poppin was not disappointed as he slipped into the alleyway. The fifty year old priest was walking slowly towards him, eyes down on his Bible. The priest stopped abruptly when Poppin stepped up in front of him.

"Are you Father Iman?" Poppin asked.

"Yes, I am," the simple answer came quietly

The priest spoke softly. "I feel a great deal of evil present."

Poppin snickered, "Is the evil in me or in you?"

"Young man, I have made peace with the evil within me. I don't know if I can say the same thing about you."

Poppin froze. He was unable to move to put his hand under his suit jacket and pull out the pistol. He saw too much peace in the man's eyes. Poppin looked down at the Bible in the man's hands and brought his quickened breathing under control. Promises had been made. The deal was done long ago. The man had to come down.

Poppin reached under his jacket and pulled the thirty-eight out. He pointed it directly at the man's chest just as the priest pulled the Bible up over his heart. The bullet struck the Bible. White flakes of paper covered the priests black cassock around where he still held the Bible. Amazement crossed the faces of the two men. The priest raised the Bible up and over to look at the front cover where the bullet had struck.

The priest spoke slowly. "God has had mercy on my soul."

Poppin recovered quickly. "Maybe so far, but you're sure going to find out if he will in the end." He fired a second shot just below where the priest held the Bible. The bullet shattered the priest's cassock and hit him directly in the heart. The priest slumped to the ground, the Bible landing at Poppin's feet.

Poppin stared at the Bible a moment. He almost bent to pick it up, but decided not to. He reached into the paper shopping bag he carried in his left arm and pulled out a bag of white bone meal. He sprinkled it liberally over the body of the priest, paused a moment, and then spread the powder over the Bible as well. He turned from the priest and walked slowly away.

Back inside the Taurus, Poppin felt lost in another world. He fumbled for his keys and started the car. He drove slowly away, his mind seeming to be in some state of meditation. Good and evil, so mixed up, so intertwined. He felt for the first time that he was indeed evil. Evil begets evil, he thought, and that was the end of his meditation. As he leaned back in the seat to make himself more comfortable an image popped into his head. He could see the young faces gathered around him in a semi-circle, faces age seven to thirteen, four boys, and two girls. Faces that were pleading for help, for justice. He heard himself making the promise, and then he let the faces fade from his mind. When he drove off in his gold Taurus he swallowed an Oxy and cracked open a beer. It would be a quiet, peaceful ride home.

*****

Shawn Jones sat in the grass, picking up blades of green and rolling them through his fingers. He looked down and there it was. A four-leaf clover. He had spent hours looking through the grass by Harrison House. One trip to Madison, sitting outside of Joan Wendtworth's apartment, and there it was. It stood up high and strong, a full two inches above the rest of the grass. Shawn picked the clover, pulled out his wallet and carefully put the clover between the plastic sheeting inside. He was careful to make sure the center of the four strands was not broken, and that they remained visible.

It seemed his luck was due to change, but he wondered what Joan would think of his being here once she arrived. He had the clover now, and somehow, he knew everything was going to turn out all right.

Collins pulled the gold Taurus to the curb in front of Joan's apartment. He put a frozen stare on Shawn. He didn't recognize him at first, but when he did, his stare turned into a frown.

Collins stammered. "Do you want any help with him?"

Joan looked at the young man sitting in the grass playing with the blades. "No, that won't be necessary. I'll take care of this little problem myself." She could barely hide the excitement in her voice.

Collins shrugged and pulled away once Joan had exited the vehicle. Joan walked slowly up the sidewalk; she stepped off the walk and stood directly in front of and over Shawn. "What are you doing here?"

Shawn looked into Joan's eyes. "I turned eighteen last week. I'm free to live on my own now. I really have no place to go, so I thought I could stay with you awhile." Shawn had gotten right to the point.

Joan smiled. "Come on. We'll talk about it inside."

The couple approached the front door, stopped, and looked down at the large green duffle bag that sat on the steps. The four foot long, tattered bag contained all of Shawn's worldly belongings.

Shawn let out a deep sigh. "That's it. That's my life, all there is to it."

"I'm sure you're exaggerating. I know there's a lot more to you than what's in that bag," Joan answered.

Joan's living room was decorated in black, modern decor furniture. The glass-top end tables had black legs and sides. A large, black lamp with arms that extended up to the ceiling and out about six feet into the room sat arcing its way out of the far corner. A black-faced stereo rested below the long arms. A soft, black velvet couch sat on the opposite wall.

Shawn threw his bag down next to the couch and took a seat. He leaned back and breathed a heavy sigh of relief. He felt confident that he would be staying in this apartment.

Joan spoke firmly. "I'll get right to the point. What makes you think that I'm going to let you stay here?"

Shawn didn't hesitate. "I get a good feeling out of you. I think you're one of those women who would readily take in a stray cat. Well, I'm a little more than that, but I think you're the kind of a woman who is willing to take a chance and help a young fellow who's trying to make his way."

Joan laughed. "You think you have me pegged pretty well. What gives you that idea?"

"I don't know, I guess it's just that when I look into your eyes, I see warmth, love, and giving there. I don't know if it would exist for everyone, but I can see that it exists for me."

Joan crossed her arms. "You're right. I don't know what it is about you, but I know that I trust you, and I know that I'm ready to help you out. I don't know why, but I know that I am ready to help you."

Joan sat down on the couch next to Shawn. She put her right hand on his left knee. She gazed deeply into his eyes. She could feel a heat rise in her and the young man next to her. She had to slow this down. It was a big decision, but it seemed she had already made it. She was incapable of making any other decision, but she had to slow herself down. She had to slow this down in case it really was a mistake.

Joan took a deep breath. "I'll make you something to eat. You must be hungry."

"I sure am, I've been sitting outside for three hours waiting for you, but a miracle happened."

"A miracle, what was that?" Joan asked incredulously.

"I found a four-leaf clover. Everything is going to be fine now. God answered my prayer. He proved to me that my luck is going to change."

"Yes, I believe that. Everything will be all right for you. I really believe that. Just relax. I'll make us something to eat."

Joan rose and went to the kitchenette. Her head was swimming with possibilities.

Shawn sat back and relaxed on the couch. He was happy that he had found such a caring woman, even if she was over twenty years older than him. He promised himself he would not take advantage of her, he would not use her; he would be honest and up-front. The situation had all the makings of a relationship, and this scared him. He calmed himself down and pulled a cigarette from his bag. He didn't think of what Joan might say about smoking as he casually lit up.

Joan spread the shrimp chop suey over a bed of rice on two plates and called Shawn to the glass table in the kitchenette. The two ate in silence, glances being exchanged occasionally between bites of food. Each tried to read the others mind, but a web of angst seemed to blind them. They finished their meal in silence.

Shawn cleared his plate at the sink. "I'll sleep on the couch."

"Good, I'll get you a blanket and pillow," Joan said softly.

She looked into Shawn's eyes after she handed him the bedding. "Sleep well," she said simply and turned to go down the hall and enter her bedroom. She closed the door and leaned against it. She thought to herself. What am I doing? What the hell am I doing? She lay down on the bed and pulled the covers up. She did not sleep the entire night.

At dawn she saw Shawn sleeping comfortably on the couch. Still, the thought remained. What the hell was she doing?

*****

Shawn unzipped the long zipper on top of the black duffle bag. He dug beneath the various sports shirts and trunks and came up with two aluminum wrapped bundles. He sat back on the couch and unwrapped the first bundle. The smell was released from captivity and rushed out to slam his nostrils. No other smell like it on earth, the smell of sativa. He almost got high just smelling it. He broke off a small chunk of the weed and put it in his glass pipe.

Shawn loved the first few luscious hits of the high powered weed. The months of pruning, fertilizing, and otherwise tending the plants had been worth it. The weed would sell for four hundred dollars an ounce and it would sell quickly. Out in the marsh by Harrison house, there had never been anyone around. There was so little risk in growing there. People never crossed the marshy bog, but he had found a good way through where the water had not been deep. On the small island of land in the middle of the bog, surrounded by a lot of small birch and poplar trees, the weed had thrived. Now it was all going to be worth it.

Shawn left the second pound in the bag. He pulled out a small digital scale and a box of sandwich baggies. An hour later, he was done, and the first pound of weed was divided into four ounces, eight half ounces, sixteen quarter ounces, and thirty-two eighth ounces. Selling for four hundred dollars an ounce, the eighth ounces alone would be worth fifty dollars each. It was one-hitter quitter and it would sell fast.

The only problem was that he didn't know anyone in Madison. Proceeding with the sales would be risky. He decided to start with a dozen of the eighths. He packed the dozen eighths in a brown lunch bag, grabbed a Pepsi from the fridge and headed for the bus lines.

Forty-five minutes later Shawn was standing on the sidewalk on the strip on Madison Street. The capitol building loomed brightly in the distance. The American flag of freedom flying lightly in a five mile an hour westerly wind coming off Lake Mendota. The strip was lined with college bars and shops. It was seven P.M. on a beautiful, sunny, seventy degree Friday night when he began walking the sidewalk.

The sidewalk was already crowded with young students in varying degrees of inebriation and fixation. Shawn took a position on the sidewalk about twenty feet down from a busy bar. He lit up a pinner joint and let the smoke fill the area. A group of four young men were attracted to the smell.

A lanky, six-foot three, black haired, white boy with a goatee and tattoos running up and down both arms approached him first. "That smells like good weed, let me have a hit."

Shawn passed him the joint, and the young man hit it deeply.

The young man's eyes glassed over, "I want some more."

"Fifty bucks an eighth and it's worth it."

"I can see that. I'll take an eighth."

One of the other young men chimed in quickly that he too would take an eighth. Shawn and the two young men went back down the street to the bar and headed into the bathroom where the exchange was made.

It took three hours, but Shawn was now five hundred dollars richer. He only had two eighths left that he wanted to move this night. He made up his mind to repeat the process the next night if the weather remained good and he even expected a few of his customers to come back and purchase larger amounts. He would switch up; make the bigger exchanges in the park a block down the street. A few of the exchanges would be made in other bars on the strip. He would move a pound quickly, and then stop for a time. Risk was risk and he figured this would be enough.

Shawn walked down the street and stopped on a corner that seemed to be a big crossing point for the young people. He lit up another pinner joint as people passed by in good sized crowds.

A black Mercedes SUV with silver spinners on the wheels pulled up to the curb in front of the crossing. Heavy bass thumped from the rap music playing on the stereo inside. A large black man got out of the vehicle, and the vehicle pulled quickly away. Shawn smiled at the black man as he approached.

The large hulk of a man stood in front of Shawn, his face came up only a few inches away from Shawn's face. Shawn looked at the gold chain hanging on the man's black t-shirt, then up at the glint of a diamond in one of the man's front teeth. He could smell a peach flavored cigar on the man's breath.

Shawn couldn't help but think that this was probably going to be a big sale. He would have to get more weed from Joan's apartment and complete the deal tomorrow.

The man let out a wide grin. "What you doing on our corner?"

"What are you talking about man?" Shawn answered quietly.

"We been watching you for awhile. We don't mind a little traffic innocently passing by on our block, but you seem to be moving quite a bit."

Shawn stepped back a couple of feet. "No, no man, you got it all wrong. I ain't selling no weed."

"First you selling on our block and then you insult me. That ain't good man. That ain't good."

"I, I don't know what to say. I'll move on. I just moved to the city, and I just want to pass some of the stuff I grew out in the country. I don't mean to move in on anybody's territory. I'm done now, the weeds all gone, I'll just get out of here."

"Look, we could really fuck you up, but I'm gonna cut you a break this time country boy. This spot is only going to cost you a hundred dollar bill today."

"Deal, I'm outtie," Shawn handed the black man a hundred dollar bill and then reached out to shake his hand.

"Man, you really are a country boy," the black man responded as he shook Shawn's hand.

The black man reached in his pocket and pushed a button on his beeper. A few moments later the black SUV was back at the curb and the black man climbed inside. "I hope I don't see you again country."

"You won't," Shawn shouted back.

Shawn headed for the bus stop and got on the next bus. It wasn't until he was back at Joan's apartment and sitting on the couch that his heart stopped racing, and he was able to breathe normally again.

Sonnentag

Chapter 7

Alyssa entered Poppin's apartment with a heart heavy with exasperation. She didn't want to be there. Her life had changed. She was a different woman now. She no longer thought of herself as the downtrodden whore who would do anything for a man's affection. For the first time in her life she had made sensible decisions about how to take better care of herself and improve her life, to actually improve her mind and expand her horizons. School was a big step and she had taken it. She could no longer see herself prostrating before Poppin or any man.

Poppin rushed up to Alyssa and gave her a big hug. "How are things going with you? How is school going?"

Alyssa let out a deep sigh. "School is tough, I've been out of high school a long time, and there's so much homework to do in college. They really move things along quickly."

"You're an intelligent woman, you'll do all right," Poppin assured her.

"Thank you," Alyssa smiled meekly.

Poppin sat down in his black, high-back, easy-chair, and Alyssa took a seat on the couch. The couple smiled at each other. They both remembered the shared sex they had always enjoyed. Poppin gave Alyssa a come-hither wink that always meant she would make herself available to him. Alyssa turned and looked down and away. Poppin was confused, what was going on here, he wondered. He paused in thought for a moment and then decided to get more brazen. He got up and walked over to the couch to stand in front of Alyssa. Without saying a word, he dropped his drawers and let his penis hang out. Alyssa smiled and took him in her mouth. What the hell, she did love doing this for someone she cared about. Taking Poppin halfway in, she froze, and a strange, still, deadness, overtook the area surrounding the couple.

Alyssa pulled back. "I can't do this. I just can't do this anymore. This isn't me anymore."

"But, but Alyssa, don't you love me?" Poppin stammered.

Alyssa stood up. "I will always love you in some way, but I just don't love you that way anymore. I can't go on pretending. I have a new life now, and have to live it. I just have to stay with the changes. I just have too."

Poppin was shaken. He had mixed feelings, a sense of incredible loss combined with a small influx of what he could only define as hatred. At the moment, he hated her for abandoning him, especially now when he felt so confused about his life. For a brief instant, he wanted to lash out and hurt her, maybe even kill her. The conflicting thoughts made his head ache. He couldn't hurt her; she had done him no real harm. He knew he had to stand up for himself. He had to remain filled with pride. He also knew he had to let the hatred and anger go. He would continue to love her in some small way. It was the only way he knew of that he could still hang onto some thread of humanity within himself.

Alyssa started heading towards the front door. "I have to go now. I've got to get back home and work on my homework. Sorry, I just don't have time for this anymore."

Poppin sighed loudly. "Fine, just go."

Alyssa ignored the hurt in Poppin's voice and left. She couldn't help but sense that something deep and important in the man had changed, but it was more than that, it was also that she had changed and she now knew it for sure. She was proud of herself as she walked down the sidewalk, jumped in her car, and took off without looking back.

Poppin went over to the bar and mixed a small snifter of brandy. What was he going to do now, he wanted a woman, and he didn't want to be alone. He felt so much more alone since the killings. He was lost inside of himself. He remembered Latoya, the young black girl with the daughter who lived in the building where he used to live. He decided that when he finished his brandy, he would go see her.

Poppin pulled the black Benz up in front of Latoya's building, now was the time to strut, hold nothing back. He knew he had made inroads with the young woman when he had given her money. He realized this had been the thing to do, at the time he was feeling generous, but now, he hoped that generosity would pay off. He felt like a total pimp. It made him feel good. He needed to relax and let his mind swirl with good times. He needed to be loved, to feel love, to push away the anger and the hatred of being a killer. The war had been raging hard inside his mind too much lately, and it seemed the killer in him was winning. He wanted to retain his humanity, and he could think of no better way than by making love to this cute, sexy, young woman.

Poppin strode down the hallway, stopped, and knocked lightly on the door.

Latoya greeted Poppin with a gigantic hug, stepped back and beamed. "I'm so glad you're here, I was hoping I would see you again."

Poppin looked deeply into the young woman's eyes and poured on his best pimpin' charm. "I just felt compelled to see you, it seems like for some reason we have a great deal in common. I don't know what that reason is, but I can't wait to find out."

"Yes, it does seem so, I don't know what it is, but after we talk awhile, I'm sure we will be able to figure it out."

Poppin just smiled. Talk, yeah, right, he didn't want to talk, he just wanted to bang her and bang her hard, but he knew how to play the game. He would talk first.

As they talked it came out again that Latoya's background had been much the same as Poppin's. She had been raised by an alcoholic father who had thrown her out when she got pregnant at the age of eighteen. Even though she tried, she couldn't convince her father that the pregnancy had been the result of a rape. He had degraded her with a lashing of slurs and told her to leave. She had left, gone on work-fare, and gotten a job as a waitress to support herself and her son.

Latoya had reached the point in their conversation where she felt she had to open up further to Poppin. "There's something I've got to tell you, it makes me different from most people. It's something very heavy and I've never told anyone before, but for some reason, I can sense that you will understand and be all right with it."

Poppin sat on the couch next to Latoya and reached out to gently put his hand on her knee. "It's okay, you can trust me with anything. I won't betray any confidence you put in me. I live by that code of honor with everyone I know. I have to do that, especially in the business I'm in."

Tears came to the young woman's eyes. "There is no other way to say this than to come right out with it."

Latoya took a deep breath. "A couple of years ago, I killed a man."

Poppin was taken aback by the bluntness of the statement. His mind swirled. He had done the same thing. He realized that he and this woman were indeed the same. She probably had a good reason, hell, I have a good reason, he thought to himself.

Poppin took his hand from Latoya's knee. He was frozen in the mystery. "Go on, tell me what happened."

Poppin doubted Latoya would go further, but she surprised him when she began to speak in a low voice. "When I was eighteen, I was raped. When the man was finished, he turned his back on me, pulled on his pants and began to buckle his belt. I was able to get my purse from the floor of my car and pull a metal comb out. I pulled up my courage and rage, got out of my car and lunged up behind him and buried the metal comb spikes deep within the left side of his neck. The metal tines hit a main artery and blood began spurting everywhere. In no time at all, he was dead."

"Man, that's rough. Didn't they want to charge you with murder?"

"At first, they thought about it, but the man turned out to have several sexual assault priors. Since the assault happened on the shoulder from a main road and a highway patrolman saw my car was still running from when I got out to help the man, they didn't push for any charges."

A strange silence ensued. It seemed to Poppin and Latoya alike that there was approval of each other in the silence. Latoya didn't understand the feeling, but she liked it.

Latoya put her hands on both of her knees and leaned forward. "I was innocent, but the thought that I killed a man has never left me."

"It's okay, it was justified, sometimes killing is justified. If someone is going to hurt you, or someone else, sometimes, there's just nothing else you can do. I know, believe me, I know."

Latoya brushed tears from her rosy-red cheeks. "What do you mean? You sound like you really know what I feel. Have you done it too?"

Poppin hadn't expected the blunt question. He took a low, deep breath. "Yes," he said simply.

Now it was Latoya's turn to have a blank expression of wonder on her face. She wondered if she was sitting next to a murderer, but she relaxed and decided she would give him a chance to explain.

Latoya sat back on the couch and relaxed the grip on her knees, bringing her hands to rest comfortably at her side. "Was it justified?"

Poppin said nothing for a moment, lost in a quandary of right and wrong. "Yes, it was justified."

"Can you tell me about it?"

Poppin put his hand to his chin and thought. "No, not right now, I just don't want to dredge any of that stuff up. I will tell you some other time; let's change the subject to something a little happier. I think we could use a little happiness."

Poppin told Latoya about his record producing and about all of his work with Big Pork Dog. Latoya quickly became enamored with him. She marveled that a man of his stature would be interested in her. She never dreamed that her tragedy would bring her together with a man like Poppin. He clearly loved the work he did. She admired the brilliance of his mind. She snuggled up close to him when he grew tired of talking. She knew she already liked this man and would give herself to him. It would be easy since she had already shared her deepest secret with him.

Latoya had an old stereo CD player on a coffee table next to the couch. She got up and put a Nelly CD on low volume. Poppin let out a small laugh. He was glad she liked rap. Latoya got up and stood before Poppin. Her eyes flashed and met his in the kiss of electricity that could only mean that she wanted to make love to him. She took off her blouse and her bra-less breasts perked up quickly. She dropped her jeans and underwear to the floor without saying a word. She turned around slowly and arched her back. Poppin looked at the young, strong, muscular legs and the staunch haunches that were a result of doing waitress work and also carrying a baby around. Back that ass up ran repeatedly through his mind. Latoya complied without having to hear the words. She knew what he wanted, and she was not the least bit afraid of him.

Poppin entered her from behind and began the bump and grind. Sweat beaded on their bodies, sweat dropped from Poppin's chin to meld with the sweat on Latoya's back. Poppin gripped her haunches hard and rubbed the sweat around on her behind. He gripped her strongly and thrust. She responded with rapid, excited thrusts back. The mating built to frenzy when both exploded in spasms of joy. Poppin fell gently forward onto Latoya again after she had lowered herself to the floor. The couple embraced and panted together in harmony.

Breaths slowing to a whisper, Poppin picked Latoya up, laid her on the couch, and lay down next to her. They covered up with a blanket taken from the arm of the couch. Slowly, they erotically embraced each other with wet kisses and coupled again in a gentle union. It was hours later before they laid together, their hearts beating as one as they drifted off to sleep.

Chapter 8

"These streets are murder. They go for two blocks turn, go another couple of blocks, and then you've got to turn again. This is crazy," Collins stated.

The two agents were traveling the streets of the south side of Milwaukee and they were a maze. The area they were in was an area of Polish descent. The streets had been laid out decades ago to bring a sense of closeness to the community. This manner of laying out the neighborhoods brought isolation, but with the isolation came a feeling of protection. Everyone knew everyone else, and looked out for each other. There was no way a crime could be done and a quick escape made in these neighborhoods.

Joan spoke up with a tone of satisfaction in her voice. "These directions they gave us at that gas station are really accurate."

Collins answered cheerfully. "Yeah, it's a good thing the guy lives in this neighborhood; he readily knew where the church was."

"A couple more blocks, turn right, then the church should be down a block on the right."

Three squad cars came into sight up ahead. Collins gunned the engine and spoke excitedly. "There it is."

The two detectives exited the car and walked slowly up to the crime scene tape. They presented their credentials and were let inside the taped off area. They walked up to and stood a few feet away from the body. In spots, the black robe showed through the white powder. The agents looked to the right of the body and saw a powdered white paper sack. The words 'bone meal' shown out in two-inch letters above the brand name Anderson's.

Collins smirked, "He's getting careless. He left us a major clue this time."

"Eventually they always do."

"Maybe we can get some fingerprints off of the bag."

Wendtworth stepped forward and leaned down to look more closely at the bag. "There doesn't seem to be any prints, he was probably wearing gloves."

"At least we have the brand he is using. Maybe we can pin down a location by the brand and lot number."

"Maybe, but maybe he's too smart for us too. He may have bought the product somewhere other than where he lives, still, we'll have to check it out and find out the outlet where it was bought. The computer science research division will get on it."

Collins stepped forward and picked up the bag with gloved hands. He turned it over. "Hey, there's a note written on the back of the bag." Collins bent forward and peered at the note.

"What does it say?" Joan asked excitedly.

"This deed is done, I've had my fun, so I'm on my way to slay on another day."

"Slayer Player," Joan exclaimed.

Joan took the bag from Collins and put it in an evidence bag that was handed to her by a nearby crime scene technician.

The detectives stepped back over in front of the body.

"That looks like a book lying by the side of his body," Collins said.

The crime scene had already been photographed so Wendtworth pulled a pair of latex gloves out of her blazer pocket and put them on. She bent down and picked up the book. She dusted the cover off to confirm her suspicions. The book was a Bible, and in the center of it there appeared to be a bullet hole.

Wendtworth shook her head slowly. "Will you look at this? How do you suppose this happened?"

Collins spoke quietly. "The man was probably trying to protect himself."

Wendtworth turned the book over with her gloved right hand and caught the slug in her left hand before it fell to the ground. She looked at it carefully even though she was pretty sure she knew what she would find. The slug was a thirty-eight. The nearby technician handed her an evidence bag, and Wendtworth dropped the slug inside.

Collins sensed something behind them and turned to look. "We've got company."

An old woman stood near the yellow tape. She stood no more than five feet tall and was hunched over from osteoporosis. She wore a heavy burgundy coat even though the temperature today was a perfect seventy degrees. Thinned white hair peaked out at the edges of her burgundy bonnet. A large, yellow rose pattern adorned the center of the bonnet. She had a taut, thin, wrinkled face. Collins guessed she was in her seventies. She smiled meekly and raised her right hand to beckon him forward.

Wendtworth and Collins looked at each other and smiled. Both were thinking, what was this all about. The old woman seemed to be mouthing words but no sound was coming out.

"Let's check this out," Collins said.

The agents walked slowly up to the yellow tape. Joan took the old woman's hand and gingerly shook it. "I'm Joan Wendtworth, and this man is Paul Collins, we're agents with the FBI."

The old woman spoke in a weak but excited voice. "My goodness, the FBI. I guess it is taken very seriously when a priest is killed."

Joan released the old woman's hand. "All murders are taken seriously, but we believe this one is tied in with others we are investigating."

The old woman looked into Joan's eyes. "He was a good man, a very holy man. This is terrible, a shame."

Collins spoke smoothly. "Yes, it is a shame. Is there something you wanted to say to us? It seems like you were trying to say something a moment ago."

The old woman pulled her coat tighter around her. "I'm so cold. I just feel so cold all of the time. Poor circulation, you know, I'm eighty-three years old."

Joan smiled. "You been blessed with a long life."

The old woman smiled. "Yes, Yes I have."

Collins sighed. This was getting them nowhere.

103

Joan got back to business. "Is there anything you can tell us about Father Iman that can help us?"

"Yes, maybe, I saw something strange this morning at services. My bladder control, you know, it's not so good anymore," the old woman groaned.

Collins matched her in a groan of desperation while Wendtworth just smiled.

After a small grin, which looked like the woman was passing gas, the old woman continued. "I had to leave during the middle of mass to go to the bathroom. The old school has the bathrooms in it; there are none in the church itself. When I came to the vestibule in the back of the church I saw a black man standing near the holy water fountain. It startled me because I have never seen a black man in the church, and I have been going to this church all of my life."

Joan's eyes sparkled at the old woman. "Did he say anything to you?"

"No, he just turned away and looked at the floor. I don't know if it means anything, but I don't know what he was doing there in the back of the church. It seemed strange and out of the ordinary."

Wendtworth took the old woman's hand again. "Thank you for your help, and if you'd be so kind, my partner here will take down your name, address, and phone number in case we need to contact you."

The old woman stammered. "That would be fine."

While Collins was occupied with the old woman, Joan left them and entered the church. She walked slowly down the center aisle. She had quit attending church when she was eighteen years old. She had become disillusioned with the Catholic faith. She couldn't conceive any longer of such a vengeful and retribution seeking God. As she walked slowly along, a lot of memories came back to her. She saw the Stations of the Cross along the sidewalls, the vivid depictions of Christ's journey to death made her shudder. She paused to look at the stained-glassed windows. They were beautiful in the morning light, especially the high one in the top corner above the altar. She looked at the words below each window. They appeared to be in Polish, and she couldn't understand them.

There seemed to be emptiness in the church, but she was unsure if the emptiness was coming from inside her or coming from the fact that the priest was dead. She finally decided it was the death of the priest that made her feel that way. She walked up to the front pew, sat down, and contemplated quietly. Five minutes later, Collins rushed up and joined her in the pew.

Joan spoke softly. "I was raised Catholic, but I follow no religion now."

Collins shifted in his seat. He didn't know what to say. He let the silence linger.

Joan finally broke the silence. "We have the head of a group foster home, a counselor, and a priest, what's the connection? Why kill these three different types of men?"

Collins chuckled. "You know, that almost sounds like the beginning of a joke."

"You're right. It does sound like that, but it's kind of bizarre isn't it? These men are from totally different walks of life, and from different places. Why kill them. What do they have in common?"

An eerie silence filled the church while both agents looked up behind the center aisle at the large statue of the cross with Christ crucified laid upon it. Joan looked to the small altar on the left side and saw the statue of an altar boy in a black robe and cassock holding a small cross.

She had an idea. "Maybe the priest sexually abused the perp."

Collins was amazed. "Where did that come from? What makes you think that?"

"I don't know, it's just that when I looked at that statue, the statue is of Saint Stanislaus in altar boy robes, I got that idea, you know, the thought of a priest abusing an altar boy. Maybe our perp was an altar boy here."

"I guess it's possible, but what do you make of the information that a black man has been on scene at two of our murders. Coincidence, or a lead?"

"I think it's a lead, but what I don't think is that he was an altar boy here. So, how come here? What does the killing of a priest in an all Polish neighborhood have to do with a black man?"

Collins slicked back his ever troublesome strands of hair and rested his hand under his chin. "It has to be something. The black man is probably our killer."

Joan paused for what seemed an eternity. The memories of her childhood faith were crowding her mind. She managed to brush them aside. "We'll have to go back to Harrison House. We'll see if there were any black residents that were ever there. There couldn't have been too many up there in that all Caucasian atmosphere. Then we'll run a computer check on them and see if anything criminal turns up. Maybe we'll find something interesting."

"Okay, let's go," Collins said happily.

"You go out and wait for me. I need to sit here a minute."

Collins gave Wendtworth a puzzled look. He couldn't imagine what she was feeling for he had never had any religious upbringing of any kind. He felt he should say something but felt helpless to find any words. He touched his partner gently on the shoulders as he rose and then walked slowly out of the church.

A small tear came to Joan's eyes. She couldn't identify the feeling that was causing it. Maybe this was what was missing from her life. Maybe she was reaching an age when she needed to take God into account again. She had been so self-sufficient for so many years. It could be time to take a look at faith again, but then all of the doubts came back, all of the feelings of hell and eternal damnation. Damn this faith business. She decided she didn't need any of that. She would shop around for a faith, a religion that she felt more suited to. Wasn't that what everyone did now.

She lowered her head and found herself saying a Hail Mary. A childhood habit had slammed back into her head. She stopped herself in mid-prayer and rose from the pew. The hell with all this religion shit. Not now. She hardened herself. It was time to catch another killer. It was who she was. It was what she did. She knew she would kill the killer if she had too. She banished the conflicting thoughts from her mind. Now was not the time to get mushy with faith. The trail was getting hotter. Now was the time to act. She picked up her pace and almost sprinted out of the church.

She smirked when she passed the Holy Water basin in the entrance to the church. Holy Water, she thought, it just wasn't holy enough. She knew it never could be. Still, it was hard to resist putting her hand in the water. She stepped forward and splashed the water around a little. It just seemed like water, and murder was murder. She composed herself and walked briskly out the front door to join Collins who was sitting patiently in the LTD.

Collins turned to her. "Are you alright?"

Joan sighed. "I'm fine. We'll have to get to Harrison House and check their records. God only knows how many more deaths may be forthcoming."

The agents remained silent as Collins worked the vehicle down the maze of streets and back onto the freeway to exit North leaving Milwaukee behind them.

Wendtworth dropped Collins off at his apartment in Madison and then headed west on Highway 94 back out of the city. Collins' jaw had dropped when Joan told him that she would be taking a day off to spend out in the country, and she wouldn't be able to be reached. Collins warned Joan that their superiors would not take kindly to her taking a break when she had such an important assignment to work on, but Joan had just shrugged and said that was the way it had to be.

As Joan took the Hawthorne Road exit and began to head south, she could already feel the tension leaving her shoulders. She would be turning forty-one the next summer and she had her twenty years in at the bureau. She had invested her money well in the stock market, and now it was going to pay off. She hoped the real estate agent she had been dealing with was truthful of her appraisal of the old homestead she wanted to buy. Joan Wendtworth, country girl, what a switch it was going to be. She could track her investments by computer and spend the rest of her time just working on and enjoying her new homestead. She knew the place would need a lot of work, but she had decided that at this time in her life, this was just the kind of work she wanted to do.

She didn't worry about her superiors, she knew how to work a case, and this case was going to go cold until the killer could plan another kill. Forensics had found nothing at the scene. This was a quick kill situation and there was nothing to be found. Sure, they would get a possible face of the suspect from the old woman at the church, but that face could fit a million young black men. Unfortunately, the case would not progress until there was another kill, and maybe, the killer would make a traceable mistake. It was the time to rest, she knew that. She would call Mortisson, her superior in the morning and fill him in. He trusted her instincts on any case, and she knew that he would not balk at giving her a few days away from work. Like any job, one always came back refreshed and with a renewed outlook when they could get away. Sometimes answers stared a person right in the face, but they couldn't see them because they were too close to the work. Time off on a farm. What a wonderful idea. She knew she would love the place and would soon buy it.

In her headlight beam, Joan could not see much of the farmhouse but then there really wasn't much to see. It looked like what the real estate agent had described it as, a large, white box of a house that was over one hundred and fifty years old. As she approached the house, she saw that the lapboard siding still looked solid, but she could see where gray shown through the top coat of white paint in places. She wondered how many times in its many years of life this house had been painted. It didn't matter, it was in the country, away from all that she had lived with the past twenty years, and she knew there would be peace here.

Joan walked up the creaky wooden steps and put the key in the lock. The key was stubborn in its turning and began to break off at the base where the cutting started, but it lasted long enough for her to finally get the door open. Just another thing to fix she laughed to herself. Nothing was going to break her good mood.

Had it been another woman, she supposed, not used to the life that she had led, she would be afraid to go into this old house alone in the middle of nowhere, but Joan knew that her danger lay elsewhere, her danger lay in the eyes of the serial killer she was tracking. She knew he wasn't here and once inside the house, she flipped the lights on in the front living room and felt immediately safe.

All the furniture was in place and she felt as though she had just walked into her grandparents' home. All the furnishings were circa nineteen-fifty, musty, worn, and faded. She loved the look and smell. She knew she would destroy most of these pieces in a bon-fire once she brought her own furniture in, and she smiled at the thought of how much fun that would be.

Joan walked up the steps towards the upstairs bedroom. In the center of the far wall across from the door was a large, oak poster bed. The wood was dark with age and had a deep, beautiful sheen that shown through many years of polishing. This was obviously a love and favorite piece of the old couple that had lived in the house previously. Joan thought herself lucky to find such a jewel of a home. The old woman, Mrs. Bilsey, had reached the age of ninety-one and had no longer been able to take care of herself. She was in a nursing home now. The farmhouse had just hit the market the day that Joan found it on an internet real estate site, and she had acted quickly. The real estate agent sent someone in to clean up the living room, kitchen, and bedroom, so that Joan could stay there that night. Unusual perhaps, but Joan thought that was the only way she could really get a feel for the place. She knew she would love it right away. It was plain, simple, and isolated, and the twenty acres of land it came with would give her plenty of space to get rid of the grizzly images from the last twenty years that now seemed to swarm more and more frequently in her mind.

Joan went back down the stairs and into the old kitchen. A table with a Formica top sat in the center of the kitchen. An old yellowed, white stove and refrigerator sat off to one side. The refrigerator kicked off and the motor made a loud rumbling, vibrating sound as it came to a halt. No matter, she had her own appliances to replace these old broken down ones. She fired up a gas burner on the stove and took a small pan from below a cupboard. The pan was battered and dented and had burn marks etched in the bottom, but she was grateful it had been left behind. She thought of how ill-prepared she had made herself for her first night in this house.

The water came to a boil on the stove, and Joan took a bag of Lipton tea from her jacket pocket. She let the bag soak for a moment and took off her jacket. The furnace she had turned up after entering the house was doing its job fine and the house was warming to a nice seventy degrees. Joan spooned the tea-bag out with an old, wooden, kitchen soup spoon, and she saved the bag in the spoon on the counter for when she wanted a second cup. Her mother had taught her this. Age old wisdom from mom, a bag is always good for two cups because you don't want the second cup so strong anyway, otherwise, it will keep you up all night.

Joan took her cup of tea and went into the front living room area to sit in a large, gray, overstuffed, herculon chair. She stared momentarily at the empty space where the television set used to be. It felt good not to be able to grab the remote and switch on CNN to see what was going on in the world. For the first time in a long time she didn't care about the constant tragedies in the world. She took a small sip of the tea and let the soothing warmth circulate through her entire body. She leaned back and relaxed.

A small, timid knocking sound came at the front door. She wasn't really sure that she had heard anything at all. It was probably just a branch from the tree in front of the house knocking against the side of the house. A few moments later, another small knock sounded. She was sure this time that the knock came from the front door, but who could be knocking at her door? Who would even know that she was at the farm right now?

Joan set her cup of tea on the ledge of the table lamp next to the overstuffed chair and walked up to the front window that was four feet away from the door. She peered through the dust-encrusted window and tried to see if someone was outside. She could barely make out the back of what seemed to be a very small person. She strode over to the door and swung it open. The hinges squeaked noisily, and she made a mental note that she would have to put some WD-40 on them.

Standing on the stoop was a small girl about four feet in height. Curious, sparkling, hazel eyes peaked out from under a blue stocking cap. The girl wore a matching tattered, blue, heavy-wool coat, and around her neck was a white, home-made, knit scarf.

"Hi, I'm Holly," the girl chirped happily. "Can I come in?"

"My name is Joan." Joan smiled broadly at Holly. "Well, of course Holly, I wasn't expecting any visitors, but this is a pleas-ant surprise. Come on in and sit down, you look kind of cold. By the way, my name is Joan Wendtworth. Joan reached out her hand and gave a soft handshake to the tiny, fragile hand that was extended to her.

"Yes, thank you, it is a cold night out there tonight."

Holly took off her hat, scarf, and coat and threw them over the sheet on a nearby chair. She bounced across the floor and plopped herself in the white, sheet covered chair next to the un-covered chair where she assumed Joan had been sitting.

Joan sat in the uncovered chair. "I have some tea on, would you like a cup to warm up?"

"Yes, that would be wonderful."

Joan was glad she had saved the tea bag for a second cup. She had second thoughts about giving the young girl a cup of tea so late at night. She didn't want her to have trouble sleeping that night, but she figured the lower caffeine content in the bag now would be just fine for this young girl. Joan went to the kitchen, soaked the tea bag in hot water for two minutes, and returned to hand the cup to Holly. Holly took a sip and Joan could see the warmth of the beverage rise in the girls face. Holly perked up immediately.

Joan took another sip of her tea and set it down. "How did you know I was here?"

Holly laughed a diminutive giggle. "I live just across the road and my bedroom window looks over this way. I saw the light on in your living room. I was excited right away. I just had to come over and see who was here. I just had too," the girl sounded desperate.

Joan felt concern rise up in her breast. "You sound so frantic, is something wrong, is something the matter?"

Holly groaned. "It's my horse; I don't have anywhere to put him. He's just outside tied up in our backyard and standing under a tarp. I'm afraid for him. I don't like him being outside like that."

Joan sighed. "No, no, that is not good. Doesn't he have a stable to stay in?"

A small tear came to Holly's eyes. "No, our barn burned down last week and so we just set up the tarp for him. I don't know what we're going to do. I know there is a barn here on this property, and I saw your light. I thought maybe I had found a solution. I was excited that someone was going to buy this property. I couldn't think of anything else. I just rushed right over."

Joan smiled at the young girl. "Holly, how old are you?"

The young girl bounced up from the chair and almost did a curtsy when she responded. "I'm eight years old."

Joan thought, a pretty young country girl, so young, so trusting. She thought of the horrors she had experienced in the world, and she thought how it was such a good thing that she was the one who was going to buy this property, and not some old pervert who might take advantage of the girl's youth and naiveté.

Joan's voice took on a comforting motherly tone even though she had never had a child. She had no idea where the tone had come from. "I feel that I am going to buy this place, and I'm sure there is a way I can help you out. I won't need the barn for anything; it would be nice if it could be of some use to someone."

Holly's face brightened immediately. "You mean you would let me keep Sneakers here."

"Oh, what a great name for a horse, how did you come up with that?" Joan asked, although she thought she already knew the answer.

"Sneakers has golden hair everywhere except for his mane, the tip of his tail, and the bottom of each of his four legs. Those areas are all white. I got him when I was six, I'm eight now. The first thing I blurted out of my mouth when I got him was the word sneakers. It stuck, and my family and I have called him that ever since."

Joan laughed. "Yes, I just love that name. Okay, I've decided, it looks like you could use this farm as much as me. I'm going to buy it, and you can move Sneakers in some time in the next couple of days."

Holly jumped up from her chair and ran over to give Joan a big hug. "That's wonderful, just wonderful, you're such a nice lady, I don't know how I can thank you."

Joan put her hand to her chin and thought for moment. "I know, you can let me ride Sneakers some time. I have never ridden a horse, and it has always been a lifelong dream of mine. Sneakers could provide the reality of that dream for me."

Holly bounced up and down in front of Joan. "Sneakers would be more than happy to let you ride. He loves it when I take him out for a ride. He's really fast, though my dad makes me take it slow on him, but you can ride him as fast as you want. I'm sure he'll love it."

"No, I'd take it slow, like I said, I've never been on a horse before. I'm kind of afraid of it."

"You don't have to worry, Sneakers is very gentle. He has a beautiful, soft spirit. He would be great for your first ride."

"Okay, it's settled then." Joan got her purse from the kitchen and came back to get a pen and a piece of paper out. "Put your name and phone number down on this and I'll call you as soon as I finalize the deal. It will be only a day or two."

"Oh, thank you Joan, Sneakers is going to be so happy here, I just know it. And now I won't have to have him go far away. I can still see him every day. I'm just so happy, you're such a nice lady," Holly's eyes sparkled with happiness.

"Okay then, have you finished your tea?"

"No, I'm just too excited. I don't want any more."

"Okay, well, you better get back home, you're father probably has discovered you missing and might be worried. Do you want me to walk you home?"

"Oh no, it's just across the road. I'll be fine, and thank you again, so much, I'm so excited I don't know if I will be able to sleep tonight."

Joan had second thoughts about having given the girl some tea to drink, but then she thought of how her niece could be so fired up one minute and then fall asleep anywhere the next. She figured Holly would calm down and be asleep in no time now that the biggest worry in her life was being taken care of.

Joan led Holly to the door. Holly turned and gave Joan another big hug. "Thanks again Joan." For a moment Joan thought Holly was going to say I love you as the young girl half mouthed the words. It was alright, Joan thought, she could have said it, but it was better that the young girl wait. Joan knew that she and this young lady where going to develop quite a friendship. It would be nice to have the vibrancy of youth around her. It was something she always felt she was missing since she didn't have any children of her own.

Joan closed the door behind Holly and went back to sit in her chair and have another sip of tea. The tea felt extra warm and comforting as it slid down her throat. She knew for certain now that this was the new kind of life that she was seeking. She knew that she would be happy on this farm. She knew in her heart that she was making the right choice about her life.

Chapter 9

"The underdog is in the ha-zouse," Jelly-Fish stepped forward and slapped Poppin's hand across mid-air.

"Yo, my niggah, whas-sup." Poppin laughed.

"Hangin low, I'm ready to go, glad you rang me up."

"Yeah, my niggah, I got work for you to do, a lot of work, we gonna get ripped on it."

"Shoot the works, go to the show, the big game is on, Big Pork Dog will be big on screen."

"Yo man, he is big, gettin' bigger, gettin' bigger."

Jelly, as he was known for short, had gotten his name when he was young because of his ability to bend all the fingers of both of his hands back until he could touch the back of his hands. Wiggly like a bowl of jelly, someone had said and the name had stuck.

Jelly popped himself down on the black leather couch. "Can't be too big, cause nothin' lasts in the game. Always a downside."

Poppin grinned. "Upside, downside, always on the slide, keep it movin' and either way you stay in the game."

"Oh yeah, brother, oh yeah."

Poppin took on a serious expression. His brows furrowed, his smile smirked. "I got the shit man, the best shit money can buy. This here's the new shit." With that, Poppin got up, motioned for Jelly to follow him and walked over to a shiny, black, side-door next to the wet-bar.

Poppin opened the door and walked inside with Jelly in tow. Poppin flipped on a light. The room was filled with photography studio lights. The bright lights were blinding. Jelly squinted. It was difficult to see the video-camera that sat on a tall, four pedestal table directly in the center of the mass of lighting.

"Man, I could really shoot some sex-shit up in here. Throw in a bed, a tapestry, and a couple of big-tittie blondes, and I'm all set. Bump and grind, get it on ladies."

Poppin rolled over with laughter, Jelly had always been the shit, and he'd never change. "Okay man, whatever, this shit is for the rise of BPD video. See to it that you get that done, and what you do on your own time is your shizzness. Deal on that and this shit is yours."

Jelly walked up and stroked the camera lovingly. "I love you baby, you too Poppin, you the man."

Chapter 10

Lean low, lean low, put that fucker down. Lay him on the ground. Bullet in the brain, center of the forehead, dead before he hits the ground.

The words ran through Poppin's head over and over again. He worked himself up into a frenzy of death. This man had been hard to find. It seemed he had vanished from the face of the earth. He had become a self-styled hippie, a polygamist, the head of his cult, the father and abuser of a dozen children, not to mention his three wives, and four concubines. The man thought he was at the center of his world, but the police had taken him down. If not for the police, Poppin would not have been able to find him.

They had printed several of his aliases, among them the name that his young victim from Harrison House had known him by. The thirteen year old victim had managed to run away. She never gave her last name to anyone. She had become one of the faces in the group in Poppin's memory. She had filled him in on the man he was about to kill.

Baby momma would have her justice. She was only thirteen and already a mother because of this man. The baby was hopefully living a good life through adoption, but this victim pissed Poppin off more than any of the others had so far. She was so young and innocent to have to go through a pregnancy. It was going to be a pleasure to bring this fucker down.

Lean low, lean low, breath slow, rest the rifle against the concrete, and deliver a death blow. Poppin looked through the three to nine variable Weaver scope. He had filed the serial numbers off of the barrel. There would be noise this time. It didn't matter. He had his escape planned. He would be gone before anyone could get near him. He had sat on the top of the building opposite the city jail for three hours already, but it was all right. He had learned to be patient in his stalking.

Poppin ran the image of the man over in his mind. Six-foot two, heavy-set, and muscular, the man presented a large target. Long, thick, graying-black dreadlocks cascaded down onto his shoulders in a fuzzy mat of hair. The hair looked dry and brittle. The man had a thick mustache that covered large lips. The man looked evil, and he was.

The back door to the city jail opened and two officers preceded forward, the man being held on each side by the arm. The orange jail jumpsuit stood out in sharp contrast to the two navy blue-uniformed officers. The officers scanned their surroundings as they walked to the awaiting transfer van.

Lean low, breath slow, squeeze softly.

The sound rocketed around the surrounding buildings and built in an ever reverberating echo. The bullet struck the man in the center of the forehead. Through his scope, Poppin saw the bullet strike flesh. The man crumbled to the ground, pulling the two officers over on top of him. The two officers at the van rushed forward to assist the fallen officers, wondering if they had been hit.

Poppin was on the move, the rifle dropped. Down the steps round and round, spinning rhymes in his head. Gotta go, gotta go, the job is done, I have won, the man is down, down on the ground, blood spilled all around. Cops in frenzy, I'm off to my Ben-Z, blowin' down the road, killin' in my soul.

Poppin smiled as he pulled onto the road straight away from the building. He was gone in the blink of an eye. Free to travel to anywhere he chose. No one had been ready. There was no pursuit. The transport officers had all been focused solely on the evil within their grasp. They had no idea an evil lurked on a near-by roof-top.

The kill had been brazen and bold. Different for Poppin. An outright sport. It had been fun. He really enjoyed it. This man was bad, maybe the worst of all. The world was a better place without him.

As he drove along, he saw the face of the young, abused girl in his mind as she had been back at Harrison House. He remembered the tears and the big smile on her face after he had made his promise to all of them. The smile grew bigger and brighter and seemed to burn into his mind. Four happy smiles now, made happy forever, but there were two more to go. Then, he told himself, he would stop. Slayer Player would stop the play.

He smiled to himself at the name the press, or was it the police, had given him. It seemed like a good, clean name. But this time, there would be no bone meal spread on the man. This bothered Poppin. He had liked the ritual. He wondered if the police would be able to tie this killing to him. Maybe not. There wasn't that definite tell-tale sign on the body, but the man was an abuser, and they would eventually make the link. But maybe not, he knew he was protected by the secrecy that incest brought with it. It was a hard nut to crack. No one talked freely about sexual abuse. Not in this society, not even in the new millennium. He was counting on the fact that a shroud of secrecy would protect his identity.

Poppin wanted to make sure the police knew, that the press knew, that this kill was the work of the Slayer Player. He had thought long and hard about it, and the simple solution had finally come to him. He had come up with a way to leave his signature without actually covering the body. When the police examined the roof-top and found the weapon, they would be surprised to find it covered with white powder.

He felt safe as he leaned back in the car seat and lit up a J. The cloud of smoke surrounded him and filled the Benz. He watched the clouds of smoke swirl in front of him, and for a moment he felt as though he drifted in the clouds. This was good weed, straight from Hawaii, sticky sweet.

By the time he got home, he was so high he couldn't remember anything for more than a moment. He went into the living room, fixed himself a glass of whiskey on the rocks, and sat down in his comfortable, black leather recliner. He drank the glass quickly and was soon off in the dreamland of a sweet nap.

He awoke two hours later to find Alyssa sitting on the floor in front of him. His mind began to flow. Do the bump and grind, hit her on the floor, hit her from behind. Poppin slid to the floor next to Alyssa. She looked into his eyes, and she knew what he wanted. Alyssa relented. She rose, dropped off her clothes, and took her position on the floor. Poppin never felt more alive and powerful in his life.

After it was over, the couple cruised to the special invitation only show at the Riverside Theater. The show was to be shot for a music video. They took their seats in the luxury balcony box that had been reserved for them.

Poppin leaned back with a large smile on his face. Alyssa cuddled in close next to him. She knew she had hitched herself to him for better or worse. She just couldn't help herself. She was addicted to the man. He had such power it was intoxicating.

Poppin fidgeted nervously in his seat. He worried about yesterday. There had been no drop as usual and when he tried to make contact with his supplier, there was no response. He needed the money drug dealing was providing. It helped everything move faster and more smoothly. Any glitch in the concert and production business was easily handled with the drug money. Something was terribly wrong, but he had taken precautions. He was always a cautious man. He would find out what was at the bottom of the problem.

Alyssa caressed Poppin's right thigh and cooed. "Big Pork Dog's so good, he's going to be a big star. He's going to make it Poppin. It's going to work."

"Yeah, it's going to work," Poppin said absentmindedly.

Poppin's gaze was fixed on the front luxury booth opposite them and across the crowd. A lone black man sat in the booth. Poppin caught the man's eyes with his own and bored deeply into them. He saw a look of hatred there. He saw death, a look he had become very familiar with when he looked at his own eyes in the mirror every morning. The man held Poppin's gaze for what seemed an eternity before he finally looked away. Poppin knew death was going to try and knock.

Big Pork Dog was drenched in sweat. He stepped forward and blared into the microphone. "Drug Deal gone bad. Bullets through the door. Coke on the floor. Blood, guts, and everywhere more."

The broad, black stranger in the luxury booth opposite Poppin pulled a black pistol from underneath his black, leather jacket. Poppin saw the flash of metal and froze in a cold stare. He met the man's sinister eyes again as the pistol came up to the man's face in aim.

A wide smile crossed Poppin's face, and the assailant froze.

What was this, he wondered, why was Poppin smiling. The answer came quickly when he felt cold steel against the back of his neck. He knew the cold steel feel of a gun when he felt one. A frown came to the assassin's face.

Poppin laughed.

"Let's you and me take a ride," Rolly said softly.

The assassin shrugged. "Okay, no problem."

Rolly led the man out of the booth. Once inside his white Cadillac Rolly talked frankly. "You might as well give it up right away. Make it easier on both of us. This was a bad play. We saw it coming."

"You sure did," the assassin sighed. "Now, what are you going to do to me?"

"It's simple. We want you to turn. You keep the money you've already been given. We'll match it. You turn around and take out your employer."

"And if I don't."

"You die now."

"That's a hard deal to refuse. But how do you know I'll do what you ask?"

"If you don't, I guarantee I will find you and that will be the end of you. I'm giving you this chance now because we're big, and we're going to be huge. You might as well be on the right side of things."

The assassin thought quietly for a moment. "You've got a deal. I'll take out the boss."

Rolly smiled. "Where can I drop you?"

121

"Here, now, this is fine. I'll make my own way."

Rolly pulled the Cadillac up to the curb. The assassin rose slowly and opened the door.

Rolly touched his shoulder. "We'll be watching the news. Don't disappoint us."

"I won't," the assassin said and was quickly gone.

*****

The next night, Poppin's Jet Black Benz pulled up to the curb in front of the Milwaukee arena. The sidewalk was crowded with screaming throngs of rap admirers preparing for the public arena show. Big Pork Dog sat quietly in the backseat for a moment and basked in the glory. He had the time. He had to wait for the security men to position themselves next to the car. Security was already in place along the sidewalk opening up a pathway to the front entrance of the building.

Poppin had said it was best to enter from the front. Face the crowds and cross them, revel in the glory and fun. BPD stepped from the Benz onto the sidewalk and was greeted by a giant roar from the crowd. Several young women immediately tried to push forward but were held back by the large, black, male security guards wearing black t-shirts. Their t-shirts bulged against their chests and biceps as they held the women back. BPD strolled forward swinging his arms up and down to a rhythm that was already playing inside of his head.

BPD was in the groove now. The cheering and shouting built to a crescendo, but he could barely hear it above the sound that was playing inside of his head. Half-way down the sidewalk and through the thronging masses, BPD reached out his hands towards the sidelines and touched the hands of a few of the faithful. The crowd lunged forward and the security guards had difficulty controlling them, but even against such a crushing rush, they were able to hold the people back. BPD stood still and reached his arms out toward the sky, reveling in the glory that was all his. He smiled widely when he saw his name in two foot high letters up in lights.

A new assassin had his target fully in the center of his sight. He had picked the building across the street for the perfect access it provided to his target. He now had the rifle scope centered directly in the middle of BPD's back. He breathed softly in, held his breath and pulled the trigger just as a young woman broke through the security guards surrounding BPD and grabbed him by the right arm to spin him around. The bullet ripped through the left arm of BPD and spun the couple down to the ground, the large bulk of BPD landing directly on the woman.

The head security man reacted quickly as the stunned crowd grew still and silent. He hustled BPD ahead and into the auditorium entrance. He led BPD down a side hall and into a back dressing room. He saw the blood pouring from BPD's arm, pulled a bandanna from his back pocket, pulled BPD's shirt up and examined the wound. It looked like a flesh wound so he wrapped the bandanna tightly around the bloody area. Big Pork Dog waddled over to a black leather couch and sat down. His eyes were glazed over, but after a few minutes a sharp clarity and brightness returned to them. He looked around the purple dressing room and focused his eyes on a colorful Chinese vase overflowing with a multitude of colorful flowers. He smiled as the colors calmed his racing heartbeat.

"Are you alright?" The head security guard asked.

"For shizzle my nizzle, it's just a drizzle, I'm gonna sizzle tonight. The show must go on. Are we ready?"

"Are you sure? Are you sure you can do it?"

"Right as rain, ain't no pain, I'm in the groove now, more than ever, let's get to the stage and I'll spit out my drizzle."

The security guard opened the door to the dressing room and the duo was quickly flanked by six other security guards as they led Big Pork Dog to the curtain at the back of the stage. Big Pork Dog took a deep breath and stepped out.

The explosion from the crowd was deafening. The crowd threw their arms in the air and pushed to the stage in a mammoth rush. The security guards were nearly overcome but somehow managed to keep the crowd back. BPD began to circle the stage, pumping his arms in the air. Ending at the arc of a large circle, he stepped up to the front of the stage and pulled the microphone up to his lips. The crowd built to frenzy in a hurry. BPD knew how to work a crowd. The words flowed in an endless stream of rhyme, rhythm, and reason. They hung on his every word.

Outside some clown
Tried to gun me down
But I ain't through,
I'm still here to spit for you.

I'm a slayer player
Come play along
Bullet through my arm
But there ain't no harm.

Gonna count my stack
Then hit em back.
Come sing along.
Slayer Player is doin' this song.

Come along
Freedom with a song
Got me some fame now
Fifteen minutes long.

Crossroads of life
Heavy with strife
I seek a way out,
Give a primal shout.

Out, Out.
Sing along
Say yah, out, out out.

Slayer Player

To hell with fifteen minutes of fame
Can't get rid of my shame
I want to take out a lease
On fifteen minutes of peace.

I'm gonna be rollin' in my
  Royce
Clothes of my choice
Bling in my ring
My fame is my voice.

Damn there goes my beeper
Makes me grim like the reaper
But rhyme is my pleasure
And I'm a pleasure seeker.

I'm here for you tonight
And we're gonna sizzle.
So let's get it on
And thunder this snizzle.

After the show Poppin sat down with BPD in the purple room. Purple had replaced green in the traditional green room waiting area because rappers preferred the dark, relaxing, and yet invigorating color.

BPD sat on the black leather couch and wiped the sweat from his forehead with a handkerchief. He took a series of deep breaths to bring his breathing back under some sense of control.

"You alright man?" Poppin asked.

"I will be shortly, cause first you gotta breathe man, ya gotta breathe."

Poppin walked over to the couch and sat down. He put his right hand behind BPD's neck and massaged the tense muscles slowly. Pork Dog looked up at Poppin with a mist in his eyes.

"Man, I don't want none of this. I don't know what the hell that was all about. Why would anyone try to do a hit on me Poppin?"

Poppin took his hand off of BPD's neck and sighed. "It ain't about you man, it's about me."

BPD let out a small sigh. "What do you mean?"

Since we're alone in this room, and considering what you've just been through, I'm going to tell you what it was all about. They tried to hit me last night at the Riverside. I was ready for that. My man was on the assassin and stopped him. Unfortunately, I didn't know they were going to try to get to me through you. I'm really sorry about that."

"But why, why would anyone try to do a hit on us?"

"I'm going to tell you something I never told you before. I deal drugs. I've had a big network for years, and now someone is trying to take over my territory. Hitting you was just another way to hurt me financially."

BPD stood up and paced wildly about the room. "I don't want this shit on me, I just want to rap, get my shit out there. I'm an artist man, not a drug dealer. I don't want to be involved in this shit."

"I know, I know, and I'm sorry, but because you're with me, you are involved in it. I'll protect you from here on out, give

126

you round the clock security. I don't want to lose you. I don't want to lose what we got. It's important to me that you succeed. I just want to be legitimate, to do something good and right with my life. It's been a long road."

Pork Dog sat back down on the couch. "I don't know man, I just don't know."

"You gotta stick with me. There may be some bad things coming yet, but I'll see to it that they're all on me. Stay on your dreams, keep moving on with your life. We're about to succeed beyond our wildest dreams. What happened here tonight will give us all the free publicity we can possibly stand. You don't realize it, but tonight you made it. You're a genuine rap star now. Someone tried to gun you down, and the public will never forget. Hang on tight, the ride has just begun."

BPD started laughing uncontrollably. His belly jiggled along with his shaggy jowls. It was several minutes before he could bring himself under any resemblance of control.

"Hell yeah, I'm a star. A star. They will want more of me now than ever. I'm with you Poppin. Next show even bigger."

"Oh yeah, and pay for view too. You're gonna be rich and bigger than you ever dreamed."

"No, not possible. I always dreamed large. I even dreamed about this hit attempt on my life a few days ago. I'm in, let's get on with it. I'm with you brother."

Pork Dog rose from the couch along with Poppin and gripped him in a large bear hug. Poppin momentarily lost his breath, but when the hug was over he just smiled at BPD. BPD smiled back with a sharp twinkle in his eyes. Poppin gave Pork Dog one last hug and left the room.

Pork Dog sat alone on the black leather couch, a large smile on his face. What a lucky man I am, he thought, what a lucky man.

Poppin stood lankly in front of BPD and a broad smile crossed his face. "Time to go talk to the world my man, time to go talk to the world."

Big Pork Dog smiled broadly and rose slowly from the couch. "I'm ready for fame, play the game and make a name. Tell them all how it is, fill the world with joyful bliss. Let's go."

Jelly was set up to film. He could barely contain his excitement and bounced around crazily. He had gotten the assassination attempt and the aftermath all on tape. He was gonna be rich.

Poppin and BPD, and BPD's press agent, Angie Constantine, walked into the press room with Rolly and the other body guards surrounding them. They took seats at the long oak table on the stage. Just over thirty press people crowded in front of the stage. The four eighteen inch built-in spotlights were switched on. Poppin, Angie, and BPD were set ablaze in a light brighter than the coming day could ever hope to be.

Angie called the first name of a reporter on the right side of the group and the crowd quieted down so the man could ask his question.

"BPD, what's your condition?"

"Hole through my arm, but I'm still full a charm. I'll be fine, still do some grind." BPD let out a large belly laugh.

"Have you seen a doctor?" The same reporter asked.

"No, no, just got a wrap on my arm, get stitched in the flesh later, I had to talk to y'all now, let the world know that BPD is fine and still spittin' his rhymes," BPD's smile was wide and happy.

Angie called a female reporter by name, and the woman wasted no time in asking her question. "What can you tell the world now in your fifteen minutes of fame?"

"Forget fifteen minutes, I'm staying in this game. Kill the beast, live in peace, keep getting high, make love on the fly. Love yourself and love one another."

The woman shot back. "Lofty goal, with all the violence around you, how can you feel that way?"

"I didn't do the violence, I only absorbed it. I'm still a man at peace, and I still love myself. I love all of you too. Peace out," Big Pork Dog finished as he rose from the table and without saying another word walked out of the room.

Rolly and the bodyguard followed BPD outside. A crowd of over one hundred still lined the runway where they had to pass through. Big Pork Dog repeatedly pushed past his bodyguards and shook hands with fans. Many he told, I love you.

Finally, two of the bodyguards surrounded BPD at the black Mercedes and bent down with him until he was inside. Cameras flashed in only half-successful attempts at getting pictures of BPD in the back seat. The driver pulled the Mercedes quickly away and out into traffic. BPD was big time now. He had been on every video music station and all the major news networks at the same time. Nothing like a gang hit on a celebrity to bring fame. How long, BPD thought, I know one thing, fifteen minutes ain't that long. Ain't anywhere near long enough. Somehow he would prolong it, build on it. Five years, yeah, that's what he wanted. Five years.

Slayer Player

Chapter 11

Shawn crept quietly onto the property at Harrison House. It had been three months since he had been there. He knew the marijuana he had tended so carefully the year before would be there, growing up as a second year crop. It wouldn't be as good as it should be, but if he was careful and only picked the tops of the female plants, and could find only those that had not cross-pollinated, the pot would still sell for a good price.

The full moon made visibility good. The warm early September temperature of seventy degrees kept the swamp alive with life. A dingy muskrat scurried away from the bank when Shawn got near the small, moss-colored Jon-boat. A small mink with golden fur came up to the boat and sniffed around. He was surprised the mink remembered him. They had become good friends when Shawn visited the plants the previous year.

"Sorry my old friend. I didn't think you'd be here. I didn't bring you a fish," Shawn laughed.

Shawn paused and smiled at the lithe, little creature for a moment, and then remembered that he had a packet of trail mix in his jeans pocket. He pulled the packet out and spread the mix on the grass a couple of feet away from the boat. The mink sniffed at the air and almost seemed to smile before he bounded forward and pounced on the mixture. He ate heartily as Shawn pushed the boat into the shallow water of the swamp.

Mosquitoes buzzed around Shawn's head, but beaten back by mosquito spray, they refused to land. Shawn was no amateur in the marshes. He knew they would be there. The marsh was alive with the sound of croaking frogs and buzzing, mating insects. A group of eight large, black crows sat in a large oak tree and cawed their shrill cries as Shawn passed under their perch.

He heard the chatter of a gray squirrel. It felt good to be out on the marsh again, away from the city. Shawn hadn't realized how much he missed the freedom.

Six hundred yards into the marsh, Shawn came upon the small island of land where he had grown the plants the previous year. He landed the boat and walked through a small copse of cedar trees and thick underbrush. As he approached the clearing he could already smell the vividly fragrant odor of the plants. He reasoned the plants may be better than he thought. They sure smelled good.

He took a quick count and found there were eighteen seven to eight foot tall plants present. He rapidly stripped the branches off the stems with a knife and shoved them into two plastic garbage bags he had brought with him. In less than an hour he was done. He headed back to the boat and crossed the marsh back to the backyard of Harrison House.

Shawn stood for a moment in the moonlight and looked at the old house that he had once called home. He remembered the feeling of deadness the abuse of the children had placed on the house. He wished there had been something more that he had been able to do about it when he lived there, but at least someone was doing something about it now. The Slayer Player, the newspapers called him. Well, that was just fine with Shawn. Even at night in the moonlight, the house seemed more at peace then it had ever been.

At the appointed time of two A.M. Shawn walked up to the road in front of Harrison House and began to walk away to the west. The old, orange, Seventy-two Ford pickup pulled up behind him, and he turned around, threw the two garbage bags inside, and climbed into the cab.

His friend, Freddy, threw him a big smile. "Looks like you did all right. Looks like you got a lot."

"Yeah, I'm guessing about two pounds per bag. One bag or two pounds for you, like we agreed. Happy selling," Shawn laughed.

Freddy laughed back at him, pulled out a joint and lit it up. The two men relaxed and hit deeply on the joint. Shawn blew out a large cloud of smoke and looked over at the front of Harrisson House. All was quiet there. He reached over and turned the stereo up loud to the sounds of a song called Twisted Transistors. The loud bass crowded out the noise of the patrol car that pulled up behind their vehicle.

Sheriff Griskey sauntered up slowly to the right side of the vehicle with his gun drawn. He tapped on the window and aimed the gun directly at Freddy's head. Even though he knew it was coming, Freddy's eyes grew wide at the sight of the gun pointing at him right between the eyeballs. Freddy unrolled the window to a vacillating swirl of marijuana smoke. He smiled. Grisky smiled back.

Grisky stepped back from the door. "Both of you, hands on your heads."

The two men followed instructions.

Grisky swelled with pride, almost popping the button off his shirt when he let out his breath. "Now, out of the car, keep your hands on your heads until you get to the front hood of the car, then lean forward and place your hands on the hood."

Shawn swore a blue streak, but he complied. He knew there was nothing else he could do, but he wondered how Grisky had known he would be there. It could not be coincidence.

Grisky walked around the car to Shawn and frisked him. "Have you got any weapons on you?"

Shawn answered quietly. "No."

Grisky grimaced. "How about in the car?"

"No."

"Well, we'll check that out later," Grisky said as he brought out his cuffs and cuffed Shawn's hands behind his back. "Freddy, you just stay put right where you are, I'm going to put Shawn in the squad, and then I'm going to come back and cuff you."

Grisky finished with Shawn and Freddy and had both men sit in the back of the squad. He flipped on a psychedelic strobe light that rested above the front dashboard. The strobe was intoxicating in its eccentricities. It showed a wide variety of different directional lightings. Shawn and Freddy became transfixed on the light quickly. Shawn found himself wishing that he owned just such a light. He leaned back and relaxed and stared intently at it. The light was doing exactly what it was designed to do. It tranquilized the captives in the back seat.

Grisky drove Freddy and Shawn to the station. They were separated, Shawn was booked, and Freddy was let go with a handshake. Freddy's previous arrest for dealing drugs was expunged. He left the building with a big smile on his face, but in his chest was the nagging feeling and wonder as to whether Shawn would one day strike him back for his betrayal of him. It didn't matter. He was free from his past arrest charges, and his present problem.

Shawn sat quietly in the holding room of the jail and knew he had been betrayed. He knew there was no way out of the mess. He had been caught red-handed. Grisky had wanted him and he had got him. He knew he would be let go soon and charged later. It would be a couple of months before he was formally charged and the case was brought to court. The wheels of justice in drug cases usually moved slowly, but separate drug courts were being established now and cases were beginning to move much more quickly through the system. Shawn leaned back on the bench and relaxed. He might as well go with the flow, there was nothing else he could do. Just go with the flow.

*****

Poppin was feeling low and alone. Lean back, let it slide, let it go. He was doing his job. The killing was easy, but the aftermath was hard. He wondered, was he insane for keeping this promise to these children that he had made so many years ago. He felt alone. The promise didn't seem to loom so large any more as he remembered the looks on the faces of the men he had killed. Still, he had made the promise, and he had carried more than half of it out. Might as well finish it. Avenge them all. Free them and free his self. He felt so alone, lost in a different world. He decided to turn to the one woman who had always been there for him, the one woman who had always comforted him when he was frazzled and confused. The one woman he felt still believed in him. He picked up the phone and called Alyssa.

Alyssa sat in the whiteness of her apartment, surrounded now by a growing influx of colors. Flowers adorned the apartment everywhere. The living room was heavy on red roses. Strands of petunias and daffodils where everywhere, a flower garden even shone from the screen saver on her computer. She wore a purple, silk nightgown, emblazoned with large, red roses as she sat on the couch and answered the phone.

Poppin's voice was low and husky. "Poppin here."

Alyssa was surprised. She hadn't heard from Poppin in three months. "Hello, long time no hear."

"Yeah, it's been a long time. I just needed to call. I've been feeling kind of lost, and I think that you're still the one person that knows me best."

Alyssa worried at the sound of depression in Poppin's voice. "I thought you had the world by the tail. I thought everything was going fine with you. I've noticed how BPD's career seems to be taking off. I figured you'd be happy and full of pride."

Poppin let out a huge sigh. "Yeah, that's all fine and good, but there's something else. I need to see you, to talk to you."

"Poppin I can't, I'm too busy with school. Its finals time and I have to get a lot of papers done before the end of the semester. I just don't have time to spend with you."

"I'm your friend ain't I, you should make the time. I'd really like to see you. I have some deep shit to talk to you about."

"You can talk to me now, what is it?"

The silent drone of the phone connection between them went on for what seemed an eternity.

Poppin broke the silence. "I feel lost. It's the promise. Fulfilling it is bringing me down, way down, down so low, I have nowhere else to go. I had to come to you. I love you."

Alyssa was surprised at the words, she had heard them before, but they seemed as sincere as ever. "I love you too, but not how I used to. I have my own life now. I will always love you in a different way."

"What the hell do you mean, different. There's only one kind of love, isn't there?"

"No, Poppin, there are many different kinds of love."

Poppin paused in thought. He fought hard to try and accept what he felt was a betrayal. Anger arose in his breast, but he suppressed it. He was impatient. He liked to have his love requited. He trusted Alyssa, maybe she was the only person he had ever trusted.

Poppin spoke quietly. "Alyssa, I have to tell you what's bothering me."

"Go ahead, you can trust me. You always could and always will be able to."

Alyssa's words comforted Poppin. "Alyssa, it's the promise, I've been keeping the promise, and it's taken me into a different world, a different place. My mind is whirling all the time. Right verses wrong, I didn't expect this."

Alyssa looked at her computer screen as the screensaver switched to her favorite rose garden scene. She wondered why Poppin was being so cryptic. "I don't know what you mean. The promise, what is that?"

Poppin fought the blankness in his mind. "The children, the promise to the children."

"What children?"

"The children so many years ago. The abused children."

"Poppin, what are you talking about. What have you done?"

"I can't tell you."

"You trust me, don't you?"

"Yes, but I can't tell you. It's our secret, me and the children. I just can't tell you."

"Then why did you call. You want me to help you, but you really can't trust me. You can't tell me the truth. There is nothing I can do for you."

Tears rolled down Poppin's cheeks and his voice broke. "I wanted it the way it used to be between us, but I see that can never be. I can't share this secret with you. I'm sorry I called."

"No, Poppin, I'm glad you called, I just wish you could tell me the truth."

"That's just it Alyssa, I don't know what the truth is," Poppin hung up the phone.

Alyssa sat back and gazed at her flowers. She had built such a place of work and peace for herself. She didn't need the confusion this man brought into her life. She realized how happy she was without Poppin in her life. She had to forget about this call, forget about his needs. There was no room in her life for his misgivings. She got up and walked over to the balcony window. What was the promise, she wondered, a promise to the children. It had been in the papers, the Slayer Player avenging abused children by killing their abusers. He hadn't come right out and admitted it, but he might as well have. She knew the words hidden between the words Poppin spoke. She knew him better than anyone. At that moment, she knew, Poppin was the Slayer Player. She had once been his woman, but not anymore.

Alyssa sat back on the couch and wondered what she should do. She found yesterday's paper with the article about the Slayer Player. At the bottom of the article was a number to call for the FBI if anyone had any information about the killer. She picked up the phone and dialed the number. Her hand shook and she was unable to still it as she spoke to the recording. She relayed her thoughts, hung up, buried her hands in her face and cried.

*****

Mrs. Gunderson had been ill for a few days, but she felt better as she shuffled into the precinct reception area. The area was bustling with people being booked and released. She almost turned to leave, but she was the kind of person that always kept an appointment. She turned and went back to stand in front of the main desk. The sergeant on duty looked dolefully down upon her.

The sergeant's voice came out in a surly growl, "Can I help you?"

Mrs. Gunderson shifted her weight and with a great effort raised her head. "I was asked to come down here and work on a sketch."

The desk sergeant surveyed the old woman. He knew she must have been pushing eighty. She would never be able to find the room where the artist awaited. He picked up the phone and called the artist to come down so he could lead the old woman to his office.

A thin, young man who appeared to be in his mid-twenties, with blonde hair and tinted black highlights streaking the ends, walked up to the old woman. Large Amethyst earrings dangled loosely from both of his earlobes. At six-foot two, he towered over the five foot, hunched-over, old woman. A broad smile crossed his face when he looked into the old woman's eyes. She smiled back warmly.

The tall blonde man took the old woman's hand. "I'm Tom Adams, and I'm a sketch artist with the FBI. I've been waiting for you. You can come with me and we'll go to an open office."

Tom stepped to the left side of the old woman and took her elbow. He lead her gingerly along. He had great respect for the elderly for his great-grandmother was about the same age as the old woman. In a soft, gentle voice he asked, "How are you feeling today?"

The old woman let out a small giggle. "I guess I'm as good as usual, there's always aches and pains when you're in your eighties."

"Yes, but you look pretty spry for your age."

"I get by all right. My faith in God keeps me going. He'll call me home when He's ready."

Adams led the old woman into the office he would be using. He guided her to a chair in front of a large desk and then took a seat opposite her.

"You're not going to sit behind the desk?" The old woman asked.

"No, we need to work closely together."

"Are you a good artist?"

"I like to think so. My sketches are usually a great help in finding perpetrators."

Mrs. Gunderson sighed. "I hope I am a help to you. You know, I'm pretty old, maybe my eyes aren't what they used to be."

Adams looked at the shiny bright eyes peering through the matriarchal face that sat before him. "There is a great brightness in your eyes. I think you will do just fine. To get started, can you tell me what type of face we are looking at here. You know, a general description. We know he was a black man."

"What do you mean, how do I start?"

"Was his face long, round, how were the eyes and mouth set, big nose, little nose, you know, just a general description."

Mrs. Gunderson looked out the window and appeared to be lost in thought. A few minutes passed before she finally spoke. "Are you a Navy Seal?"

"What...wha...what?" Adams stammered.

The old woman smiled. "Are you a Navy Seal?"

"Umm, no, what would make you think that?"

"I thought all of you FBI people were former Navy Seals."

Adams laughed. "No, no, I'm not a Navy Seal. I've never been in the service of any kind. I'm just an artist."

"Are there any Navy Seals here in your FBI unit?"

"No, I don't think so."

"It seems like everyone's an ex-Navy Seal in all the detective suspense novels that I read."

"Yes, well, those are just stories. There really aren't that many Navy Seals to go around. Most of them stay in the service for years, and police work is a different business. Books and movies, they kind of overdo it."

"That's too bad. I really wanted to meet a Navy Seal," Mrs. Gunderson looked out of the window again and lost herself deep in thought.

"Mrs. Gunderson, let's get back to our sketch. Can you give me a general description?"

Mrs. Gunderson fixed her eyes back on the sketch artist. She smiled and her eyes beamed with light. "Denzel Washington, he is such a handsome, fine looking black man."

"Yes, yes he is. Did the man look like him?"

"Yes, he was a handsome black man, he looked kind of like a young Denzel Washington, but Denzel Washington would never kill anyone would he?"

"No, I don't think he would, but let's start with that look. I'll sketch in a broad outline based on Denzel Washington's appearance when he was young. We can adjust it from there."

Adams picked up a charcoal pencil and began sketching in an outline.

Mrs. Gunderson bent over in her chair and grunted.

"Are you okay?" Concern showed in the artist's voice.

A pink flush came over the old woman's face that made her look almost girlish. "Oh, it's just these damn foot stockings. They won't stay up. I should really get some new ones."

Adams smiled and finished the roughing in of the sketch.

"Now, how does this look. Does it look anything like him?"

"Oh my yes, but it's not very distinguished. It seems like you left a lot out."

"That's where you're going to help me. Now, I'm going to ask you a series of questions that will help better define the man's features. Are you ready?"

"Ready as I'll ever be."

Adams laughed and then calmed himself. He had to try and concentrate. "His nose, does his nose look right?"

"No, it was a little broader at the tip, a little wider on the sides."

Adams sketched the changes in. This wasn't going to be so bad after all, he thought to himself. "What about his eyes, closer together wider, thicker lashes, or thinner."

Mrs. Gunderson seemed to be all business now. "His eyes were closer together. His eyebrows were a little thicker, and his eyes seemed a little beadier, but of course, maybe that was just because of what he had just done."

"Yeah, maybe, but I'll sketch it in anyway," Adams went back to work on the drawing.

Mrs. Gunderson went into a coughing fit.

"Would you like a glass of water?"

"Yes, that would be so kind of you."

Adams left the room and went down the hall to the water cooler. When he returned, he saw Mrs. Gunderson rifling through a desk drawer.

"What are you doing?" He said incredulously.

"Oh, I'm sorry, I'm really just a nosy busybody. I didn't think you would be back so soon."

"Let's put those papers back and get back to our drawing."

"Okay, you're such a fine young man, a fine young man," Mrs. Gunderson stammered and then retook her seat.

"Okay, let's continue with the drawing. How was his hair compared to the drawing. His chin, jowls, forehead, any detail you can tell me."

Mrs. Gunderson now seemed more focused on the details. Question after question came from Adams, and this no doubt kept the old woman more focused. After an hour had passed the drawing was done.

"That looks just like him!" Mrs. Gunderson exclaimed.

"Good, we'll make copies and distribute them."

"I'm glad I could be of help, but isn't there just one Navy Seal at your headquarters that I could meet. Just one."

Adams smiled. I'll check into it and give you a call if I can find one. How would that be?"

"Oh, that would be wonderful."

Adams took the old woman by the shoulder again and led her out to the front door of the precinct. He watched her as she climbed into a taxi. I hope her memory really is good, was all that he could think of as he turned and walked back into the precinct.

Sonnentag

Chapter 12

Collins drove the silver Crown Victoria down Highway 116 and once again passed the sign for the Waukau nature preserve. Wendtworth looked to the right and saw a large parking lot.

Wendtworth was amazed. "What are all of those cars doing over there on the right? You know, it looks like this preserve is bigger than I thought. Pull into the parking lot there on the right."

Collins pulled the vehicle into the gravel lot and drove to the middle of the parking area. Wendtworth got out and surveyed the surroundings. The area was full of fishermen, there had to be at least thirty of them on the creek and pond that formed this part of the preserve. Wendtworth walked up a small knoll with Collins following close behind her.

"This is interesting. I guess there is something to do out here after all. Reminds me of when I was a little girl and used to go fishing with my father," Wendtworth finished.

Collins grunted. "That's very touching, but what does it have to do with us?"

Wendtworth glared at Collins. "Nothing, it just brings back memories of going fishing with my father when I was young, that's all. Let's go."

Collins spoke up as they traveled further along the highway. "Maybe we'll find some information on the murder of the cult leader when we look through the files at Harrison House."

"Let's hope so," Joan responded softly.

Five miles down the road Collins was pulling the Crown Victoria on to the drive in front of Harrison House. The old dog was nowhere to be seen. Wendtworth figured the dog was out chasing birds, or cats, or something. After a few minutes, Mrs. Larsen opened the door to the house and ushered the two agents in. The frown on her face told them she was not happy to see them.

Mrs. Larsen led the agents to sit at the large dining table. Clearly, she did not want the agents there and did not want to make them any more comfortable than she had to.

Wendtworth remained standing and got right down to business. "We're here to check the client records for the last ten years or so. We're looking for a client that was black. Do you remember any black clients in the past?"

Mrs. Larsen rubbed her jaw, and it appeared that she was not going to answer. She let out a small huff of air. "I don't like this business. Can't you just leave us alone. We have a lot of changes we're making. New owners. New management. I don't even know if I'm going to be kept on."

Collins snarled. "Don't you want justice? Don't you want to know who killed Mr. Harrison?"

"Justice would be fine, but leave us alone. Find your justice somewhere else. There is no justice to be found here," Larsen responded.

Wendtworth finally took a seat cater-corner from the old woman. She stared deeply into her eyes. "What are you hiding?" She asked bluntly.

The old woman sat back in exasperation. She ran her hand through her thinning white hair. Her eyes began to tear up slightly. "Go ahead then, search the records. I don't care."

Collins spoke firmly. "Where are the records? Are they on computer?"

The old woman shifted in her seat. "Some are, some aren't. Mr. Harrison didn't get a computer until about five years ago. Any records beyond that are paper records. They're kept in the basement in a locked room."

Collins continued. "Do you have the key?"

The old woman shook her head and dropped her chin in her hands. "I don't know where the key is. Mr. Harrison was the only one who had a key."

Joan's voice was firm and businesslike. "Can you show us to the basement?"

The old woman grunted as she rose. She stretched out like a cat, her bones creaking as she stretched. Without saying a word, she rose and walked away. The two agents followed her through the kitchen where she stopped and pointed at an old, varnished door.

Mrs. Larsen spoke quietly. "Down there, the basement is down there."

Larsen turned around and walked briskly away from the two agents.

Collins opened the door and a musty smell of mold assaulted their senses. He stepped into the stairway and flipped on a light. The basement walls were encrusted with dirt and cobwebs. The stairs creaked with the weight of the two agents as they descended.

"Like being in an old horror movie," Wendtworth laughed.

"Yeah, I wonder if there's someone down here with a chain saw."

"A chain saw huh, you sure do have a vivid imagination. Wouldn't a knife or an ax do just fine?"

"Oh yeah, that would be just fine," Collins laughed.

The agents crossed to the center of the basement floor and surveyed the surrounding walls when their eyes came upon a dirty, golden, oak door on the far side of the basement. They walked up to the door and saw that it was locked.

"The door is locked," Collins stated glumly.

"Brilliant Sherlock, what did you expect. Larsen told us the records were kept locked up. How are you at lock picking?"

"Never done it, and you?"

"Ditto."

The agents stood and stared at the door a moment. Wendtworth finally spoke up. "We can just take off the hinges."

"Sounds good. There's a work bench over there on the far wall. Maybe there's an old screw driver there."

"Go check it out," Wendtworth said quietly.

"I'm not going over there. Look at all those cobwebs. How am I supposed to get through those?"

"Oh, you big baby, I'll do it," Wendtworth said in annoyance.

Joan walked ahead, brushing the cobwebs aside. She stood in front of the battered, old workbench and searched the shelves above for contents. Her eyes came to rest on an old, rusty, wooden-handled screwdriver. She brushed more cobwebs aside and picked up the antique tool. I hope it doesn't break, she was thinking as she walked back across the basement to the golden, oak door. She handed the tool to Collins.

Collins looked at the rusty tool in his hands. "I hope I don't cut myself. There is probably all manner of germs and disease on this old thing."

Collins began prying at the hinges. With a lot of effort he soon had two of the hinges out, but the top hinge didn't want to budge. He wedged the door open with a near-by two by four and began prying at the screws inside the door jam. With sweat dripping down his face, he grabbed the door and twisted it back and forth until the screws finally gave away. With a loud huff, he threw the door aside.

"Good work, Mr. B and E," Joan laughed.

"Yeah, quiet as a mouse, wasn't I?"

The two agents stepped into the room. They were surprised to see it was rather large, about sixteen by twenty feet. It was also neat and clean. Collins flipped on a light switch on the right-hand wall. The room became brightly illuminated.

"Look at that, it looks like a photography studio. A large, clean bed, spot-lights."

"Yeah, and I'll bet that over behind that curtain is a dark-room."

"This is getting interesting, very interesting."

"There's the file cabinet over there."

For the next half an hour, the two agents rifled through the paperwork. They found that in the previous ten years, only five black children had resided in the home.

"Only five, that's not too bad. We should be able to check them out easy enough," Collins concluded.

"Yeah, that's not too bad. I didn't really expect to see too many black, male children staying at a place like this out in the country. It's too bad there are no photographs of the children.

We might be able to match a child up with the forensic artist's sketch."

"Yeah, well, we'll just have to do some legwork and track these men down."

Wendtworth stood up and stretched. She lit up a cigarette.

"So, you're smoking again."

"Yeah, too much stress in my life. I made a bad choice and here I am, smoking again."

"It smells like gas down here. I hope you don't blow us up."

"Yeah, right. Hey, let's check out that darkroom behind that curtain further," Joan said as she pointed to the left and to a dusty, burgundy curtain that covered a doorway.

Collins nodded. The two agents entered a small, four by six foot room. Collins waved his hands in the air searching for a pull-cord. He hit Joan on the side of the face.

"Ouch, damn-it. Watch what you're doing."

"Sorry, wait, here it is. I've got it," Collins pulled on a dangling cord.

The room was lit up dimly by the forty-watt bulb in the loose hanging fixture above them. Collins stepped up to the darkroom table to look at the trays that lay before him. He bumped his foot on something below the table. Bending down, he took a closer look.

"There's an old locked chest under here," Collins said excitedly.

Collins pulled the chest out from under the table. It was clean and cobweb free. He saw that it was an army footlocker.

Collins grabbed the leather handle on the side and pulled the chest out into the larger, bright room.

"Whatever this is, it's been visited often. It's clean, and look at the way the finish by the latches has been worn away from frequent use."

"See if you can pry the lock off?"

"I don't know; it looks pretty tough. I need a hammer or something."

"How about an ax?" Joan laughed.

"You're kidding, of course."

"No, not really. There's an ax by the sidewall back outside by the entrance to this room. I'll go get it."

Joan went back into the first room and retrieved the ax. She returned and handed it to Collins. Collins put the screwdriver in behind the clasp and steadied himself. "I hope I don't hit my hand."

"You won't, just be careful."

Collins took aiming strokes three times and then brought the ax down hard on the end of the screwdriver. The wood shattered, a small fragment embedding itself in his left arm.

"Ouch, damn-it."

"There's goes another antique," Joan laughed.

Collins pealed the wood away from the metal of the screw-driver and was left with a nice metal wedge. He placed the wedge behind the hinge again, and without any practice swings brought the ax down on the metal. Four more slams and he was able to work the latch free with the metal wedge of the screw-driver.

"Porno, lots of porno," Joan said calmly.

"You don't sound too surprised."

"I kind of expected it, what with the studio surroundings and darkrooms. This guy was abusing kids and photographing it."

Collins flipped through the pictures.

"He wasn't too particular on which sex he abused, was he?"

"No, it doesn't seem he was. Maybe our killer is in one of these pictures."

"Could be, but he would be a child. How could that help us?"

"We'll take the pictures back to headquarters, take any of black male children, and have them run a computer enhancement aging program on them. Then we'll compare the aged, black faces to the artist drawing and see if any look the same. We might be able to have a better look at the face of the suspect."

"Yeah, it might help. Let's get this stuff out of here."

The two agents sat quietly in the car in order to catch their breath.

"No wonder Mrs. Larsen didn't want us around. She must have known about this," Collins said.

"We'll never know. There's no reason she would implicate herself. She probably has a don't ask-don't tell policy concerning Harrison. Needed her job, in love with him, who knows. We'll never know, but that's not important. We got what we needed. Maybe this will be a big help."

"It probably will. More clues. The gap seems to be narrowing."

Joan stated with finality. "It always does. It always does."

Slayer Player

Chapter 13

The knock on the door was less timid this time. It came in a rapid staccato of bursts separated by only a few seconds until another burst came. Wendtworth knew it had to be her little friend from next door. She had seen her through the kitchen window when earlier the young girl had entered the barn to feed Sneakers.

It was a beautiful late fall morning of amber, orange, and yellow-golden colors that had only half-way fallen from the trees. The sun delivered a burst of warmth that by ten A.M. had brought the temperature to fifty-five degrees. A cloudless, windless sky promised an increase in warmth throughout the day. If there was such a thing as an Indian summer in mid-November this day was surely it.

Wendtworth opened the door to the beaming white smile of the young girl. Holly bounced up and down in happiness and bounded into the house. Holly pulled her bright, Christmas red scarf from around her neck and threw it over Joan's favorite chair. Joan noticed the stitching was not very tight in some places.

"Good morning Holly, how are you this fine morning?"

"Joan, I'm just great. Sneakers is really happy too, he can't wait to take you for a ride. I could see it in his eyes when I went out to the barn."

Joan looked at the red scarf again. "Holly, did you make that scarf?"

"Oh yeah, I didn't do a very good job though, it is the first piece of clothing that I have ever knitted," Holly said somewhat dejectedly.

"Oh no, on the contrary, it's wonderful, it's nice that you are learning such an art and hobby. Who is teaching you?"

151

"The mother of a friend of mine."

"Holly, for a first effort the scarf is very nice. I'm sure you will get better with more practice."

"Yeah, the stitching is a little loose, but I like doing it. It relaxes me and gives me something productive to do."

"You know Holly. You're a very wise young lady."

"Thank you Joan, but hey, let's get back to the plan for today," Holly bounced up and down and let out a small cheer. "Are you ready to ride?"

Joan was a little unsure of herself. "I guess, I don't know. I am a little scared. As you know, I have never been on a horse before. I want to, it's just that, I don't know, I don't want to fall off."

"You won't fall off, Sneakers is as gentle as any horse can be."

Joan believed Holly's words and found them soothing. Since the horse had moved into the barn, Joan had several chances to watch the young girl with the horse. She was so gentle and loving with the animal. Holly had the horse since it was a pony, and it was easy to see the love the two shared. Joan only hoped that Sneakers would take to her as gently and as lovingly as he had taken to Holly.

"Let's get to it Joan. Sneakers is chomping at the bit to get going."

"You mean you have him saddled already."

"Yes, after I fed him and brushed him, I saddled him. He loves going for runs. He kept bumping up against the stall in excitement."

Joan walked towards the coat hooks by the door and grabbed an old, brown, cloth coat. She swung the coat on and shrugged. "Now is as good a time as any. Let's go."

Holly bounded out of the back door in front of Joan. She raced to the barn with Joan doing a slower stroll behind her. Joan was still a little apprehensive. What was a woman of forty doing riding a horse for the first time? In her heart she knew this was the best chance she would ever have of fulfilling the childhood dream of what was nearly every female child in the country.

The two entered the barn and Sneakers let out an excited whinny. He lifted his front legs, and then he brushed up against the front gate of the stall. His eyes sparkled. It was easy to see that he was happy and ready to go. The rusty hinges creaked as Holly opened the dusty, wooden gate and led the horse out by the bit. Joan could smell the freshly brushed coat of the animal as she drew closer to it.

Holly beamed. "Joan, give Sneakers a few pets on the top of his nose, he loves that."

Joan stepped forward in front of the horse's head, lifted her right hand, and began to stroke the horse softly on the top of his head. Sneakers neighed and shook his head up and down with glee. She blinked her right eye as if to say that everything was going to be okay.

Joan smiled. "Okay Sneakers, be gentle with me, this is my first time."

Holly took Sneakers by the bit. "Okay Joan, it's time. Just go around the side and put your right foot in the stirrup. Step up and swing your left leg over his back."

Joan stood beside the horse and was glad the mustang was small in stature, but a mustang it was she thought, and she knew the history of mustangs was that they were a horse tamed from the wilds. She wondered how much of a wild gene would still be left in this one. He seemed tame enough though, and she knew the horse knew a great deal of love in his life. She convinced herself that everything would be fine. She swung herself up on top of the horse and braced herself for movement. The horse remained motionless. Sneakers had been well trained by Holly.

Joan felt an unknown source of strength arise inside her. She felt proud to be on the back of the strong animal. Six feet off the ground, she felt on top of the world. She tightened her legs tighter than she should have and Sneakers took that as a sign to go. Sneakers stepped forward brusquely. She was quickly restrained by Holly.

"Okay Joan, loosen you legs, Sneakers will respond to a very little bit of pressure on his sides and be ready to go. He will walk slowly for you if you just squeeze his sides gently. Usually, I ride him pretty slow, because I just like the feel of the slow jumble of his body as he moves beneath me. He's used to that. He likes to go slow and look around."

Holly stepped back from the horse, her face filled with joy. She was happy to give Joan a chance to ride. It reminded her of the first time that she had ridden Sneakers. Joan gave a gentle pressure to Sneakers sides and the horse began to walk slowly out of the barn yard.

"Holly, I forgot, how do I stop him?"

"Just pull back a little on the bit and he will stop. Pull right or left to get him to change directions. He will obey just fine. He won't be any problem," Holly assured Joan.

Joan pulled right on the bit and turned Sneakers right onto the edge of a hayfield. The horse walked slowly through the tall grass. Joan felt a sense of freedom she had never known in her life. For a moment, she felt like a young girl, the young girl who had always had a dream of riding a horse so many years ago.

Joan pinched Sneakers sides a little harder. The horse broke into a small gate. Sneakers became a little excited and wanted to go faster because he sensed the heavier weight on his back was an older person. Joan pulled gently on the bit to slow the horse down and he readily responded. Joan was not surprised at how easily the horse obeyed commands. He was indeed gentle, and it was easy to see that Holly had trained her horse well.

Coming to the end of the hay field; horse and rider came upon a small forest. Joan saw a path leading into the center of the woods where there was an opening. She pulled right and back on the bit again and Sneakers followed the path into a clearing in the center of the woods. Joan pulled back and stopped the horse. It was now time to get off.

She had no instructions from Holly to follow, but she guessed instinct would be enough to work for her this time. She let go of the bit, Sneakers stood still, and Joan lifted her left leg up over the horse, swung it around, and stepped effortlessly down to the ground. I'm glad I did this before I got too old, she thought to herself.

Sneakers stepped off about twenty feet into the distance and lowered his head to graze on some tall, fresh, green grass. Joan walked back about ten feet and sat down against a tree to watch the animal graze. She looked at the sleek body of the animal and felt a slight sexual attraction. Sneakers was so young and strong, and she couldn't help but notice his large penis sheath. She sighed and realized that maybe now, in this new life on the farm, she would need a man more than she had in a long time. She laughed to herself. She would have to wait, but out here in the country, where would she find one. Maybe a handsome, strong, young farmer would come along, but what would she have in common with him. Her life had been so different than the one she was about to jump into now. She could change though, couldn't she? It was never too late to change your life.

Joan stood up and brushed herself off. She thought it would be a good time to see if she had made any headway making friends with Sneakers. "Sneakers, come here," she said strongly yet trying to sound friendly.

The horse picked up its head and perked up his large ears. His eyes twinkled.

"Sneakers, come here," Joan commanded gently again.

Sneakers trotted happily over and nuzzled his nose against Joan's chest. Joan stroked his head and the horse neighed happily.

"It's time to go again," Joan said softly and the horse shook his head in agreement.

Joan got up onto Sneakers more easily this time. She was beginning to feel like a real rider now. She turned Sneakers around and headed back to the hayfield. She squeezed Sneakers sides and he picked up his gate. Now was the time, she thought, this is my chance, I have to go at least a little fast.

"Okay Sneakers, this is it, what the hell, let's stretch it out a little. The worst I can do is kill myself. Sneakers, there's some spunk in me yet. Let's go," Joan pressed hard on Sneakers sides and rapped his bit.

Sneakers picked up speed quickly and Joan wondered at the wisdom of her decision to make him go fast. She could feel his strong body moving wildly below her. The horse was fast, faster than she had expected. She fought the urge in her mind to panic and squeeze him tighter. She relaxed herself and pulled back slowly on the bit. Sneakers responded and pulled back, but then he increased his speed again. It was plain to see that he did not want to slow down. Joan pulled back again, and the horse slowed to half the speed it had been traveling, but it was still at a run. Joan adjusted to the movement and found she liked it. It seemed to take only a few minutes and horse and rider were back at the farmyard. She pulled back on the bit, probably a little too hard, and Sneakers stopped in a cloud of dust.

"Hey Joan, I've been watching all this time. You're a good rider," Holly laughed as she rushed up to rider and horse.

Joan looked down with a frown on her face. "I don't know about that, but it didn't feel too scary. It was fun. I seemed to adjust to him rather quickly."

Joan got down off of Sneakers, walked over to Holly, and gave her a big hug. "He's a wonderful horse. You trained him well."

Holly smiled and just kept petting Sneakers' head.

Joan patted Holly on the head. "Holly, thanks so much. It was wonderful. Someday we'll have to borrow another horse from somewhere so we can take a ride together."

"That would be wonderful, you can ride Sneakers, he likes you, and I'll ride the other horse. It would be fun for me to ride another horse."

"Okay, it's a deal then, for now, you put Sneakers away, and I'll go into the house and start some lunch for us."

"It's a deal Joan, all of it."

Joan watched Holly lead Sneakers into the barn. She watched the strong, young haunches of the animal as it disappeared into the barn, and she marveled at the wonder of how her childhood dream had come true. Life was so strange, she thought, so unpredictable, but this was the kind of unpredictability she could come to love, the kind that had been missing from her life for so many years. Joan felt unaccustomed warmth in her chest as she walked into the house. She liked the feeling.

Chapter 14

  Coach Erickson had coached the eighth grade Boys football
team for twenty years. He had won half a dozen conference
championships. Taken the boys to state twice, and come away
with third and second place finishes. He was somewhat frustrated that he could never get over the hump and take the title.
He always had a happy and disciplined squad, but there was always one boy who was withdrawn on the squad, one boy who
would eventually quit the team. He didn't think the sacrifice
was too much. After all, it was only one boy.
  Poppin had surveyed the school several times in the last three
weeks. He noticed that it was usually about eight o'clock before
the coach left the building, and by that time, there was no one
around. But how to get in. The building was always kept
locked. He was going to have to take a chance he didn't want to
take.
  Poppin stood around the outside door closest to the locker
room. He had noticed that the boys always left by that door, and
there was always one straggler among them. The boy would
never get out of the building until six-thirty or six forty-five. At
six-twenty-five, he left his car and went to stand beside the door.
Poppin stood flat against the side of the building. Five minutes
later a young boy with blonde-hair raced out of the building.
  Poppin grabbed the door and slipped in behind the young man.
The boy turned to look and see who was behind him, but it was
too late. All he saw was the back of the head of a black man
holding a briefcase. The young boy shrugged, he wondered
what a black man was doing slipping in the door at this time of
night. He jogged along home, quickly forgetting and not caring
about what he had seen.

Poppin slowly opened the door to the locker room and slipped inside. A heavy humidity from all the showers the boys had taken still hung in the air. He recognized the smell of sweat and remembered his own days in a locker room after he had finished high school basketball practice. He took a deep smell, savoring the memory. He was surprised at how vividly the memory had crowded in given what he was about to do.

He gazed around the locker room and saw a large, six by eight foot glass window. He looked at the sign above the office; Victory begins when each individual player plays to the best of his ability as the member of a team. The glass window beckoned him forward. He knew that behind this glass rested the coach's office. The office door was open. Poppin pulled out the silenced Smith and Wesson thirty-eight and quietly slipped through the open doorway.

The coach was bent down over the playbook on the desk designing a play.

"That's the last play you'll ever design," Poppin said softly.

The coach looked up to see a black man standing before him with a gun. His eyes widened and his jaw dropped. "What are you doing in here?"

"Justice has come for you today. This is for all the young boys you picked out each year to ruin their lives. This is for one boy in particular you picked out ten years ago."

Poppin aimed the pistol and fired two shots into the man's chest.

The shots flung the coach's body back in his chair, arms flailing wildly. He leaned forward and then sat straight back up. He put his hands to his chest and came away with them covered in blood. Blood began to ooze out of the corner of his mouth. He took a deep, gasping breath. "I, I didn't mean to hurt anyone. I love children."

"You loved some of them the wrong way," Poppin fired another shot that hit the coach right in the center of the forehead.

The coach's head fell with a loud thump on the desk, and he was dead. Poppin set his briefcase on the desk and opened it up. He removed a paper bag and spread white powder over the body.

He placed a note on the desk in front of the coach. The note
read 'Game over, Game on.' He closed the briefcase, turned and
walked out of the office, leaving the smell of gunpowder, blood,
and bone meal behind him. He shoved the pistol in the shoulder
holster under his jacket. He didn't notice the smell of the locker
room this time as he fled through it and out into the hall. The
hall was empty, good, he thought, so far so good. He slipped out
the side door and back into the parking lot. No one was around.
He crossed the lot, got in his car, and drove away. Another successful kill, only two more to go.

Poppin sat back in the leather recliner and laughed to himself.
Some of them out there, the public, thought he was a thrilla killa,
but he knew what he really was. He was a man on a mission.
The troubling thought though was the violence from his past that
welled up inside him. He had a reason to kill, a good one, he
thought. But his father, he hated when he closed his eyes and
saw the raging, evil, almost green eyes that stared at him after he
had just been physically and mentally abused by him. He wondered, was he killing his father, over and over again. The rage
seemed to dissipate only briefly after a kill, and then it seemed to
come back all the more intensely later for the next one.

He was doing the right thing, he reasoned, bringing justice to
those who had been helpless children. But the children, they
were all adults now, couldn't they seek justice for themselves.
No, not this kind of justice, not sword for sword, stone for stone,
blow for blow, gun for gun. When he thought of it this way, he
was happy. These low-down pieces of shit didn't belong on this
earth. They had brought hell to so many children so hell was the
place where they had to be sent. Fuck-it, Poppin laughed, too
late to get goody now.

Poppin sat back in his favorite black leather recliner and took a
sip of Hennessey. The liquor cooled his throat and calmed his
racing heart. He wiped the sweat from his brow with the sleeve
of his white dress shirt. He needed to watch some rap videos,
connect with the street. It seemed that sometimes he felt just too
far removed from it. Maybe, he thought, that is what he liked
about the killings. It was so raw, so street. And yet here he was,

basking in a life of luxury. The irony of it all. He seemed to have everything he wanted so why did he jeopardize it for something else. Why did he have to keep the promises he had made to these children so many years ago. He took another sip of the whiskey, best not to think about it, best to float off into some kind of oblivion. Most of his life he felt that is where he was anyway.

Chapter 15

The rap-song doorbell played BPD's most recent number.
Poppin stirred from the depths of his oblivion and wondered
who would be intruding on his home at three A.M.
Could be anyone, should he rise and answer the call or just ignore it and let his mind float back out there. What the hell, he
thought, it could be fun, could break the state of his lost mind.

He reached over to the console on the table and hit the talk button. "Yeah, what's up?"

"It's Peter. I need to talk to you."

Poppin sat quietly in thought for a moment. He knew a half a
dozen guys named Peter from being in the business, but he
couldn't place the voice. Maybe the speaker was distorting it.

Poppin leaned forward, hit the talk button, his voice coming out
in a low guttural tone. "Peter who?"

The static cleared as if by magic. "Peter Miller; I'm from from
the old days, from Harrison House."

Poppin sat bolt upright in his chair. What was this, he thought,
and in the next moment, he knew. One of the children from
those days long gone by had caught on. What to do now. There
was nothing else he could do. He reached over to the talk button. "Come in, come right on in."

Poppin reached over and hit the button to release the electronic
gate. A few moments later a knock was sounded on his front
door. He hit the release button and the door swung open. Peter
Miller walked slowly into the room and stopped six feet in front
of Poppin.

Poppin surveyed the man who stood before him. He remembered him as being big as a child of thirteen. He had been a
farm kid, years of totin' bales of hay had already made him tall
and stocky by that age. He was bigger now, six-foot three and

close to three hundred pounds. Huge biceps were surrounded by a tattoo of barbed wire on each arm.

Poppin addressed the young man. "What are you doing here; have you come to thank me?"

"Thank you, hell no. I want you to stop what you're doing." Peter flexed his biceps in a show of strength, the barbed wire expanding and standing out against his white skin.

"Stop, why the hell should I stop, I made the pact for your and the others benefits."

"Yeah, maybe then, in your warped way, you did, but now, you're just doing it for yourself. You have to stop."

Poppin shook his head no and grinned. "Can't stop, won't stop."

"Then, I'll make you stop," Peter answered angrily.

"Son, you better stay out of this if you know what's good for you. This trip is rollin' strong and it ain't gonna be over until it's over."

Peter stared straight into Poppin's eyes. He saw a swirling rage there that scared him. He turned around and headed for the door.

At the door, about to leave, he turned back. "Watch your back Poppin, I may be back, and you ain't gonna like it when I am."

After Peter had left, Poppin sat back in his chair and took a whiff of his cigar. What a bitch, he thought to himself. What a little ungrateful bitch.

Chapter 16

Shawn sat on the couch and leafed through the most recent copy of Rolling Stone magazine when Joan entered the living room.

Joan had a sexy pout on her lips. "Would you like a glass of wine?"

Shawn put the magazine down. "I guess a glass of wine would be fine, but Joan, I wonder, what is it you're trying to do, seduce me?"

"You're pretty blunt aren't you? I really hadn't thought about that no." Joan was lying.

Joan went to the kitchen and poured two glasses of wine. She returned to the living room and sat down on the couch next to Shawn. She could feel the heat of the young man, smell the masculinity surrounding him. She must be crazy, she thought, but she couldn't get out of her mind the thought of what it would be like to have the young man taking her sexually.

"Anything interesting in the magazine," Joan began nervously.

"No, not really, just a lot of the same old stuff."

"Are you interested in music?"

"I'm not a musician if that's what you mean, but I like music a lot, and I hope to work in some kind of editing and production some day. I want to attend some kind of school for it."

Joan leaned forward and put her right hand on Shawn's left knee. "Shawn, I don't know how long you can stay here with me. I'm used to living alone. I don't know if I can stand having someone around a lot."

"That's okay, just let me stay awhile until I can get on my own two feet, get a job, get enrolled in school. We can see how it goes. You're gone a lot. I won't be a bother, and I can help you pay rent."

"We'll see, you can stay awhile, we'll see how things go. I've been looking at buying a farm out in the country. I want to retire from the FBI. If I let you stay here, maybe by the time I move you can take over this apartment, but I've got to think about all of this." Joan put down her glass on the coffee table nearly knocking it over as she did so.

"Do I make you nervous Joan?"

Joan hadn't expected the blunt question. Her cheeks flushed, and she turned slightly to the right to look Shawn directly in the eyes. Shawn inched closer to her, taking her hand into his own two hands and rubbing it gently.

"I don't mean to make you nervous, but truth be told, I'm kind of nervous myself. I think we both know what we feel between us."

Joan smiled and put her other hand over Shawn's hands. Shawn leaned over and kissed her on the cheek. He brushed her blonde hair back and moved his mouth over to softly brush her lips. Joan let out a small sigh. She took the side of his head and brought it tightly against her mouth. They enfolded each other and began to kiss passionately, Shawn putting his right hand under her sweater to reach up and caress her breasts.

Joan pushed away and stood up. She removed her clothes and then knelt before Shawn. She removed his manhood and gently kissed it. After several minutes of foreplay, she climbed up on Shawn's strong, young body. She shivered as he entered her. Joan felt young again as she pushed herself again and again against Shawn's body. She climaxed to a nightfall of shining stars swirling within her brain.

The two lovers lay together breathing in unison.

"What have I done?" Joan panted.

"You've done what you wanted to do for a long time. Maybe since the first time you saw me. It's all right. We're both adults. We can handle this."

Joan sighed. "I'm not going to think about our age difference. It's been a long time since I made love. You made me feel wonderful."

"Let's do it again," Shawn said happily.

Joan laughed. "Youth, oh yeah, youth, I feel pretty young right now myself. You're on, but let's go to the bedroom."

By the time the sun was coming up they had made love two more times and slept for hours in each other's arms. Shawn got up from the bed and went into the kitchen to make some coffee. On the counter he saw the artist sketch and the computer enhancement of the suspect Joan was chasing. Joan entered the kitchenette and sat on a stool. Shawn poured Joan a coffee, added cream and sugar, and set it before her.

Joan began to take a sip, but pushed the cup away because it was too hot. "How did you know I liked cream and sugar?"

Shawn giggled. "I don't know, I just figured."

Joan sighed. "We fit together well, almost too well."

"Don't worry about it, just enjoy what we have right now."

The couple sipped at their coffees in silence.

After a couple of minutes, Shawn spoke up. "I was looking at these composites you have of the suspect you are looking for, and I was struck by the resemblance of someone I saw in Rolling Stone magazine, but I doubt that the man could be who you're looking for."

Joan perked up interest. "Really, who do you think it looks like?"

"It looks like this guy named Poppin. Rolling Stone magazine did a feature on him two months ago. He's a record producer in the rap industry, up and coming and all of that."

Joan was only slightly excited. "Let me see his picture?"

Shawn went into the living room and retrieved the old magazine from his duffle bag. Back in the kitchen he opened it on the counter and put one composite drawing on each side of the large opening feature picture of Poppin. The couple stared in study.

Joan put down her coffee cup. "He sure looks like the picture on the right, the picture that was done by our forensics artist. In fact, he looks a little like the other one to, but the forensics sketch, he looks a lot like that one."

Shawn took a sip of his coffee. "Maybe it's nothing."

"Yeah, could just be coincidence, but we've got nothing so far. Collins and I will check this guy out. We've got nothing to lose."

Shawn laughed. "I can't believe someone with his credentials would be a killer."

Joan's face took on a stern expression. "You never know, serial killers can cross all types of boundaries."

The two sat quietly for awhile looking at the pictures and sipping their coffee.

Shawn smiled. "Let's go back to bed."

Joan giggled like a schoolgirl. "I'd love to, but I have to get to work, and besides, I think I'm going to have sore muscles from what we have already done. I'm not as young as I used to be."

"I never once have thought of your age. I just connect with you, and that's all I can think of."

"I connect with you too Shawn, but I'm going to shower and get to work."

Joan left Shawn sitting at the counter. While she showered she thought of the wisdom of what she was doing. Shawn was so young, but what did it matter. She made him happy. He made her feel sexually alive again. She would deal with their age differences some other time. She felt too good and complete right now to spoil it. She felt alive again. She couldn't wait to get to work, giving off to everyone the warm glow she now possessed. Shawn and I, time will tell, time will tell, she thought as she left the apartment and headed out to the curb to be picked up by Collins.

*****

Shawn's court date arrived and he would have to face it alone. Joan wanted to be there for him but she had been full of mixed emotions, and there was a lot of work to be done yet to catch a killer. Shawn caught a ride from an old friend from Harrison House to the Green Lake County Courthouse. He went up to the courtroom on the second floor and sat on an old wooden bench opposite the room number that he had gotten off his summons papers. He waited patiently for his lawyer to arrive. Joan had pulled in a favor from an old acquaintance and gotten him an associate of one of the better drug lawyers in Madison.

The bench was filled with a wide variety of ne'r-do-wells, several black men were grouped together on Shawn's far left side, and several Mexican men sat on the far right side of the bench. Several family members were grouped around the alleged criminals. One of the Mexican women was swearing and another Mexican woman was crying. Shawn turned and looked away, shaking his head, he was glad he was alone.

Slowly, one by one, people were called into the courtroom and sections of the bench emptied. Shawn looked to his right and saw his lawyer Sam Stone coming down the hall. He had met him only once so from a distance he wasn't quite sure it was him. The man walked up, stood in front of Shawn, and smiled. Shawn rose to shake the man's hand and noticed his hand was sweaty.

Mr. Stone seemed excited. "Come with me, we'll go to a conference room and talk things over quickly."

Shawn rose and followed Stone. Stone was only about five-foot seven inches tall, about the same height as Shawn, but he had the heavier build of a man in his mid forties who had spent most of his life sitting on his butt. He was not overly heavy though and Shawn took this as a good sign. The man must be active in doing something besides lawyer work, maybe he worked out a little. Stone had surprisingly soft blue eyes, and somewhat unkempt long blonde strands of hair that fell wildly over his forehead. Shawn reasoned that maybe this was the way a drug lawyer was supposed to look.

Stone's voice was cheery. "Well, at the pre-trial conference I got them to agree to six months in jail and four and a half years probation. Various fines that aren't too high in their amount. All in all, you're going to get off fairly good since you've had no prior convictions. This could have gone a lot worse for you, you could get up to four years in prison. I'm pretty happy with what I was able to bargain out for you at the pretrial conference."

Shawn leaned back in the chair and let out a large sigh. "I don't want to do no jail time man, I told you that. I just don't want to do no jail time."

Stone smiled. "I know, nobody does, but that's just not the reality of it. Manufacturing THC, a controlled substance, is a serious crime. They could really lay it heavy on you, in fact, there is no guarantee that the judge will go along with the recommendations of the District Attorney's offer from the pretrial conference. Be happy we got this deal, be apologetic and polite and you'll get this deal. Don't mess it up in there by saying anything inflammatory. Things could get a whole lot worse for you if you do."

Shawn shrugged. "Fine, I'll do what I have to, I'll be a sympathy gathering idiot in there."

"Okay, lose the anger, calm down, everything will be all right. Let's go back out to the hallway now and wait."

The two men went back to the bench and sat across from the courtroom door. A grisly- looking, unshaven, white man in a flannel shirt came out of the courtroom. "Two years man, damn, two years in jail. This fucking sucks."

Shawn had to stifle a laugh. From the man's appearance, it looked like he deserved two years, maybe more, no matter what his crime was. Shawn was glad he had worn a gray suit, white shirt, and tie. Appearances mattered, especially in court. A half an hour later another group of ten cases, Shawn's among them, was called into the courtroom for their cases to be heard. Shawn sat quietly, and listened to several cases being heard and charged, a battery, an OUI, and a burglary, the man in cuffs and jailhouse orange jumpsuit being lead to the stand by a jailhouse guard. After two hours of waiting, the bailiff called Shawn's name and case number.

Shawn and his lawyer went up and sat at the chairs behind the desk reserved for the accused. It felt different being up here to Shawn. He already felt guilty. He knew he was, but he had somehow convinced himself that all of this was no big deal up to this point. He couldn't deny it, the finality of it was breaking into his mind.

The judge was a rotund middle-aged man with a beet-red face and neck stretching out from his black robes. He sat at a station four or five feet off of the floor overlooking the domain before him. Shawn looked closely at the man's shiny red face and tried to look into his squinty eyes, but the judge was just too far away to make good eye contact. A sheen of sweat beaded up on the judge's face. The man looked tired and overworked. Shawn did not take this as a good sign, and he resigned himself to being fully apologetic and polite.

The bailiff read over Shawn's charges. Shawn's lawyer began his defense. Shawn's mind rambled. He was barely able to pay attention to the words that were being said. Sam Stone talked for awhile about something, but all that stood out to Shawn was that he had no prior convictions and the mention of the sentence recommendations that he had been given at the pretrial conference.

Silence reigned for a brief moment in the courtroom. A palpable tension surrounded Shawn, it was D-Day for him.

The judge wiped his forehead with a handkerchief and placed it back on the desk. "Mr. Jones, you have the options of guilty, not guilty, or no contest pleas to these charges, though with a no contest plea, this court will find you guilty as charged. How do you want to plead?"

Shawn managed to maintain a deep firmness in his voice. "Guilty, your honor."

"Okay, the guilty plea is accepted by this court. I'm inclined to go along with the recommendations of the District Attorney in this matter, but before I pass sentence, do you have anything you want to say."

Shawn cleared his throat and his voice sounded weak even to his own ears when he spoke. "Yes, your honor, I want to apologize to this court and the people of the State of Wisconsin. I know what I did was wrong, and I'm deeply sorry for it. Call it the ignorance of youth if you will. I was going through a very emotional time, trying to grow into adulthood, and I blew it. Again, I'm truly sorry, and nothing like this will ever happen again."

The judge paused for a moment. "Okay, Mr. Jones, I'm glad you've apologized, and I hope that you realize in the future that there are better ways to go through the transition from child to adult than by growing marijuana and selling it."

Shawn almost blurted out that he had never sold any, but he knew that was a lie, and he knew it would have been incredibly stupid at this point.

The judge continued in words that it seemed he had said a thousand times and probably had. "The only change I'm willing to make to the pretrial conference is to the amount of time to be served in jail. Since this is your first offense, and you seem truly apologetic, I'm willing to reduce sentence of jail time to four months." The judge went on to read the rest of the sentence and terms of probation. He finished in a drone. "That is my final verdict. Next case."

Shawn got up slowly from the chair, his head still ringing with the finality of the last sentence. Four months in jail, it seemed like a long time, but at least he had saved himself two months. He always got through everything alone in life anyway. He would miss Joan though, and he wondered if she would come and see him, or be disgusted by him and just blow him off for good. He was in a daze as he shook his lawyers hand and went out into the bright afternoon sunshine. He was going to miss that sunshine, miss the fresh air, he was going to miss his freedom. Shit was the one word that kept running through his head. Shit. Shit. Shit.

*****

Shawn stood outside the jail and took his last breath of fresh air for awhile. It wouldn't be too long before he got another breath though for he had gotten Huber work privileges at the time of his sentencing, and in the four week wait until there was an opening in the jail for another inmate, he had managed to get full time work across the street from the jail at the Duck Blind restaurant. He would be in jail two days before he worked his first full shift.

He wanted it this way. He figured he needed the two days to adjust to his new situation. He didn't know if this made sense or not. Maybe he should have scheduled a work shift sooner. He didn't know what the jail experience was like. Well, he thought, what was done was done.

Shawn had a fit of a night of tossing and turning. He had taken six sleeping pills before entering the jail, but the pills seemed to have almost no effect on him. Now, standing in front of the jail door and readying himself to ring the buzzer, he could finally feel the pills beginning to take effect. He smiled when he hit the buzzer and looked up and to his left into the camera.

A female voice came through a speaker out of nowhere. "Yes, can I help you?"

Shawn kept looking at the camera. "Yes, I'm Shawn Jones, I'm here to begin my jail time this morning."

The voice answered. "I'll buzz you in. Go up the stairs on the right and take a seat in one of the chairs. We'll be with you shortly."

Shawn did as he was told He took a seat on a light green, vinyl chair and stared at the Pepsi machine in front of him. The colors were bold and vibrant. The ice and soda looked refreshing. He was reminded of the light in the police cruiser the night he had been arrested. The Pepsi machine seemed to fade into the distance as the sleeping pills and twenty minutes of boredom began to take their toll. He was about to nod off when the door opened and a short, thin, female officer with page-boy cut black hair told him to come in. Shawn followed her silently. Once inside the outer door, the officer pulled out her keys and opened yet another door. Shawn couldn't shake the unmistakable feeling that he was now getting deeper and deeper locked inside. Reality was hitting him like a brick, and so were the sleeping pills. He was as calm as could be, and he was glad he had taken the pills.

Past the second door, the couple turned right into an office. Two computers sat on a desk, and a young male officer sat in a chair in front of the desk.

"So, you're the new guy, huh," the officer laughed.

Shawn looked at him, smiled, and said nothing.

"Take a seat," the female officer stated flatly. She was used to giving inmates orders, and it shown in the roughness of her voice.

Shawn complied and took a seat on the right side of the seated male officer. The female officer went through a long list of personal questions about Shawn's physical description and legal history. Shawn answered them all politely with the only sticking point being that the female officer couldn't believe he didn't have any tattoos. It seemed everyone had a tattoo or two now-a-days. She even boasted a rose tattoo on her hand. The questioning came to an end, and Shawn was about to nod off to sleep right in the chair when the male officer asked him to rise for fingerprinting. The man smeared the ink on Shawn's fingers and placed them on the appropriate places on the fingerprint card. Shawn was given a rag and a cleaner and wiped his hands.

"Now, stand facing the opposite wall behind that red line, it's time to take your photos," the male guard commanded.

Shawn complied as he faced forward and then in profile.

Shawn laughed. "Do I get a number?"

"Hell no, this ain't no prison, this is county. We know who you are. We remember everyone's name, we spend so much time keeping track of you, especially you guys on Huber."

Shawn smiled and spoke to the female guard. "Just one big, happy family, that's the size of it."

The young woman laughed. "Oh yeah, we're all family here, and you're one of our bad kids, but we'll take care of that for, oh, let me see, says here, four months."

The male guard stood up. "Okay, that's it, follow me. I'll show you where your clothes locker is, and introduce you to your new home."

Shawn followed the guard across the hallway and into a small, ten by twelve foot room filled with orange lockers. He was shown his locker and asked to undress to his underwear. Then came the part he had dreaded, the part he had heard about from other friends who had gotten in trouble, the strip search.

The guard spoke blandly as if he had said the words a thousand times and still dreaded saying them. "Pull down your underwear. Lift up your balls. Turn around and bend over. Okay, fine, now put on this orange pants and top and these slippers."

Shawn complied with all the commands and felt like a robot. The sleeping pills were hitting him hard now and he just wanted to sleep. He was led out of the locker room and down the hallway where he had first entered the building. Getting to the secondary locked door, the guard instructed him to turn right.

Shawn stammered. "Is it open?"

The guard laughed. "This side is, but the other side sure isn't. It's easy to get into jail, but it sure ain't easy to get out."

Shawn and the guard walked past a bathroom with shower stalls, and past a heavy metal table that was painted tan with thick, industrial paint. They took a left, and Shawn gazed upon a large room with seven double bunk beds and three single beds in it. The cold, steel gray frames of the beds shown out in blunt contrast to the institutional tan that everything else in the place was painted. Three heavy metal round tables with steel benches went down the center of the room. Everything was bolted to the floor. There was nothing else in the Huber dorm. Nothing.

Shawn was shown to his bunk. He was to get an upper.

The guard spoke quietly. "This is really strange. No ones in right now. No one to welcome you. Don't worry, as the day wears on you will have lots of company as people arrive from work."

With that the guard turned and walked abruptly out. Shawn heard the outer door slam shut and felt the finality of his situation. He climbed up on the top bunk and looked around. Everything looked so cold, barren, and hard. He sighed, and thought, what a mess I've gotten myself into this time. He lay back on the bed and put the pillow under his head. The bed and pillow where as hard as rock and seemed to be filled with a hard, straw material. There was not one shred of softness in this place. So this was jail, Shawn thought, not so bad, maybe he could just lay around, write some rap songs or something, he laughed to himself.

Sonnentag

Shawn tried to gain some resemblance of comfort on the hardness, but he couldn't. It didn't matter. The nervous tension of going to jail was ebbing from his body. It was over, he was here now. He closed his eyes and let the sleeping pills do their job. It would be dinnertime before he awoke again.

Chapter 17

Holly bounced into Joan's apartment with her usual childish glee. She was happy that Joan was packing to move and had made the deal to buy the farm. She was happy that Joan was soon going to be her neighbor for good.

Joan looked around at all the half-packed stuff. She hadn't realized that she had bought so many trinkets and keepsakes over the years from her travels to different parts of the country. Luckily for her she had stayed away from the state-insignia type stuff and stayed with buying strictly art and homemade crafts. She thought for a moment that maybe she should have had a moving sale, but then again, the farmhouse was big and had a lot of room. There was a lot of wall and storage space.

Holly started in to help wrap Joan's various glass knickknacks in paper tissue for transport. She carefully wrapped and put Joan's glass bird collection, which numbered almost a hundred, carefully in the boxes with cardboard dividers. She stopped occasionally and identified a local bird.

"Holly, I'm surprised you know so many of these birds, are you a bird watcher?"

"Yes, my mother and I used to have several bird feeders and we would watch the many different birds that would come to the feeder, though most of them were just sparrows and finches." Holly mentioned her mother without even the slightest tone of sorrow in her voice.

Joan was glad to hear that Holly was no longer sad over her mother's death. She didn't know how long it was since Holly's mother had died, and she supposed the girl still had sad moments on anniversaries or holidays. She said a small prayer of thankfulness that the two of them had come into each other's lives.

After about two hours, Joan carried the tenth box over to the pile of other boxes by the door. Just as she put the box down, a gentle knock came at the door. Joan figured it would be her partner coming to help out. Joan slowly began to open the door. The door was pushed violently against her, and she was flung back hard against the wall.

Holly turned in a blur. "Joan, are you all right?" Holly ignored the man standing over Joan's slumped form and pushed by him to kneel beside Joan.

Joan had hit her head on the wall. Her head pounded and her vision blurred. She looked past Holly and saw the large, bulky form of a man with a jean-jacket standing before her. She expected the man to say something, but he said nothing as he looked down at the little girl beside Joan. As Joan's vision cleared, she was able to see a crooked smile on the man's face as he looked down at Holly. She couldn't help but read his mind, bonus situation.

Rudely, the man pushed Holly aside, leaned down, grabbed Joan by her blouse and arm and pulled her to her feet in front of him.

The intruder spoke roughly. "Lady, I am going to fuck you up. You're going to wish that you had never sent me away twenty years ago."

Joan's mind flew into FBI mode. "Fine, bitch." She snarled. "Just leave the little girl alone."

The man hissed in Joan's face. "I might do that, I might not. Depends how much fun you are first."

The intruder, his grip hard on Joan's shoulders, grabbed her and banged her head several times into the wall. Holly began to cry and covered her eyes. Joan slunk half-unconscious to the floor.

The evil man stepped back from Joan and looked at Holly. "Now, what are we going to do with you? We can't have you gettin' in the way of all my fun."

Holly took her hands away from her eyes and trembled.

The man reached down and grabbed Holly by her right hand to raise her to her feet. He half-dragged, half-pulled her along until he was in the doorway of Joan's bedroom. He looked around the room and saw that everything was pretty much packed in there except for some blankets and towels. He looked back at Joan and saw that she was still slumped on the floor.

The intruder walked around the bed with Holly in tow. He saw the empty phone jack and felt satisfied that he could leave Holly in the room.

"Now, little girl, you just stay in here and cover up with some blankets and we won't have any problem. This ain't got nothing to do with you. I've got a granddaughter your age, so they tell me, but I've never seen her. You be quiet in here and stay in here until somebody comes to get you out."

Holly ran over behind the bed, grabbed a blue blanket from the bed and lay down on the floor to cover herself up. The attacker smiled and left the room, slamming the door loudly behind him.

Joan managed to pull herself to a kneeling position and was about to try and stand up. The attacker rushed up in front of her, snarled his right fist, and brought it up to hit her smack in the mouth. Blood flew from her shaking jowls to spatter on the off-white wall. The large man was proud of himself. Waiting seventeen years for his vengeance was worth it. The violence, the sex, he felt like a god who had finally been freed from the confines of hell.

The man pulled Joan to her feet, ripped open her blouse, and cut her bra off with a knife.

He paused for a moment but held Joan firmly. "Now, relax bitch, I know our re-introduction here has been kind of harsh, but it's time for you to relax so we can get a little romantic. I haven't had a woman in seventeen years, and you get to be lucky enough to be my first one since getting out."

Joan tried to breathe deep and bring herself under control. She could barely understand the words the man was saying. Her ears were ringing from her head hitting the wall so many times. It didn't matter that she couldn't really make out the words. As her eyes cleared, she recognized the man who stood before her. He was a sadistic rapist. It was never proved that he had killed some women, but everyone back then figured that he had. Joan was pretty sure that he meant to kill her.

The attacker lightened his grip on Joan's arms as he looked at her breasts. "Man, seventeen years later and I finally get to see them. You know, I used to fantasize about your breasts during the trial. Hell, I've fantasized about them for the last seventeen years. You were one of the last civilian women I ever saw.

"Lucky you, lucky me," Joan said quietly.

Her attacker didn't know what to make of Joan's statement. His warped mind half-way believed Joan was happy she was going to get what he was about to do to her. In his bewilderment, he lightened his grip on Joan's shoulders, barely holding onto her at all. In a moment of twisted gentleness, he brushed the wetness from Joan's cheeks and brushed the hair up off of her forehead.

Joan felt the loosened grip. She lowered her head down so her chin rested on her upper chest. Her attacker took the response as a soft, gentle, sexual surrender. Joan was surprised that the man could possibly still possess such a misdirected thought in his mind. Maybe she was misreading him. Maybe he was just playing her.

She decided that it didn't matter. Quickly breaking the weak hold on her right arm, she balled her fist and brought a fierce blow up along the man's right ear. After the blow, she screamed, "Pay back you bastard."

The blow didn't have the desired effect. The man stepped back slightly and didn't bother to bring his hand up to his ear. He cocked his head and listened to the ringing in his ear. The inner sound brought a strange smile to his face. He punched Joan hard in the guts.

"Now now, agent Wendtworth, don't make me mark you up too much. It's seems your creamy, white skin is going to show marks easily. Just lie down on the floor, catch your breath and relax. I'll take your pants and panties off to help you breathe."

Joan's attacker laid her on the floor and straddled her at the waist, keeping only enough weight on her to hold her in place.

He just kept looking deeply into her eyes, willing Joan to catch her breath and at the same time surrender to him.

Holly crept to the door in the other room and listened to the sounds to try and figure out what was going on. She knew the sounds weren't good. Her dad had never let her watch any mature audience television or movies, but once in a while a bad scene would come up unexpected. She summarized that Joan was going to be raped.

Holly began to search around the room for anything, any idea that she might be able to use in order to help Joan. She began rummaging through some stacked boxes, but the noise of opening the first box scared her into believing she might be heard. Trying to stay mouse quiet, she opened box after box and peered inside. There was nothing but clothing and bedding in the boxes. She was exasperated. She walked slowly around the room, looking at the four walls. She looked out the window, but she was afraid to open it for the noise it might make. She looked outside and sighed when she saw no one was around.

Holly began to walk pointlessly around the room. There had to be something, she thought. She saw the phone jack on the wall behind the night-table stand. It was pointless; she had not been able to find a phone in any of the boxes. She thought maybe she should check the boxes again, but she had to go to the bathroom. She went quietly into the master-bedroom attached bathroom.

Joan finally brought herself to a settled stillness. She was still a little shattered, but her training and experience began to take over. She figured the only way she was going to get an edge on her intruder was to give him what he wanted. Maybe during sex, she would have some kind of a chance.

Joan smiled as best she could manage. "Relax, Tony, that is your name if I remember it right, isn't it."

Joan's attacker jerked his head back in surprise. "I'm surprised you remember it, but it did take awhile."

"No, not really, I was just teasing you. I'll be good now Tony. I'll give you all the sex you want. You want some oral sex first?" Joan chided.

"Oral sex, hell no, it was hard enough avoiding that in prison. I just want some real, live, warm cooze."

The right side of Joan's cracked lip bled a little when she attempted another smile.

"Okay Tony, I'm going to cooperate. Afterwards, you can do with me what you want. I just don't want you to hurt that young girl in the other room."

"No problem, it's like I said. I have a granddaughter about her age. For all I know, she is my granddaughter. I don't want no kid. It's you I'm interested in sugar."

"Sugar, Tony. That sounds so old-fashioned." Joan tried to giggle but gurgled a little instead.

"Yeah, well, I am out of practice. That's enough talk anyway. I'm going to let you up. I want you to button your blouse again and do a little slow, strip dance for me. I haven't watched a woman strip to get me excited in years."

Joan thought, the only women you probably ever had strip or dance for you were professionals, but she managed to keep her mouth shut. She hoped that by doing what she was about to do, she would gain some modicum of control.

Joan stepped back from Tony, unbuttoned her blouse, and then held the palms of her hands forward towards him. The mid-morning sunlight silhouetted her body and made her blonde hair glow. By the stiffness that was growing in Tony's pants, Joan could tell that he was happy with how the show was going.

Outside, Shawn saw a bright white shirt glowing through the window. In a brief glance he saw the light hitting Joan's blonde hair. He was about to reach for the door when he glanced briefly to the window and saw a red streak. He paused and looked harder, trying to figure out what the streak was.

He shrugged his shoulders, Joan was moving; she probably had just gotten the shirt dirty. He reasoned he had better enter the apartment slowly in case she had parked any boxes in front of the door. He knew Joan could be distracted a lot lately because of the major changes she was making in her life.

Shawn put his key in the lock, and it turned quietly to unleash the door. He was happy his jail time was over, and he was coming home. He poked his head in slowly with a big smile on his face. The smile quickly turned to shock. To Joan's right he saw a bulky figure dressed in denim.

Tony turned and looked at Shawn. Tony turned back to Joan. "Who's this scrawny little fucker?" Tony snarled.

Shawn simply smiled.

"Funny huh, so I'm funny you little shit, huh? Close that door and get your ass over here," Tony demanded.

Shawn stepped forward and closed the door. He took another two steps towards Tony. He turned and looked to see the disarray that Joan was in. Shawn shook his head and took another two steps towards Tony. Shawn smiled.

"You sure are happy you little shit, really happy for a little man who's about to get the shit kicked out of him."

Joan looked at Shawn and a tear came to her eyes. She didn't want him involved, Tony was so much bigger than Shawn. She would try and help but she was so exhausted. Maybe the two of them together, it would work.

Tony looked to Shawn. "Come over here, I'm going to tie you up and put you in the other room with the little girl."

Shawn tilted his head back in surprise. "Little girl, what little girl are you talking about?"

"Don't worry about it, just shut up and get over here. And you, Wendtworth, stay out of this or we will go back to pain instead of pleasure, I guarantee it."

What a warped fucker, Joan thought.

The room froze. No one knew what would happen next. Tony wasn't sure that either of these two people was going to comply with his wishes. Seventeen years in jail did cause a person to hold onto a lot of self-doubt.

Tony's self-doubt was just enough as Shawn exploded towards him, brought up his right foot and kicked him in the left knee. Tony spun towards the floor with a loud grunt, but at the last moment, he twisted his upper body around, caught Shawn by the neck with his strong, right forearm, and the two tumbled to the floor.

Tony quickly punched Shawn several times about the head. Joan lunged forward right into Tony's head, twisted his neck back, and pushed him back to land hard on top of him. She tried to hit Tony about the head, but he covered quickly with his forearms. Tony grunted in a deep breath and threw Joan off hard against the wall.

Shawn gathered his wits up about him as Tony rose from the floor, favoring his right knee, but still managed to stand up fairly straight. In a burst of anger, Tony charged Shawn, wrapped his arms around him, and lunged with him towards the large, front bay window.

The two bodies hit the window with a large crash. Shawn's body flew out the window. Tony fell back and slumped inside on the floor.

Tony writhed around. Pieces of glass were wedged in his head, chest, and arms. Blood seemed to be running out freely from all over his upper body. Joan could not see anything of Shawn.

Tony tried to get up but slumped back down to the floor. Slivers of pain were striking him everywhere. He tried to remove a sliver of glass from his face and after a fretful jerk, he succeeded only to have blood gush freely from the wound and completely cover his cheek and neck.

Joan didn't know where it came from, this new grasp of strength and clearness of mind. Later, she would suppose that it had in fact only come from God himself, but that would be much later. For now, all Joan knew was that the clearness of mind was there. She raced forward, grabbed Tony around the throat, took a large piece of glass out of his right arm, and slid the glass quickly across his throat. Blood immediately gushed outward to cover her. Tony's life was already gone as the blood slowed to a steady seepage.

Joan sat back on the floor and tried to catch her breath. The door to the apartment was kicked violently in and two policemen with guns drawn entered. They pointed their weapons at Tony's slumped form and then back at Joan. Joan managed a small smile and then slumped over sideways to hit her head hard on the floor. She was out.

One of the officers checked Tony for vital signs and found none. Shawn was dead outside. They had already checked him.

The older officer lifted Joan's head and felt a strong pulse. "Go call an ambulance, this one is going to make it. The officer put a blanket under Joan's head and covered her with several others.

Joan opened her eyes and managed a smile. The officer was surprised when Joan spoke. "I feel good now, I feel warm now."

The officer patted Joan's head softly. "You'll be all right, your pulse is strong, but if you can tell me, what about the young girl who made the call?"

Joan's eyes opened wide. "Holly, I forgot, she's in the bed-room," Joan tried to get up.

"No, no, just lie still and rest. I will check on her."

The officer opened the bedroom door.

When the young girl sitting on the bed with a cell phone in her hand saw the police uniform she gave the officer a friendly smile. The officer smiled back. He knew there was death here, but he knew there was also life. Often, that's the best that an officer of the law can hope for.

Sonnentag

184

Chapter 18

The young woman's long brown hair blew wildly in the gusts of wind that swirled around the Stanley building. It seemed her lithe body could almost glide through the cracks of the twirling glass doors at the front of the building. Once inside she brushed her hair back over her brown eyes and stepped gingerly up to the building directory. Breaking Out Productions was on the top floor. She should have known. She rode up alone, an old Beatles tune turned to Muzak played in the elevator. She laughed to herself. She bet Poppin would change this music if he had the chance.

The elevator door opened. She stepped out to stand directly in front of a set of large glass doors. The words 'Breaking Out Productions' blazed out in eight inch high golden letters. She pulled the heavy doors open and rushed inside to stand in front of the elderly black woman who sat at a large, gloss-black desk. A computer monitor was the only tool on the top of the desk. She wore a telephone headset on her head. Putting her hands on her hips, she tried to present an air of authority even though at the age of twenty she still had a baby face that looked at least five years younger.

The secretary finished typing a few words and looked up with a pleasant smile on her face. "Can I help you?" The elderly receptionist smiled.

The young woman spoke politely. "I'm here to see Poppin, I'm an old friend of his."

A surly frown came to the old, black woman's face. "Do you have an appointment?"

An enticing smile crossed the young woman's face. "No, I'm sorry, I don't, but I know he will see me, I just know he will." The woman's voice trailed off with a small hint of desperation.

185

The secretary easily picked up on the tone of voice and used it against the young woman.

"Well, if you don't have an appointment, I'm sorry, but there is nothing I can do for you. There are people trying to get to see him all of the time, and we just can't allow that to happen at random."

The young woman perked up excitedly. "You don't understand, I'm an old friend of his, my name is Melissa Parker. Please, just call him and tell him I'm here, I know he'll remember me and want to talk to me." The pleading in the young girl's eyes was almost palpable.

"Oh, I suppose it won't hurt to interrupt him and ask him, but you saying that you are an old friend of his better be true."

"Honest, honest, I am, we go way back to years ago when we both lived in a group home together."

"The secretary got Poppin on the line and relayed the information to him. She listened intently for a moment and then put the receiver to her chest. "He says he doesn't remember you."

A deep frown crossed the young woman's face, and her shoulders slumped noticeably. She was about to raise her hands in a gesture of what's the use when an idea came to her. Her eyes filled with light and beamed down a gracious smile. "Ask him if he remembers the Harrison House basement."

The secretary lowered her chin in a show of doubt and bewilderment. She thought for a moment that maybe this woman was someone Poppin did not want to see, but as she looked at the young lady who stood before her, she couldn't take her sight off of the woman's sparkling eyes and beaming white smile. A basement, she thought, maybe it had been one of his first sexual liaisons, that devil. She put the phone to her mouth again.

"Poppin, this young woman says to ask you if you remember the Harrison House basement."

The secretary put the phone back in its cradle. There was a look of bewilderment on her face. "He says to send you in, he will see you right away."

Melissa opened the large oak doors and stepped into the inner office. She walked slowly up to a large, gloss-black desk that matched the desk in the reception area except that it was twice the size. Poppin stared intently at her face for a few moments.

A smile beamed across Poppin's face. "I see the face of a child I knew buried in the young woman who stands before me. Melissa, it's so nice to see you."

Melissa nearly jumped out of her shoes with joy. "Poppin, it's so nice to see you too, I just had to come and see you. I just had to ask if it was you."

Poppin's smile faded from his face and was replaced with a serious scowl. His thoughts ran to the basement of Harrison House and the young group of faces he had stood before so many years ago. He could remember the young face of this woman as though it were yesterday. And this question she asked, he knew she already knew the answer, but he prepared himself to answer it anyway.

Poppin looked Melissa directly in the eyes and spoke in a deep, somber voice. "Yes, it was me, I promised to set you free, and I did it."

Melissa stood frozen, lost in awe. Poppin motioned to a chair and Melissa went over and sat down. There was a dead stillness between the two people. Poppin wondered if he should have told her the truth so quickly, and Melissa was shocked that he had.

Melissa leaned back in the chair and rested her hands comfortably on her lap. "Maybe I shouldn't have just come out with it so bluntly like that, and I'm sure you're thinking you shouldn't have told me the truth, but I'm glad you did. I don't know the reason why you trusted me so quickly, but I'm really glad you did. I don't mean no harm, I came here to thank you."

Poppin sat back, his mind swirling, he seemed unable to stop the confusion that reined inside of his brain. This was what he wanted, wasn't it, to avenge the poor, the helpless young kids. But never had he expected one to seek him out and thank him. He didn't know how to react. He thought it best to sit quietly and say nothing.

Melissa joined Poppin in the silence, and the silence seemed to build in ecstasy as though it where the movement of a symphony. Silent music. Music for the soul. Music they had made together so many years ago, was coming together and being played once again only for their ears, hearts, and minds. Silence seemed to go on forever, but it was so pleasant that neither one of them wanted it to end, but end it had to.

Melissa ended the symphony with sadness in her voice. "Poppin, I want to explain why I'm happy that you went through with your promise of so many years ago." Poppin silently looked at her. "I'm twenty years old now. I have tried to commit suicide three times. I've been in and out of counseling four times, in a mental hospital twice. There have been times when I thought I was never going to make it another minute in my life, many times. None of this was supposed to happen to me. None of this is supposed to happen to anyone. I think sometimes how different my life would have been had I never been abused. Years have been stolen from my life, and I have yet to offer many years up in the hope that I will someday recover from the abuse my abuser put on me. When I heard the news that he was dead, a great weight lifted from my heart. I knew that I would never have to fear him again."

Poppin sat forward and contemplated a minute. He put his right hand under his chin and rested his elbow on the desk. He looked Melissa directly in her eyes and asked her what for him was now the most important question in his life. "Do you think murder is always wrong?"

A look of dazed bewilderment came over Melissa's face. Her brow furrowed in thought. How does one answer such a question when they are full of such thankfulness; does one admit that there is any reason to justify murder. Does she take the blame for the murder? No, she had enough blame in her life to last her whole lifetime. She sighed and spoke softly. "Poppin, I don't think murder is ever right, but I'm not here to judge you or myself. I only know that whatever you did was done out of love for us. Maybe it's the only way an abused person can show love. I know you loved all of us when nobody else could or would. The depth of your love for us is being shown by the carrying out of your promise to us. I'm not going to stay awake nights wondering if what you did was right or wrong. I just know that what you did set me free. I don't have to lay awake at night anymore knowing that the man who abused me is still around and probably abusing others. I'm glad he's dead. That's all there is to it. No gray area for one who has been abused. Leave judgment for a higher power."

Poppin smiled. "Then I can trust you not to tell anyone that you think it was me who committed the murders."

Melissa went around the desk. Poppin rose and they threw their arms around each other. Melissa's response came through teary eyes and a shaky voice. "Brother, I will take our secret to the grave with me, now at least, I believe my grave is a long way off. Finally, a long, long way off."

The couple embraced for what seemed an eternity and then collected themselves. They parted with a promise that maybe someday they would meet again if circumstances provided. In the final glance at each other, they both knew that this was never going to be. They also knew that they would never really be separated from each other because they both understood that they had never really become separated to begin with.

Sonnentag

Chapter 19

Collins and Wendtworth approached the middle-aged black woman who sat at Poppin's reception desk. She looked up questioningly. They flipped out their shields.

Wendtworth smiled. "We're with the FBI, we're here to see Poppin."

The receptionist had seen many different types of people approach her but she became wide-eyed at the appearance of the shields. She had never seen the FBI.

The woman said the only thing she could think of. "Do you have an appointment?"

Collins leaned forward and put his hands on the desk. "We don't have an appointment, and we don't need one. We need to talk to Poppin now."

The receptionist leaned back in the chair, trying to get as far away from the two agents as she could. "He's with a client now, I'll see if he will see you after he is done."

Collins clenched his fists. "No, now, we will see him now."

"I'll buzz him," the black woman was shaking.

After a few moments of muffled conversation, the woman hung up the phone and smiled. "He says to let you in. He will see you."

Collins and Wendtworth walked into the inner office to see Poppin sitting behind his shiny, black-lacquered desk. Red and white lights gave the room a look of restful peace. A large black man with a red bandanna on his head sat in a chair off to the left front of the desk. Both of the men had huge grins on their faces as they looked at the two agents who stood before them.

Poppin clasped his hands in front of him. "What can I do for you agents?"

Collins put his right hand on his right hip. "Who is this man?"

Poppin smiled. "Who are you first?"

Wendtworth smirked. "We're FBI agents, Collins and Wendtworth, and we have a few questions for you."

The agents showed Poppin their shields.

Big Pork Dog rose from his chair. A frozen stillness filled the room. "I'm Big Pork Dog, I'm a rapper. I'm a rapper with Breaking Out Productions. Pleased to meet you." Pork Dog threw the agents a wide grin and reached out his right hand.

Collins and Wendtworth shook it in turn.

Wendtworth sensed a great peace about the man. Her instinct told her the man probably had nothing to do with killing. "Big Pork Dog, you can go if you wish. We're only here to question Poppin."

"No, I'd like to stay if that's alright. This could be very interesting." Pork Dog sat back down.

Poppin unclasped his hands and opened them. "He can stay, maybe he can make a rap song out of this bullshit."

Collins grimaced. "This here ain't no bullshit. We know what you've been up to."

Poppin laughed. "Oh, what is that?"

Wendtworth pulled the computer enhanced drawing and the composite drawing out of her blazer breast pocket and spread them out on the desk before Poppin. "Take a good look at these pictures."

Poppin gazed intently at the pictures. "Why that sure is a handsome black man in these pictures."

"Yeah, and he looks a lot like you," Collins grunted.

Poppin laughed. "What a lucky fellow."

Wendtworth's eyes blazed. "We know what you've been up to. These are pictures of you, aren't they?"

Pork Dog leaned forward. "Let me see those pictures." He grabbed the pictures and looked at them intently. "This could be any of a million black men. Who is this supposed to be?"

Joan looked Pork Dog in the eyes. "We call him the Slayer Player, and he has killed five people so far. All the information we have points to your boss here as the man. Take another good look, it's him isn't it."

Pork Dog sighed. "I don't know nothing about that. Poppin is a hard working rap producer, and he has made me a star. I have never seen any hint of violence in him. You've got the wrong man."

Poppin sat back and relaxed in the chair. "Unless you are going to charge me with something, I think our conversation is over. You can leave now."

Joan picked up the pictures and threw them on Poppin's lap. "We've been watching you, and we'll be watching you. We know it's you. We'll get the proof."

Poppin sighed. "Whatever, dream your dream, follow your fantasy, but right now, follow the path to the door and get out."

"We'll get you," Collins said authoritatively.

"I'll be at Big Pork Dogs shows on Friday and Saturday night, you can buy a ticket, but I don't think you'll be able to get near me," Poppin stated.

Joan smiled. "We'll get near you when the time comes."

Poppin laughed. "Whatever, bye now, hit the road, and don't you come back no more, no more."

Wendtworth turned to Collins. "Quite a rhymer isn't he, he's a regular Slayer Player."

Collins snickered. "Yeah, Slayer Player goin' down, down, down."

Joan turned to leave. "Later player, later."

The two agents strode briskly from the room.

Pork Dog looked questioningly at Poppin. "What the hell was that all about? Are you the Slayer Player?"

Poppin sighed. "No man, why would I jeopardize everything I've spent years building up. Those agents are crazy. I ain't got nothing to do with no killing, except for producing killer records."

Pork Dog remained lost in quiet thought. "I hope not, I don't need this man. I've always trusted you. Mine is a way of faith in God. I hope you haven't brought more evil into my life."

Poppin looked serious. "Don't worry about nothing. They are on the wrong track. I'm no Slayer Player. I'm too busy and too smart for anything as stupid as that."

Pork Dog noticed that Poppin looked down and left for an instant when he spoke the words. He knew the man was lying. He knew it was time for him to do a little investigating of his own. Time to cover his ass. He always had.

*****

The young man behind the wheel of the nineteen eighty-eight burgundy-red Ford Ranger's real name was Peter, but he hated the name. No one but his oldest friends had ever known his real name. That was the way he liked it. It made him feel safe. Everyone knew him simply as P. At nineteen years of age he was sinewy and strong of build. An eighth of an inch of red hair made his head seem to glow whenever a light was shone upon it. He had crazy looking hazel eyes.

ICP was playing loudly in his truck as he rolled down Highway 151 to Madison. He laughed loudly when he thought about stirring a drink with his own dick and offering it up to his latest girlfriend's mouth.

P was a nasty player, a womanizer. He knew it, and he loved it about himself. He smiled to the sing-song rhythm of ICP and turned it up louder as he put the pedal to the floor and pushed the truck to ninety miles per hour. The perfect songs to play for payback he thought to himself, now he was really in the mood. He took out a CD a friend of his had created with his drum/electronic sound machine. He knew the freaky, energetic, melded songs would put him further in the mood. He slipped the CD in the player and turned the player up to almost full volume. A little more and he knew the music would be distorted. He wasn't ready for that yet. Not yet, but soon.

A while back he had listened to CD of Indian wooden flute music. It had calmed him down, something he had needed after doing two grams of coke the day before. As the wooden flute played on it was as though at any moment he expected to see a couple of Indians making their way slowly out of a forest or field of corn. When at last he had thought he had really seen a

194

couple Indians he turned the tape off in silence. But now, as he got within only thirty miles of Madison, he knew it was time to fire up with the dynamic, sometimes eerie beats his friend had created.

The music worked quickly and his mind became relaxed. How strange, he thought, that he was still able to stay calm with loud, progressive, rhythmic music playing. He must have been a coke baby, he laughed to himself.

P was hopelessly addicted to smut, drugs, and alcohol, the last of which he loved the most. It was the cheapest and most easily available. He felt locked in a world of his own making most of the time, but it wasn't really entirely of his own making, now was it, he thought to himself. His mother must have drank a lot when he was in the womb. Fuck her, he laughed, whoever the hell she was.

He turned the music up just a hair and was surprised to see that no distortion had taken place. It was either that or the distortion in his mind was taking place at exactly the same pace as the distortion in the music. It didn't matter what the solution was. He loved it. His mind raced further on into insanity.

He was going to make Poppin pay. It wasn't that he thought that Poppin was doing the wrong thing. He knew Poppin was partly keeping the promise for him too, but rather it was that he was jealous of Poppin. He wanted to be the one doing the killing, evening the score. He was a man, he didn't need someone to do his deeds for him, and besides, killing people was wrong, he had to stop it. Stop a killer by killing someone himself. It didn't make sense. He would be just like him wouldn't he? No, this was his brand of justice, hell; the cops did it all the time. People did it daily. It was always on the news. He was insane.

Some days he would watch the world news reports over and over for hours. The killing stories being repeated until he could stand it no more. That morning had been just such a time. He was so tired of hearing the repetitions that he was way ready to become a killer himself. He wondered how many times, how many days, weeks, or even months, his story would be repeated if he were caught. After all, Poppin was a famous music producer, and if he killed him, his story would be repeated for many years to come. P needed a good buzz, he needed a line of coke. He grabbed the whiskey bottle between the seats and took two hard slugs. The whiskey hit his brain like a plunger and freed up his mind. There was no longer any doubt. He knew he could and would kill Poppin. After the buzz subsided from his brain, he could only smile. Smile and listen to what he called the New X-File song on his friends CD. His friend had not yet titled the tunes.

As he entered the fringes of the city of Madison, the chill out beat at the end of the tape seemed to relax him into an even beat with the speed of the city. The cars that were rolling by faster than he was traveling seemed to be in a daze of slow-motion, stop speed, and yet he traveled onward towards his goal. He became oblivious to anything around him in the silence when the CD ended. He smiled as he reached over and pushed the button to play the CD again. He wondered what other thoughts would flirt through his mind but not stay long in his brain as he drove down Madison avenue towards Poppin's recording studio.

The rapid staccato, then eerie beginning of the beats came on again. He pulled the thirty-eight from beneath the seat and caressed it warmly in his lap. He laughed when he felt himself getting a little stiffy. Could the two things be related. He knew that for him they were. The proof was in his pants.

He pulled his Ford Ranger up to the curb across from Breaking Out Productions. He didn't worry about getting in to see Poppin. He didn't worry about getting out of the office building after the deed was done. He didn't worry about being able to accomplish the task before him. He turned off the CD and put the gun in the front of his waist under his belt. He pulled his dark, red flannel shirt out all the way and covered the gun.

The only thing he did worry about was whether he would be able to stop laughing after he saw the look on the great and mighty Poppin's face before he killed him. After that, it didn't matter what would happen. He would deal with things as they came to his mind. He supposed that self-preservation would take over, but it didn't matter. Whatever he would do, he would just do. His brain was buzzing too much to care.

To everyone in the building, even Poppin's receptionist, he was just another young man carrying a CD in and trying to break in and get to make a pitch to Poppin. The secretary tried to stop him, but P brushed past her gruffly and knocked her to the floor. It took a moment to realize when he looked back that the woman had hit her head on the floor hard and wasn't anytime soon going to get up and give him any more trouble. P paused briefly outside the door and touched the cool handle of his thirty-eight. No time like the present to make my pitch to Poppin. He's definitely going to be number one with a bullet. He laughed gregariously at the thought as he pushed into Poppin's inner office.

Poppin sat frozen at his desk, a look of bewilderment on his face. There had been times when other people had managed to get past his secretary and into the office, but not many, and there had never been a time when a man had stood before him with a CD in his left hand and a gun in his right.

After a few moments, that could have been hours, it was hard to tell, Poppin broke the silence. "Jesus, I guess you are really serious about having me listen to that CD your holding. No one has ever held a gun to my head before to get me to pay attention."

P laughed. "It ain't to your head yet, but it's about to be."

P walked quickly around the desk and put the gun to Poppin's left temple.

"Hey man, you don't have to be so serious about this. I'll listen to your stuff. It's probably good," Poppin tried to placate the man.

"This, yeah, this CD is good, but when I put a bullet through your ears, and I mean both of your ears, you ain't gonna have to worry about how good or bad this CD sounds," P finished as he put the CD into his waistband where the gun had been.

"Okay, okay, calm down. If this isn't about some music you have, what the hell is it about? We can work it out. There are lots of ways I can help you. I'm rich niggah, and I can do a lot of things for you. What is it you want? Anything, come on man, help me out here. We can help each other out here, can't we?"

"For you man, there ain't no help, this is the end of the line for you. Your vengeance upon people ain't right. It's too much for too little that they have done. Who gives a shit about what happened to a person when they were young. I sure as hell don't give a shit, and right now, this very minute, I don't give a shit about what happens to you."

Poppin sat frozen. Heavy beads of perspiration had begun to form on his forehead. He knew he had to think of something and to think of it quick. It didn't make sense. What kind of an eye for an eye philosophy was this?

Poppin spoke low and slow. "What about that gun right there?"

"What gun? Where?"

"Right there, at the front of my desk." Poppin raised his right arm from the desk and pointed to a gun that had a long sharp, knife-like point at the end of it instead of a barrel. The gun rested in a soft, red-velvet lined, wooden carrying case and was fully open to view.

P looked more closely at the box. "That ain't no gun, man but that is weird. I've never seen anything like it. It sure does have a nice pearl handle to it."

Poppin relaxed slightly. He knew he had succeeded for the moment in distracting the young man from doing what he had come there to do. Poppin inched his hand slowly toward the fake gun in the box.

Anyone could see what was coming next. Poppin knew this, and he figured he had no chance, but he also knew the man who stood beside him was jacked up on quite a few drugs, or had at least been so lately. He could still smell the alcohol on the man's breath.

Poppin spoke calmly. "That fake gun there is really something special. It was given to me as a gift by a Spanish rapper that I have been working with. It's really quite a bit heavier than one would think. It feels like a real gun."

Poppin felt the situation was far too simple. He wondered if anyone could really be stupid enough, or fucked up enough, to fall for what he was going to do. To his surprise, P said nothing. P reached over to the box and pulled it towards him. He pulled the pearl-handled letter opener out of the box, stood up straight, and became mesmerized by the glow of the lights off of the pearl handle.

As P put the handle up closer to his face to examine the glow of lights off the pearl, Poppin flung himself up from his seat, took hold P's right wrist, and in one quick motion, pushed the blade towards P, pulling it across his throat. Poppin dropped the weapon to the floor.

P gasped as blood began to spurt out of the neck wound. Poppin stepped back and looked at P as he steadied himself. P's shirt became saturated with blood and blood dripped down onto Poppin's desk when P lowered his hand. Poppin looked more closely at the man. The wound was bleeding heavily, but it did not look that deep. Poppin looked at the gun that still remained in P's right hand. He knew that P might still be able to act. He made the quick decision to finish P with the weapon that he had started with.

He pushed P hard. P stumbled a few steps to fall to the floor, still clutching the thirty-eight in his right hand with all his might. Poppin stooped to the floor, grabbed the pearl-handled leather opener with his right hand, and glided across the floor until he stood straddling over P's chest. Poppin looked the crazed man in the eyes. He couldn't make out what he saw there. He was surprised to see that P looked back with a look that was identical to the look that Poppin saw lately in the mirror whenever he looked at himself.

Poppin figured he better end this now. He took the letter opener gun and shoved the dull point into P's chest where he hoped he would hit his heart. He was right. His shot with the letter opener was right on target. Poppin's face and chest quickly became covered with a wall of wet, running blood.

Poppin pushed hard on the floor and rose away from P's bleeding form. He slunk back over to his desk chair and watched the man on the floor bleed out and die. He took a deep, calming breath, and then he realized how glad he was that he had turned on the office cameras that morning. Everything would be on tape. It was self-defense. There wasn't a thing that he needed to worry about.

He further calmed himself when his secretary arose and entered the office. Even though taking a hard hit on the head, she seemed to be more aware of herself and the surroundings than Poppin was. She went to the desk and called the police.

Poppin sat in his chair with his head back and his eyes closed and replayed the entrance scene of the man who now lay dead in his office over in his mind. It was a strange awakening when out of nowhere it came to him that he had seen this man many years ago. In an instant he saw the young man as he was eight years ago when he was sitting in the group of children in Harrison House with which whom he had made his pact.

It wasn't until the paramedics gave him a sedative that he was able to forget the face. P's face would haunt him in the future. He would continue to take on that same strange look in his eyes that P had when he was about to kill him. He would see that same look repeatedly in the mirror as he looked at himself. He wondered when all was said and done would he be able to come out of the insanity that he himself was creating. He knew that it was death that awaited him at the end.

There was no way he could know for sure, but there was still no way he could turn back. He was beyond committing himself and this attack on him meant nothing. P was just another sick fuck that had to be taken care of. Better now than later when he wanted to be finished with all the killing. Finished, was there ever going to be such a thing.

Poppin rested at home for a few days, and felt safe. He wished this feeling could be kept for the rest of his life, but there was still a job to finish. When it was done, maybe he could commit himself to a health farm for a month. Forget about the bad things, and get on with his life. He would do what every rich celebrity always did when things got to be too much for them. He would hide out at a costly place where only the rich can go.

He would be among his own kind. Yeah, right, he laughed to himself. Was there another person like him? P, almost, but almost don't count. Almost only counts in horseshoes and tiddly-winks. He wondered as he fell off to sleep where the hell that had come from. His grandmother maybe. He would have to ask her some day, ask her what the hell a tiddly-wink was.

Sonnentag

Chapter 20

Collins pulled the silver Crown Victoria LTD up slowly to the old country house at the edge of Green Lake County. The house wasn't much to look at. The really strange thing though was that penned in cows and goats were allowed to roam right up to the house in their fenced in yards. Collins could only imagine the amount of dank odors that surrounded and filled the house throughout the warm months of the year.

Collins and Wendtworth turned to smile at each other and laughed. Joan finally calmed herself enough to speak. "You go first, check the immediate area for any globs of shit, okay." Joan couldn't help herself and laughed hysterically for several long minutes.

"Yeah, this is it. I love it. Shit patrol. I've finally made it to the big times," Collins laughed.

Walking slowly from the car, Collins did finally lift his right shoe to see how much doo-doo had gotten on it. Joan slapped Collins on the back and began an uncontrollable laugh again. "Shit patrol, you are on top of things, definitely on top of things, things that are really smelly."

Both the agents' faces were beet red by the time they had stopped laughing. Collins scraped the shit off his shoes in the near-by tall, brown, dead grass. The two agents stopped to take a deep breath to try and remain calm. This action worked somewhat, but the stench in the air prevented a good cleansing breath from taking place.

Wendtworth and Collins were glad when at last they approached the front steps. The aged planks looked weak and shaky. Wendtworth motioned you go first with her right hand and arm.

Collins smiled back at Joan. "No, no, I insist, after you, I've had all the fun so far. It's your turn."

Wendtworth put her right hand on a rickety railing and stepped up on the first step. "See, I don't think we're going to have any problem here."

Collins kept his distance from the steps. "I don't know, that's only one small step, good luck with crossing the whole porch."

Joan got brave and did a side-long, leg-drag shuffle across the porch and came to a stop in front of the red back door. The paint was pealing and blistering, large patches of weather-worn bare wood shone through. Joan turned back and motioned for Collins to come up and stand beside her.

Collins hesitated but complied when Joan let her shoulders slump.

Joan motioned towards the window to the left of the door. "Step over there by the window and see if you can make out any activity that is going on inside."

Collins shifted slowly over to the left to try and get a view through the dirt encrusted window.

Joan knocked lightly on the door and waited for an answer or any sign of movement from inside. Nothing came in response. Joan knocked hard a second time, bringing the full brunt of her fist to bear upon the door.

Collins jerked his head up to the sound of someone coming to the door from inside the house.

The stale, warm air that rushed out of the house when the door opened forced Joan's head back. Standing in the opening of the door and poking his head through was a young man of about twenty years of age. His head was shaved high and tight, leaving only a six inch swatch of quarter inch hair over the back of his head. This short hair in the back proceeded to six inches in length by the time it reached the front of his forehead. Hazel eyes peered out at Joan questioningly. The eyes were very bright. The young man appeared to be stoned on something.

Joan thought to herself. Big city gang players, and small, out-of-the way, country stoned hicks, this job was really getting ridiculous, what next?

Collins moved over to stand beside Wendtworth. Joan smiled and spoke politely to the young man in the doorway. "We're agents with the FBI. Can we come in and talk to you?"

The young man started giggling. "FBI, yeah, wow man, come on in."

Joan couldn't help but think that the man had to be buzzing on some drugs of some kind. He seemed overly happy, almost childish, or maybe it was something else causing his euphoria, who knew nowadays.

Wendtworth and Collins followed the young man into the living room and took a seat on an old, off-white, early American, heavily stuffed couch. The man sat in a navy colored easy chair opposite them.

Collins and Wendtworth introduced themselves, and the young man introduced himself as John Colmes.

Colmes' wide smile remained plastered to his face, and Wendtworth knew it would not easily be erased. She decided to go right to a difficult question and see what would happen with the young man's expression.

Wendtworth leaned forward and put her hand on her right leg. "Were you a resident of Harrison House over by Eureka when you were younger, say about the age of twelve?"

The wide smile remained firmly implanted on the young man's face. "Yes, I was a resident there. It was all right there. It was cool, I didn't have any problems living there. Why, what is this all about?"

Collins leaned back and took a relaxed posture. "First of all, I just want to say that you have nothing to worry about. We just want to show you a couple of pictures and see if you recognize the man in them. We believe you were at Harrison House the same time he was, and we believe he is responsible for a recent series of crimes."

The young man relaxed. "Sure, no problem, but it might be hard to identify him. It has been eight years since I lived at Harrison House. He probably will look somewhat different now, but I'm willing to give it a go."

Wendtworth took the pictures from an envelope and handed them over to John. John bent over and looked closely at the photos.

John let out a small chuckle. "Yeah, no problem, I know who that is?"

Collins frustration showed in his voice. "All right already, stop the suspense, who is it?"

"That's the man, my main man back then in the house, Charles Popiniero."

The two FBI agents sat back and relaxed. They were happy to have the identification, almost bursting inside. They looked at each other with wide smiles. Collin jerked his head up slightly to let Joan know that she should go ahead with the questioning when she was ready.

Joan could barely contain the excitement in her voice. "Did he have a nickname?"

"Oh yes, Poppin, yeah, Poppin, my main man," Colmes stated.

"So, you're saying you were pretty close to him then," Joan said calmly.

"Close yeah, we were like brothers, brothers of different colors, but brothers none the less," Colmes let out a boisterous laugh.

Joan gave Collins a knowing look. Both knew there was some valuable knowledge about the case that was going to be gained here, but Joan was stumped. She wondered where she should start. How could she get to some kind of confirmation of Poppin's guilt?

Collins broke the silence with a simple question. "How did Poppin get to have such a strange name as Popiniero for a black man? The name sounds Italian to me."

"Italian, no, he told me that his great-grandfather had gone to Canada after having been freed in the states as a slave, and in Canada he took the name of a friend of his who had died. The friend was French-Canadian. The name never seemed to fit the black lineage of Poppin's family, but they had always liked the rhythmic sound of it so the name had never been changed," Colmes said.

Joan wanted to get right back to the point of their visit. "So, if you were so close, did he ever give you any secrets to share, secrets about a crime that he would commit himself to completing some day in the future when he got out of Harrison House."

Colmes sat back in his chair, and his smile dissipated until it was almost completely gone. "There was a secret, he told me once when we got into a neighbor's home-made wine cellar and got drunk."

The smile disappeared completely from Colmes' face.

Collins leaned forward in his chair. "You can be a great help to us. We have put together a picture of what is going on with Poppin, but we don't know the reason why for sure. We have a good guess, all you will be doing is helping us confirm his motive for what he is doing."

Colmes let out a sigh of exasperation. "Okay, here goes. There was a time when he was just about out of the house. It was about a month before he turned eighteen and was about to leave Harrison House for good. We were sitting in a wooded area out back by the marsh. Both of us had drank a one and a half liter bottle of home-made wine and hit up on a couple of joints." Colmes paused as a huge smile came back on his face. The two agents definitely knew now that Colmes liked to get buzzed up.

"Go on," Joan said simply.

"Poppin told me that a few nights before this he had a special meeting with some of the younger kids in the house. All of these kids had been sexual abused by someone. Some of them had been abused by Harrison himself," Colmes paused and seemed unable to go on.

Collins sensed the usual deadness in the air that always came about whenever the subject of sexual abuse came up. He spoke quietly. "Sexual abuse is more common than people are willing to admit. People always want to keep it a secret. We have run into the subject many times in this investigation. You don't have to worry about anything when you answer this next question that I'm going to ask. "John, were you sexually abused?"

"Me, hell no, Harrison tried it on me once, but I grabbed his nuts and squeezed the hell out of them. I have always been kind of a crazy fucker. No one was going to force me to do anything I didn't want them to do."

Joan chuckled. "What happened then, when you hurt him."

"Harrison took off up the stairs holding onto his nut sack. It was hilarious. Of course, I had to pay for it later by doing a full month of kitchen KP duties, but it was worth it. Every time I saw Harrison after that, I just smiled at him and he left me alone. Every time in the future whenever he came near me, I just gave him a knowing grin. In time, it just became a non-issue."

A short silence ensued among the triad.

Joan broke the silence. "Let's get back to the secret, what was it?"

"The young kids, Poppin told me he had gone in the basement one evening when he saw a group of six of the younger children grouped up and sort of holding a meeting of their own. I say sort of because Poppin said that all that seemed to be going on was that the children were all just taking turns crying. He said he calmed the children down and finally, the bravest, oldest male, told him what was going on."

John looked sternly at the two agents before him. He had to go on, he knew he couldn't stop now. He brought a smirk back to his face and continued. "It seemed that all of the children had been sexually abused by someone, some of them were also abused by Harrison. Poppin told me that some kind of deep-rooted anger took hold in his heart, and he vowed to these children that someday he would avenge them by taking care of all the people who had abused any of them."

"Taking care of, what did he mean by that?" Wendtworth ventured.

"He told me straight out that he was going to kill each and every abuser, starting with Harrison."

"And the kids, they kept this secret all of these years. I can tell you that some of them know right now what Poppin is doing and they don't want to say anything against him."

"Why is that?" Wendtworth questioned.

"Poppin had stopped Harrison from abusing most of the kids, but with a couple of them, he had gotten away with it. They wanted the justice worst of all. Poppin told them all to resist any further attempts by Harrison. He would be out soon, and he would come back and take care of Harrison. Poppin said everyone believed him, and everyone was happier and felt safer after that. I don't know if any of the kids were further abused by Harrison or not, but I do know that Harrison was later killed. I heard about that."

Collins stood up. "Is there anything else you can tell us. Can you tell us the names of the children that were involved in this pact?"

Colmes sighed. "No, I never knew any of their names. I wasn't a part of the pact. All I know is that it occurred, and Poppin seemed dead serious about carrying it out some day. Is he doing it now?"

Joan shook her head up and down. "Yes, we believe he is, and it seems you just confirmed it. You've been a great help." She turned to Collins. "Let's go, there's nothing more for us here."

Joan stood before Colmes. "Thank you, you've been a lot of help. Here is my card, if you think of anything else, give us a call."

Collins wanted to continue the questioning, but Joan turned towards him and gave him a look that told him he should just shut up and not continue. Wendtworth and Collins shook hands with Colmes and left.

Back inside the Crown Vic, the car seemed to be filled with an air of peace.

Softly, Joan said. "See, I told you in time we would get to information that would help us. We know now that Poppin is definitely our man. Now the fun begins."

The two agents remained quiet until they got to the interstate highway when Joan popped an Insane Clown Posse CD into the car player.

"What the hell is that?" Collin's exclaimed.

"It's my fire up CD. The Great Malinko. It gets me into the humorous psychotic mode that I need to be into to go up against these crazy bastards when the time comes. Listen to it awhile. You'll see what I mean."

"ICP, what about rap Joan, don't you have a fire-up rap song for that?"

"Oh yeah, you'll see. When it's real close to all coming down. When I know we'll be meeting him face to face, I'll put something hard and ghetto on. I'll put on something that fires me up to take him down."

"Don't you just need silence to prepare yourself?"

"Not me man, I need to get into my zone. It has always worked for me. Heightened my awareness, sharpened my senses. I hope it doesn't bother you or mess you up."

"Don't worry Joan, I've learned a lot from you. I'm not worried about it. You do what you always do."

Collins trusted his partner completely now. As he listened to the psychotic laughter and lyrics of the Posse, he thought maybe Joan was right. Bring it on, he thought, I'm ready. He kept repeating the phrase; I'm ready, in his mind over and over again until he felt himself becoming psychotic. Oh yeah, I'm ready all right. Joan sat beside him, and she noticed that Collins was touching the handle of his gun beneath his jacket.

"Hey Collins, the secret to apprehending a maniac is simple. You got to be insane and sane at the same time."

Collin's laughed. "How the hell do you pull that off?"

"You'll see Collins, soon, you will see."

Chapter 21

Poppin slammed the Benz into fifth gear, raced down Belmont Street, and turned left onto Seymour street, the rear tires flying wildly out to the right as he made the turn. He fought for control of the wheel and pulled the vehicle straight again. He floored the car and drove down an alleyway between two warehouses. He was safely in the warehouse and factory district. He thought for a moment and realized the truth. The FBI agents had made him. They had pieced together the various glimpses of him and made him. He looked in his rear-view mirror to see if he was still being followed. He breathed a sigh of relief for only a moment when he saw the FBI agents round the corner to continue their pursuit.

He took a hard right down an adjacent alleyway and slowed the car to a crawl. He hit the automatic door opener button on his visor. The warehouse door was up in no time, and he slid underneath it. Hitting the button again, the door closed behind him. He exited the vehicle and headed toward a back office room in the warehouse. He took up a position behind a pile of crates to the left of the abandoned office. From this vantage point he would be able to fire upon the agents when they checked out the office.

Collins pulled the car into the alleyway where he had last seen the Benz turn.

"Stop, stop," Wendtworth yelled. "I don't think he's gone any farther. I don't see him up ahead. I think he has entered one of these buildings."

"Yeah, maybe, but which one," Collins responded.

"I don't know, creep along here slowly," Wendtworth said as she shifted her eyes from building to building. "There, on the right, that large door. It looks like that door has been greased recently, and the rail seems somewhat shiny. Let's check that one out."

Collins pulled the vehicle into the lot and stopped about twenty feet from the door. The two agents exited the vehicle and walked up close to the door. Upon closer inspection, the door did look like it had been used recently, but how were they to get in.

Collins lifted and grunted, but the large sixteen by twenty-foot door wouldn't budge.

Collins wiped the sweat from his brow. "Now what?"

"That bottom rail, it looks kind of loose. Let's slowly back the car into it and see if it breaks away from the side wall."

"Okay, but you file the damage report. I'm going to say it was all your idea."

"I don't care. We've never been this close to the killer before. We're going to get him if he's in there."

Wendtworth went to the car, started it, put it in low gear, and crept slowly forward. She nudged the edge of the door.

"Now, give her a little gas," Collins yelled.

Joan pushed the pedal halfway to the floor. The metal on the sides of the large door squeaked and groaned. The rotten wood began to break away from the side and soon the car had created an opening of about two feet at the base of the door. Collins grabbed a nearby wooden pallet spacer and shoved it up as high into the opening as it would go. Joan put the car in reverse and backed up. The spacer held. Joan got out of the car and looked at their handiwork. The two feet at the bottom of the door narrowed until within three feet of rise the opening stopped. It was a small triangle.

Joan looked at Collins. "I can get through it."

Collins shook his head. "If you can get through it, so can I."

Joan went down on her knees and then turned over onto her side. "I hope he's not watching the other side of this door." With a few snakelike motions Joan's midsection, legs, and then feet vanished through the door.

Joan rose, gun at the ready. The Benz was in plain sight just ahead of her. Everything was silent except for the ticking down of the engine as it cooled. She sped forward, aiming the gun inside the Benz, examining both the front and back seats. Nothing. She could hear Collins rustling in the dirt outside of the door. He was making his attempt to enter when the door suddenly let out a large squeak and the wooden spacer began to crackle. The spacer broke in half allowing the metal to twist halfway back into shape. Collins was caught in the midsection. He looked up helplessly at Wendtworth.

Wendtworth shook her head. "Are you alright? Are you in pain?"

"I'm alright, just pinched in here. I can't seem to move at all. I'm pinched in tight."

Joan turned back and ran her eyes over the warehouse space before her. She turned back to Collins and saw that he at least had his gun hand free. She began walking back towards Collins when a loud crash of metal sounded up a set of stairs near the back of the warehouse. Joan turned toward the sound.

Collins shifted half a turn and was able to see what was in front of him. His gun trembled slightly as he held it aloft. "You go, you've got to go after him now. I'll be okay. You'll get him. I know you will."

Wendtworth's instincts cried out that leaving Collins was wrong, but she had to do it for wasn't he completely vulnerable with or without her there. Her being there only made her vulnerable along with him. She decided she would forge ahead. She could better protect Collins by remaining on the offensive.

Joan walked slowly toward the office window. A heavy crust of dust fogged the window. She could see nothing but broken down office furniture and other rubble. She passed quickly by the office and proceeded to slowly rise up the stairs to the side of the office. The sky-blue industrial paint on the stairs was heavily encrusted with dirt and dust. She kept her right hand on her thirty-eight, her left hand by her side. She didn't need to use the rail as she slowly rose up the stairs. At the middle landing, she could still see nothing. She continued her rise until she was at the top of the stairs and onto the main landing.

Joan took a full firing stance. "FBI, come out with your hands up."

Nothing came in answer.

Poppin smiled as he rose from his hiding place behind the boxes and stepped forward. He took careful aim and fired. Joan spun around in a complete three-sixty and fell to the hard steel platform. Her gun flew from her hand and fell to the floor below. She writhed on the steel platform and grabbed her ankle. Even in the dim lighting she could see that the bullet had gone through her right foot. She felt the hole in the top of her shoe. The pain was excruciating.

Poppin turned and headed back to the Benz. He stood under cover on the left side of the Benz and looked at the agent who lay prostrate on the floor.

"Freeze," the wedged in agent yelled.

Poppin laughed loudly. "You're in no position to freeze anyone."

Poppin leaned on the rear hood of the Benz and took careful aim at Collins head. "Drop your gun, and I'll let you live."

Collins didn't move. He tried to get a better bead on Poppin.

Poppin laughed again. "You don't have a chance man. The only chance you have is if you trust me."

Collins grunted. "I'm supposed to trust a killer?"

"Have you got a choice man? I can drill you in the head right now. You may get a shot off, but you'll never hit me from that position. I don't want to kill you. This has nothing to do with you, just drop your gun, and I'll let you live."

Joan pulled herself to a standing position, but it was hard to move along. She couldn't get a firm grip on the dusty handrail.

"Make your decision now, live or die," Poppin commanded.

Collins tossed his gun aside. Poppin walked over and picked it up. He looked at the agent wedged between the door. He bent and took a pair of handcuffs from the agents pocket and pulled his arms out straight above his head to put them on. Collins grunted as his middle section bit into the metal rail of the door.

Poppin looked Collins straight in the eye. "I'm going into my car, and then I'm going to open the door. Stay to the side. I'm

214

going to drive out of here, and then I'll be gone. I've still got work to do, and that work has nothing to do with killing you. Just stay to the side."

Poppin ran back to the Benz and got in. He saw the other agent had reached the middle landing of the stairs but she was moving slowly. He had plenty of time. He pushed the opener and the door rose slowly. Collins gasped in a deep breath. It felt good to be free. He remained where he was as Poppin put the Benz in reverse and sped out of the building.

Collins rose to his feet and met Wendtworth at the bottom of the stairs.

Collins spoke excitedly. "Are you all right?"

"Sort of. He hit me in the foot. It hurts like hell, but I seem to be able to move and bend it all right. I hope there's no permanent damage."

Collins turned around and Wendtworth unlocked his cuffs.

Collins looked down at the ground. "I can't believe I got stuck in that door."

Wendtworth shook her hand and tried to stand up straight. "Just go bring the car inside, and get me to a hospital."

"Okay, we'll get him yet Joan, we'll get him yet."

"I know we will Collins. I know we will, but he will kill again before we can get him. We were close. He's going to act quickly now. Whoever is left on his list, he's going to finish, and how are we going to find him now. Where has he gone? Who's next?"

Collins went to retrieve the car. He helped Joan inside. Joan remained silent in the passenger seat.

"We've got to find the location of the last person in that pact. We've got to get her to confess who her perpetrator was, and we have to do it fast."

Joan gritted her teeth. "Yes, he has the advantage. He knows who he's going after. Let's hope the agents we sent to interview the last remaining sexual abuse victim from Harrison House were able to find her."

"After I get you to the hospital, I'll check it out."

Joan grabbed Collins right arm. "You don't go alone. You take back-up. I can't help you. I won't be able to walk for some time. You've got to have help. Promise me you won't go alone."

Collins sighed. "I know procedure Joan. I'm not a lone wolf. I'll get help."

"Good Collins. Get our man. Somehow, beat him to the next victim. Get him for the other victims, get him for me."

"I will Joan, I will."

Chapter 22

Jelly Fish entered Big Pork Dog's apartment and took a seat in the worn, old, large, floral patterned couch. The cushions had become warped out of shape and a zipper struggled to open up on the center cushion.

Jelly looked around the apartment and laughed to himself. What a mish-mash of old furniture. In front of the couch was a cheap table made out of two by six lumber, stained Walnut, and covered with a heavy, gloss varnish. The varnish had aged considerably now and had more of a satin sheen. Heavy nicks and scratches could be found all over the table. A pair of heavily stuffed pink chairs sat off to his left, both chairs showing heavy wear on the arms. BPD had definitely brought his ghetto furniture with him. Even with all the money he now had, the only new things in the apartment were a couple of paintings. Jelly knew that Pork Dog had not had to pay for gifts from friends of his who were good in art. The only striking new item in the room was a fifty-five inch Toshiba wide screen television. The television was tuned to MTV Jams, a Ludicrous video on the screen. The mute button was on. BPD took a seat on a ten foot long couch with a swirling color mixture of black and silver fabric covering it. A short six by six piece of lumber propped up the front leg to Jelly's right side. The couch creaked as BPB shifted his weight.

Pork Dog noticed Jelly was fidgeting a lot and kept scratching hard at his head. He was obviously very excited, but Pork Dog figured it was the being so close to the Presidential assassination when it happened that was causing Jelly's anxiety. It had just been coincidence that Pork Dog was in the vicinity where the assassination occurred.

Pork Dog leaned back and put his heavy arms behind his head. "You've got to relax Jelly, the assassination is over. He died. It didn't have anything to do with us."

Jelly smirked. "Well, there's something you don't know, it does have something to do with us. Something big, real big."

Pork Dog sighed. "With us, how can it have anything to do with us?"

"You know how often I am videotaping you for the documentary you and Poppin are paying me to do. Well, my girlfriend Jasmine was standing beside me at the parade when she said she saw a man with a gun in the opposite building. I turned the camera on the windows until I found the gun sticking out of a window on the top floor. I zoomed in and the man fired. I got it all on tape."

Big Pork Dogs eyes went wide. "You mean you got the killer of President Millard on tape.

"Yes, and a close up at that. You can see his face clearly, and I'm sure with computer enhancement, a perfect image of his face could be obtained. We got something very valuable here."

Pork Dog got up and plugged the recorder into the big screen television. On the image of the big screen TV the picture of the man's face was huge. You could see a mole on his left cheek. The right cheek pressed firmly against the stock of the gun. Previous frames and following frames gave a clear picture of the man's face. He would be easily identifiable to the police.

Pork Dog sat quietly on the couch. He wiped the sweat that was already beginning to form on his brow with his large left hand. He stayed deep in thought for some moments before he spoke. "I'm surprised you have come to me with this video. I'm sure you're aware that the video is worth a great deal of money. You could sell it to any of the major news stations for millions. I can't believe you didn't do that."

"BPD, we go way back, back to the ghetto. You and Poppin have been good to me. You brought me along, you're my best friend. You're paying me to do the documentary on your life. A chance is all I ever wanted and you gave me that chance. We can share whatever the video is worth, or you can do what you want with it. It's your choice. I know you will do the right thing, because that is the kind of man you are," Jelly took a deep breath and held the tears back from his eyes.

Pork Dog was unable to do the same. Tears flowed freely down his heavy cheeks. This kind of loving friendship he knew was worth more than all the money in the world. He was glad he had this kind of friend. He sat quietly with his hands on his chin. After several minutes he leaned forward. We need to hang onto this for awhile. This may come in handy as a bargaining tool if we ever need it. It's a nasty unforgiving world out there. This may come in handy if anybody ever tries to take me down. We may need it later. Yes, we'll sit on it awhile. I'll keep it in a safety deposit box downtown if that's alright with you?"

"Yes, that would be fine, I trust your judgment," Jelly answered.

"Okay then, let me get a shower, and we'll get off to the studio. You've got a video to make, and I have music to make. Let's stay focused. It doesn't get any better than this." BPD let the tension go and let out a small laugh.

Jelly laughed in response. "No it doesn't get any better. Let's get it on."

Jelly watched a Jay-Zee video on the television and slid into it as though it were his own. The video seemed so real, he couldn't distinguish otherwise. He was happy, soon, he would be shooting BPD's next video and all that was unreal would be real, and the real would be unreal. He waited quietly until Pork Dog came out dressed in a shiny, silken, black suit. As Jelly arose from the couch, Pork Dog gave him a big hug. The two men were all smiles when they entered the downtown studio to begin recording the new video music track. For both men, it was going to be a very fun day.

Sonnentag

Chapter 23

BPD looked around the sound stage set and marveled at how much of a circus his life had become. Maybe he should just put on a red rubber nose and do the video. He felt like a clown anyway with everyone always telling him everything he had to do. He vowed to himself that he would make a difference with this video. Ax-cepptance. It was a great title for a video, but it made him mad at people that he had to fight to even get them to accept this title. He was the big man. He was the star. Everyone had better start listening to him or else he vowed he was going to pull the plug. He just wanted to make sure he was doing something useful, something that would somehow help troubled, poor young people find a way out of their troubles other than by using violence, or by breaking the law in some fashion or another.

BPD looked around himself at the insanity that filled the stage. The city landscape behind him looked so real, just like a Johnny Carson stage of old. It even changed to different buildings and different lighting at the touch of a button. At the stage in front of him were eight scantily clad women in thong bikinis. They were indeed sexy, but he hated the image. It wasn't what he wanted to portray. No bling, and no ass shakin' or grabbing, was what he wanted.

The director sat in a chair with what looked to be a white dunce cap on his head. It was a bad image. He was a black man but he may as well have been white. Too much high level marketing was taking place here; Too much planning.

The young, scantily clad women took the stairs up to the stage and took their positions all around BPD. He should have felt that he was in heaven, but he didn't. He turned to his left and then to his right and smiled at each and every one of the young ladies.

BPD turned away from the young ladies and bowed his head. In a deep, low voice, he spoke to the women who stood before the stage. "I'm sorry, I can't do it this way, please leave the stage."

The women were confused, and they looked to the director for help, but the director was busy fussing with the light man off to the right side of the stage. The women looked helplessly at BPD's back, but then he turned back, raised his head and gave them that special look of his. It was the look that said, I ain't messin' around here.

Still, the women didn't move.

BPD let out a low growl of a voice. "Now, I mean it, get off the stage!"

The director raised his head when he heard the rapid footsteps of the women going down the steps. "What's going on here? I told you women to take your positions on the stage."

The director looked BPD in the eyes, and he wasn't sure what he saw there, but he was sure that he didn't like it.

The director moved up to the front below the stage. "Pork Dog, my man, what's going on here?" He tried to sound friendly though his voice quivered.

Big Pork Dog laughed. He laughed long and hard.

The director stood dumbfounded, a blank look on his face.

"I'm changin' things around here. This ain't what this song is about."

The director stammered. "But, but, I thought we agreed on how this shoot was going to be done."

"I didn't agree with you about anything." BPD pointed his finger menacingly at the director.

The director flinched and stepped back a couple of feet.

BPD grimaced. "Now, I'm going to fix this."

"How?" said the beleaguered director.

"Just watch me man, just watch."

BPD walked slowly down the steps and off the stage. Everyone was careful to stay clear and wide of him. He walked over to a table upon which rested a large bamboo basket of apples and oranges. He took one of each in each of his hands and turned back towards the stage. He looked at the surrounding audience with a broad, childlike, glee. He began to throw.

Apple after orange, and orange after apple hit the expensive city background at the back of the stage. Glass and plastic shattered and spewed all over the stage. It looked sharp and dangerous and it was, but not as dangerous as BPD seemed to be.

BPD finally emptied the basket and threw the empty basket up on the stage. He grabbed a fifty-five gallon metal garbage can that sat next to the table that the apples and oranges had been on and hurled it up on the stage. The can spewed its fast-food and candy wrappers everywhere as it rolled and hit the back city wall. There the can wedged into the bottom of the city scenery. A large slice of the city scene dislodged and fell forward crashing into numerous pieces over the top of the garbage can.

Pork Dog laughed. "All I need now is a Muppet in that can and this could turn all the way back to stupid, but that ain't gonna happen. You better get ready to shoot this video because I'm only going to do it once."

Pork Dog grabbed a broom as he headed up the stairs. The gaping audience thought for a moment that he was actually going to clean some of the mess up, but then he twirled the broom in his hands and took aim. To the director's surprise, he found the audience clapping. BPD plunged the broom handle right into the center of a building section that remained unbroken on the stage set. Two large, gaping holes now filled the set of the remaining city scene.

The broom handle stuck out at a forty-five degree angle towards the ceiling.

"Now, and I mean now, I'm ready to shoot this shit my way. Ax-cept it or get out. This is take one, the only one. Jelly, let's do it."

Jelly started the cameras rolling. BPD stepped to the center of the stage amidst the garbage and began the number.

"Ax-cept, Ax-cept, but don't cut yourself on the way up or down....." BPD began.

During the entire rest of the song, BPD barely moved anything but his arms. His face told the story. He wanted to portray a story about how to accept the conditions in someone's life, and bad though they may be a person must rise above them.

The powerful words of the song came to an end, though the audience and even the misplaced director weren't sure. BPD had changed half of the lines and made up new ones as he went along. The song was no longer about gangsters getting over on people. The song was about changing one's life and surroundings for the betterment of themselves and the betterment of all.

The director was angry. "I don't know what you think you're doing but that shit ain't gonna fly."

"Oh yes it is, and so are you. You're fired, get the hell out of here."

At the exit door to the sound stage, the director heard a loud round of clapping. He looked back to see what was going on, and he saw that the cameras were still rolling.

Big Pork Dog had taken off his leather jacket, rolled up his sleeves, and taken the broom out of the background building scene.

Just before the director left the stage, he heard these final words in a lull in the clapping.

"We'eze all got to clean this shit up, now let's get to it."

BPD put his head down and began to slowly sweep the stage. The lights on the stage dimmed and BPD disappeared into blackness.

A tumultuous ovation came from the crowd that gathered before the stage.

BPD walked to the front of the gathering. "Don't worry, I'm paying you all double what you would have been paid with this video. I only want one thing from all of you. Don't mess this shit up. Remember it, and try to keep it right in your own lives."

The large man walked silently away from the crowd, and the crowd returned his silence, only turning to murmurs once Big Pork Dog had finally exited the sound stage into the outside hallway.

Big Pork Dog almost bumped into two rotund, young women who were barely able to step back from the door as he exited. He took in the smell of their perfumes in an instant. He smiled when he saw the flowery dresses that they wore. One wore a dress of large sunflowers, the other a dress of large, red, daffodils.

"I suppose you saw all of that?" Came the simple question from the large man.

"Um-hmm," said the red daffodils.

"All of it, you saw it from the beginning when I wrecked the stage?"

"Oh yeah, honey, we saw it, and we loved it. It ain't never too late, or the wrong time to spite Satan," Yellow sunflowers stated.

"That's right, um-hmmm, never the wrong time, never," red daffodils said firmly.

BPD stood in awe of the two women. His lower lip was hanging down to leave his mouth agape in a moment of wonder.

He gathered himself together. "Well, I just had to do what I thought was right."

The two women spoke in unison. "That's right honey, you just gotta do what's right no matter what the cost. No matter what," the two women finished emphatically.

BPD let down his shirtsleeves and wiped his brows. "Hey, you ladies sound like you're from the south, are you?"

"That's right honey, we'eze, fine southern bells. Women through and through. God-lovin' southern Baptists and you're the first sensible person we've seen since coming north to this city for a vacation." The slightly heavier and slightly older woman with the dress of sunflowers seemed to be taking the upper hand in the conversation.

"Well I hope you enjoyed what you saw, because I sure enjoyed doing it. Thank you, and maybe I'll see you again sometime," BPD began to turn and walk away.

"Yo, oh no, don't be so fast to go honey. My name is Sunflower, and my sister here, Daffodil, has wanted to meet a man like you for a long time." Sunflower beamed into BPD's face as she grabbed his shoulder and spun him back towards her sister.

"A man like me, do you two ladies even know who I am."

"Yeah, we know, you're the man who just went to war with the devil. What could be a better foundation to get to know someone than that," Sunflower said.

BPD noticed how bright the ladies dresses were. He didn't know what to say. He just looked above the brightness and into the eyes of Sunflower.

"No, no, young buck, not me. My sister, Daffodil, she's the one you ought to get to know. I'm married, but she's single."

Daffodil remained quiet on the sidelines.

Pork Dog looked at her and he did feel a tinge of excitement. The young woman was large, but she was sturdy, and she was cute. Her black eyes were a deep well of warmth. It was the kind of warmth that BPD had been looking for for a long time. He had never been able to find it in this city. He had come from the south at the age of eight and he knew what a good southern woman could be like. His grandmother was a good example.

Without further examination, he took Daffodil's hand in own. "Would you and your sister care to join me for dinner?"

"That would be wonderful, wouldn't it sis?" Sunflower beamed.

"Yes, I guess it would," came Daffodil's shy response.

"Fine, that's great, I'll pick you ladies up at your motel at about seven tonight. Where are you staying?"

Daffodil began to wonder away from the group. Sunflower spoke quietly. "Don't worry about her. She's always been shy, but trust me, you'll like her, she's a diamond in the rough. All she needs is the right man. Maybe you're it."

Daffodil was now some twenty feet down the corridor and almost out of the building.

Sunflower wrote the particulars of their address and phone number down and handed it to BPD. Sunflower hurried to catch up with her sister. "We'll see you later, you big lovable man."

Pork Dog watched the two women leave the building and he wondered. Had he been fighting the devil with the video production, or was he just beginning his fight with him. It was only dinner, he reasoned, but he couldn't forget the smile and the twinkle in Daffodil's eyes.

He only had one thought as he got in the limo to be driven back to his apartment. His life was more than just a video; it was an entire damn movie.

Sonnentag

Chapter 24

Wicked clowns, Joan couldn't get them out of her head. Was it the ICP she kept listening to or was it the book Life Expectancy by Deane Koontz that kept affecting her. Wicked clowns, wicked people.

It was time for a trip to the farm. The puking all the time was getting old, especially in the morning. This was definitely something new. Forty-years old and she didn't want to face the truth, and yet, every time she did, she was happy. She was forty years old and pregnant. She knew it, and she loved it. Only problem was, she knew who's baby it was. She knew who the father was. It was definitely time for a little rest and relaxation at the farm.

She wondered, would she see Holly's father when she went to the farm, would he come right over when he saw her there, or would she have to make the effort. She wanted to talk to him, but she didn't know just how or when.

She was scared. At times when she was alone, she would hear the voices inside of her head. It had been so many years since her first troubling years with the FBI when she had heard that one strange one. The one that always made all of the hair on her arms stand up straight. Kill yourself; kill yourself now, the voice said; over and over while she listened to some techno music. She wondered if the voice was real. No it couldn't be. This was strictly techno music. There were no words on the CD. She had listened to it many times before. She had never heard any words. Why now? Why did she now hear the words that upset her.

Kill the baby, kill the baby, came the words in the exact spot where they used to say kill yourself. No, she screamed to the emptiness of the car after she had turned the CD off. Killing the baby would be like killing myself. She wanted this child, no matter how the conception had come about. The child was growing inside of her. She would retire to the farm and she would have the child.

Joan looked across the road at the house of Holly and John Adamsley and saw that many lights were on. She got a sense of warmth just from looking at their house and realizing how much she had grown to love Holly, but John, she just didn't know yet. He seemed like such a good man, but she had never shared her deepest secrets with him. As she turned into her gravel drive-way and traveled up slowly to the house, she vowed that she would share with him this trip, share her deepest new secret and see how he reacted. She didn't put anything on the outcome. After all, she didn't have the faintest idea about how she would bring it up. She vowed to herself not to judge John too harshly.

Joan pulled her shoulder harness off and wrapped it around the gun. She placed her weapon in the drawer of the desk by the hallway that led back to the bedrooms. After she closed the door, she stepped back and thought of how many times she had fired the gun in the line of duty. Was it seven or eight, ten or twelve, she didn't want to think about it too long, but then a worse thought intruded. What about the men she had killed? It was four wasn't it, no, it was five, she was sure of it.

But these thoughts, why did they intrude now? Maybe it was because of the life that grew inside of her. Before she had had only past impressions of deaths buried deep within her, but now a new impression was forming as she lay down on her bed and touched her womb area. Forty years old and bringing a life into this world. She had to remind herself that her life was about to change. There would be no more crimes and criminals. She could end it, and tell her superiors she was pregnant. She knew they would let her ride out the final weeks to retirement. She didn't know how long it would be until she took down this last serial killer. She cried for awhile. She had a coming child to think about. Her death would mean the death of a new life. She didn't know what to do. She lay on the bed and sobbed until physical weakness put her to sleep.

In the end, after she had lain awake in her bed for over an hour the next morning, she made the final decision that she knew she must make. She couldn't quit now. She was the only one who saw inside the inner circle of fear Poppin had been causing. She had to stay involved in taking him down, for what good was a world that she would bring a child into that contained such a man. She paused, she knew there would be others. There would always be other murderers, but this man knew her. She would never feel safe for herself or her child until this man came down. She would finish what she had begun.

Joan sat in a new, blue recliner that had been delivered to the house during her absence. Holly's dad, John must have let the delivery men in as she had asked him to when she called him. She had also asked him to stop over and see her whenever he realized she was at the farmhouse.

Joan was thinking of John just as a knock came at the door. Joan opened the door without fear or questioning. She could sense the goodness of the man who stood outside.

Joan said a quick hello and went back to slink down in the blue recliner. John stepped forward to stand in front of her.

Forty-five years old, John was still a young man. He looked five maybe even ten years younger. Joan supposed it was the deep warmth that emanated from his dark brown eyes.
There was something special about this man, something holy. He had strong, broad shoulders and a strong, overall build. His arms were muscular and full of hairy curls to match the curls on his head. His moderate mustache always turned Joan on. She was sexually turned on every time she saw him. This was a new feeling for her. Maybe it resulted from the new life growing in-side of her. Too bad, the baby wasn't Johns'. She broke down crying and couldn't look at him.

John stepped forward and knelt before Joan, putting his right hand on her left knee. He didn't say a word but just waited.

Joan sobbed and then sucked the next sob back inside of her. She calmed herself and finally was able to open her eyes and look at the man who knelt before her.

John thought her blue eyes were more beautiful than ever.

Gently, he spoke. "Joan, I know we don't know each other totally yet, maybe two people can never know each other totally, I don't know, but one thing I do know is that in the past times that we have spent together I feel I have come to know you quite well. I do know that I think a lot about you, about the courage you possess, as well as, well maybe, as well as the love I know that is inside of you. I think your job is tearing you apart and you need to get out now."

Hearing the words made Joan calmer. She could tell by the gentleness in his eyes and voice that this man truly did care for her. She thought for a moment and calmed herself further. Oh no, she thought, I think this man loves me. If only this new life inside of her were his. How can I tell him all of the truth?

John took Joan's hands in his and stroked them warmly. He gazed deeply into her eyes. "You can tell me Joan, tell me anything you need to tell me. I don't know how to say it other than to come right out with it. I've fallen in love with you Joan."

Joan couldn't help herself as she broke down once again into uncontrollable sobs. The once, always in control FBI agent, was in control no more. Suddenly she stopped sobbing and started laughing.

John pulled back away from Joan and stood up. He felt crushed that she would laugh at his admittance of love. When the shock began to ebb away a tear came to his eyes.

Joan stopped laughing. "Oh John, no, I'm so sorry, it's not what you said that I'm laughing at. It's me. I've gone and done it this time. I'm so mixed up I don't know whether to be happy or sad. You see, I know that I am falling in love with you, but there is something else. Something so absurd that it may ruin any chance we have of being together."

John wiped the tears from his face and looked in puzzlement at Joan. "Joan, you know something, you are a complicated woman. I don't know what you're talking about, but I'm willing to listen. Is it about finishing your job and still being alive?"

"John, no, I wish it were that simple. That is a part of it, but it is only a small part. There is something more, something much more complicated."

Only the ticking of the grandfather clock on the wall broke the silence of the room. Neither one of the couple knew what to say next. Tick-tock until the front door opened and the silence was broken by the bouncing, joyous, jumping of a small child. Holly bounded into the chair next to Joan and smiled at Joan and her father.

"Holly, what are you doing here? I thought you were in school."

"Dad, we got out early, they say the snow is going to come down harder in the next few hours, and they wanted to get us all home safely. After the first hour after mid-day the day counts as a full school day anyway."

"Oh," was all John could manage.

Joan felt good seeing Holly; it somehow felt right that she should be here. Maybe what she was about to say would be too much for Holly to handle, but then again, the wisdom and readily acceptance of things that youth can accept could come in handy. Or else, Joan thought, maybe she was just using Holly as protection. If John rejected her, Holly probably wouldn't. She suspected that a young girl would be happy to know about a baby no matter where it was coming from.

Joan sucked up her courage and blurted out the truth. "There's no other way to tell you two except to come right out and tell you. I'm pregnant."

Holly bounced out of the chair like a rocket. She was quickly in Joan's arms and giving her a hug.

John turned and walked away from the hugging females. He went to stand by the old, eight-pane farmhouse windows and looked out at the falling snow. He didn't know what to make of the new announcement. He knew he loved Joan, but it was a different kind of love, an older, more mature kind of love. It was the kind of love he had always hoped that he would one day have in his life. A child, whose? He knew it was too soon in their relationship to be his, but if not his, then whose? Had his love been misplaced? He looked out the window again and saw that Holly's school had been right. It did look as though there was going to be a very heavy snow before it was finished snowing outside.

He calmed himself and prepared to hear Joan out if she was ready to tell the rest of the story. He wondered if she would with Holly there, but then he figured it out. Joan felt safe with Holly present, and that was a good thing. He didn't want the ladies to see the tears in his eyes. He wiped them away and put a smile on his face before he turned around away from the window and the softly falling snow.

After Holly's excitement died, she got off Joan and went to hug her father by his knees.

Joan looked past the two at the white snow swirling outside. It somehow felt so safe and warm in this house with these two people present. She wished things could have been different, but they weren't. She had to tell the whole story.

She began slowly. "John, Holly,..." Holly slowly turned to face Joan. "I have to tell you guys, the baby inside of me is not from John. Do you understand what I'm saying? The baby is Shawn's, the young man who died trying to save Holly and me."

Holly stood frozen, a perplexed look on her face. She looked as still as a completed jig-saw puzzle.

Holly slowly walked up and stood in front of Joan, looking at Joan's belly. She turned and looked somberly at her father. After a long pause she spoke. "What do you think dad, does it matter whose; do you love Joan?"

Holly was such an intermediary at such a young age. Joan and John didn't know whether they should laugh or cry. John stepped up past Holly and took Joan's hands to pull her up from the chair. He gave Joan a big hug.

Holly joined in the warm embrace before it ended.

John let out a deep sigh and hugged Joan tightly. John took a step back from Joan and looked into her eyes. "Joan, I do love you, I still love you, and I suspect that I always will. I never expected something like this, but I'm okay with it as long as you love me. Do you love me Joan?"

Tears came to Joan's eyes as she threw her arms around John and hugged him tightly.

"Oh, John, yes, I do love you, I was just so afraid that you would reject me when you found out I was pregnant by someone else. I didn't mean for it to happen. I was lonely and afraid. The sex just happened. It didn't mean anything to me, but the result of the child inside of me does. It is a prayer that has been answered."

Joan stepped back a little and brought Holly back into the embrace. "I love you both, and if you'll let me, I want you two and this baby to be one with me. I want to be a family."

Holly and John both said yes at the same time. The trio embraced and cried tears of joy together.

After a short time, Joan was able to pull away from the embrace. She went to the kitchen to get some warm tea for the trio. John followed her into the kitchen while Holly went out to feed Sneakers.

John walked over to the kitchen table and took a seat.

As the tea brewed, Joan turned to face John. "John, I hate to break a good mood so quickly, but I'm a little worried at how readily you accepted the fact that I am pregnant."

John sighed. "Joan, there is something I have to tell you. I had a bad accident once. I fell from the tractor and crushed my testicles when I was still quite young, only a year after Holly was born." John paused to let Joan soak up the new information.

"You mean," Joan paused.

"Yes, after Holly, my wife and I were unable to have any more children."

"And that's why, why you don't mind," Joan said nervously.

"Yes, that's why. I always wanted to have another child. I suppose you don't fully understand it yet, it took me a long time to realize it and forgive myself. You see, Holly's mother committed suicide. It was vehicular suicide, but I believe it was a suicide none the less. She couldn't deal with the fact that we could never have more children.   She drank heavily and there were other things, I suppose, but that was a big one."

"Oh, I'm so sorry," Joan said quietly.

"No, its okay, what has happened here today is an answer to my prayers. I love you Joan, and a child coming from you, any child, I will love as my own. Another child is something that will help me heal; help me to fully love again. Of course, I will need your help with that."

Joan smiled. "No problem, you've got it. I love you John."

"I love you too Joan."

John and Joan entwined in a long embrace and then sat in silence at the kitchen table and sipped their tea.   After finishing feeding Sneakers outside, Holly entered the kitchen and brushed snow off of her clothes.   She sat down at the table.   Her hazel eyes flashed a question mark. The adults seemed so happy, but she didn't know the whole story.

Holly didn't know that Joan and John would make love the entire night long.

Chapter 25

Collins stood with his back arched and took in a deep breath of the fresh country air. A windless, clear blue sky stretched out overhead.

Wendtworth gave Collins a quick tour of the house.

Collins stood and looked out the kitchen window towards the barn. "Needs a lot of work Joan, but it's beautiful out here, nice and peaceful. I think you're making a good choice, but you are going to see this present case through aren't you?"

Joan was surprised at the question. "Yes, one last time. We'll get this one, and then I'm done. I've had enough of that kind of life. I've had enough of death around me. This place is full of life. I can only imagine how full of life it will be in the spring.

"Yes, I'm sure there will be new birth everywhere. I'm happy for you. After so many years of working in this business, I know you need a rebirth in your life. You need to focus on the living," Collins stated without knowing the full truth of his words.

Joan was happy with Collins. She had grown to like the young man over the past months, and she hoped he would stay a part of her life from time to time in the future.

Joan walked up and put her arm on Collins' shoulder. "I hope that after I retire, you come and see me here at the farm, especially if you need to chill out. There's plenty of room here and you're always welcome for a visit."

"Thanks Joan, I'll take you up on that. I feel less stressed just being here today. Closing in on our man is making me pretty jumpy. Hey, I noticed a fence line about fifty yards behind the barn. Do you think we could put something on the fence posts and take a little target practice?"

"You've done your qualifying this quarter, haven't you?"

"Yes, I'm jumpy, and I want to stay fresh. I think the memory of shooting out here in the calmness of the wilds will carry through with me if I have to pull the trigger on a human being. I've never killed anyone."

"Neither have I," Joan lied in order to keep down Collins anxiety level.

Collins was awestruck. "I know we never talked about it before, but I always assumed that in all your years of work you probably would have."

"No, I've had to draw down on a lot of perps, but I never killed one, I've wounded a few. You've got to remember, these people are used to having the advantage. Most are confused when they lose that advantage. It's not hard to subdue them."

"Yeah, I can see where that would be true, but I really want the practice."

Joan wondered at the wisdom of bringing anything in connection with her job to the peacefulness of the farm, but she knew her partner was being sincere. She could see where the peace and quiet of the farm could stick with him in his mind in a tense situation.

"Okay, I think your idea is good. There is a case of old Point beer bottles in the barn. We can line them up on the fence and take turns taking them out."

"Great," Collins touched the pistol in his chest holster out of excitement.

The couple walked out to the barn. Pigeons cooed at the top of the old, cement silo. Sparrows flitted from the barn overhang as they approached. Joan went inside the barn and returned to Collins with the faded, dusty, old case of empty beer bottles. They walked behind the barn, and Joan set the case down. Collins picked it up, walked over to the fence and affixed three beer bottles on separate posts that were six feet apart. Walking back, he joined Joan twenty yards from the posts. They would compete with their standard issue FBI Smith and Wesson thirty-eights. Both weapons were already loaded.

"You go first," Joan stated flatly.

Collins stepped forward and clicked off the safety. He took aim quickly and fired three shots in rapid succession. Two of the three bottles broke. He looked back at Joan.

Joan's face was blank. "Take it out."

Collins fired again, breaking the last bottle.

Collins went to the fence and placed three new bottles on the post. Now it was Joan's turn. She stepped up into position and fired three rapid shots. All three bottles were shattered.

"That's great shooting Joan."

"Thanks, you're not so bad yourself. Try it again."

The next time, Collins shattered all three bottles. Joan hit her first three, but missed her last one of the second three.

"We're tied," Joan laughed. One more time together. We each draw from the sides and try to take out a bottle."

The agents pulled their firearms up from their sides and fired. Both bottles shattered simultaneously.

"One bottle left Collins. From the side, let's take him out together on the count of three. You count."

Collins looked at Joan and smiled. "One-thousand-one, one-thousand-two, one-thousand-..., the shots rang out in unity, the bottle shattered. Both shooters hit the bottle simultaneously.

The couple stood still and listened to the dead silence around them. They had an impending sense of the future as it would unfold. It was good that they had hit the target at the same time. They had the sense that soon they would need this unity. Soon, this act would be for real.

The two agents holstered their weapons. Joan turned around to see Holly staring blandly at them. The girl's white, ashen face was wrinkled with worry, her hands stretched out in a gesture that asked what was going on.

Joan walked calmly up to Holly.

The girl began to cry. "What's going on Joan, you're scaring Sneakers, he's circling his stall and bumping into the sides."

Joan took the girls small hands in hers. "Oh, Holly, I'm so sorry, I never thought of that. I didn't realize we were going to bother Sneakers."

Holly pleaded. "Don't shoot anymore, please."

Joan gave Holly a hug. "No, we won't, let's go in the barn and calm Sneakers down."

Collins watched as his partner and the young girl talked calmly to the horse, and entered the stall to pet him. He was surprised at how the young girl and the woman fit and worked together. It was as though they were mother and daughter, and maybe they already were but just didn't know it. He had the feeling Joan had found more than just peace on the farm. He knew she had found the new life she needed.

Chapter 26

The text message read what it always read. Go Rolly, Go Rolly. Rolly would know where to go. Poppin gave him the allotted hour to arrive and then pulled up in front of the bus depot. He was surprised to find that Rolly wasn't there. He waited.

A Greyhound bus unloaded and reloaded a group of new travelers. He watched the old, bent over travelers along with the young, near-penniless ones. Poppin was thankful that he lived the high life and never again had to use public transportation as he did when he was several years younger.

He waited. A nervous tension began to fill him and his hands shook on his lap. Rolly had never been late in the five years they had been making these exchanges. Poppin looked up and down the barren streets. Twenty minutes seemed like an eternity to wait. Rolly had always been at the drop-off point ahead of him. Something was wrong.

He found himself sweating, and he didn't have a pill to pop. Ten more minutes passed, and the reality that Rolly wasn't going to show set in. Poppin put the Benz in gear and drove the two miles over to the Sizzle. He saw Rolly's white Cadillac parked in the parking lot. To the usual greetings by the bouncer, he strode inside.

Rolly was throwing back a shot at the bar.

Poppin approached him cautiously.

241

Rolly gave Poppin a look of reproach when Poppin stopped and stood next to him.

Poppin glared at him. "What happened?"

Rolly grunted. "It's over. It's over between you and me."

Poppin was not surprised. He had seen it coming. His world seemed to be falling apart. His sanity was on the brink. It figured that his best friend would now betray him. Poppin had made a call from the Benz. He had come prepared for a problem. Rolly didn't notice the two large black men who walked up to stand beside him until it was too late.

The thumping sounds of the rap beat came to a halt as a comely blonde stripper finished her set to a hearty round of applause. Dead silence. It was unusual for the Sizzle.

The husky black man on the left side of Rolly took him by the left arm. "Let's go, you're coming with us."

"Where are we going man?" Rolly asked while looking at Poppin.

Poppin grinned weakly. "We're going to the back office. We're going to talk this over."

The ill-lit cluttered office was small and smelled musty. The two black men on each side of Rolly looked even bigger as they set Rolly down in a chair in the middle of the room. Poppin came around to stand in front of Rolly.

Anger flashed in Poppin's eyes. "Why you want to do this man. After all these years, why do you want to mess with the way things are?"

Rolly stared glumly without answering.

Poppin slapped Rolly hard across the right cheek. Rolly shook it off, looked up, and saw that Poppin had tears in his eyes.

Rolly gathered himself together. "I grew tired of being second man. I got into gambling trouble. I needed the money."

Poppin's tears disappeared and his eyes shown with anger. "Bullshit man, you could have come to me. We've worked together for years. You're my family man. I'm your brother. How could you betray me now? Why didn't you just come to me again?"

"I've been to you so many times, I just can't stop gambling. I'm a sick fuck."

"I'll say you are. You betrayed me. You betrayed your own family. I'm sick at the sight of you." Turning to the two burly guards Poppin said slowly, calmly. "Take him out of here."

The two guards jerked Rolly to his feet.

Rolly broke down in tears. "What are you going to do to me. Don't kill me."

Poppin let the words hang in the air.

Poppin sighed. "You're like a brother to me man. I'm not going to kill you, but I don't want to ever see you in this city again. After all that I've done for you. Man, just get lost forever, and don't even think about getting in the middle of my business here."

"Thank you Poppin, thank you," Rolly stammered through tears.

Poppin shook his head. Tears flowed freely when he was alone in the room. Poppin rang a buzzer, and the manager of the Sizzle appeared at the office door.

Poppin wiped the tears from his eyes. "Send me that last blonde stripper. I want to party. I've got to party. I've got to somehow forget about this."

"Consider it done," the manager left the room.

Poppin smiled. He would go on. He would get by. Have some fun and forget about it. His life was bigger than any one man, any one betrayal. He would balance the balls, juggle things, keep things going. Another would fill Rolly's slot. Game on again.

Keep it going player, he thought to himself. Keep it going.

Sonnentag

244

Chapter 27

Traveling down the country roads, the sound of the bass emanating from the speakers of the gold Taurus pounded in Poppin's brain. The resounding, repetitive beating was life-blood to his body. Pounding, pounding, keeping him from going insane. He had chosen the Taurus instead of the Benz so that when he cruised through the countryside he would remain inconspicuous. Out on Highway 23, in the middle of nowhere, it didn't matter how loud the music was. There was no one around to hear it.

The snows of winter had given way to the greening of the landscape. Soon the trees would be fully into their spring budding, but soon also another man would be dead. Poppin turned north onto Highway 49. Seven more miles through the greening landscape he turned left on County trunk H and followed the signs through the winding country road until he reached the edge of Camp LuWisama. It had been easy to find the place. All he had to do was read the paper and find out that the Scout leaders would be taking their troops on a spring retreat to the camp. He hadn't scouted the camp before arriving because it was so far from his home, but he wasn't worried. He knew that out here in the country there would be nothing but wide open spaces. All he needed to do was find a place where he could get the man isolated, and he could get the job done. It was time for his next kill.

Poppin drove past the wood-carved sign announcing the entrance to the camp. He drove slowly forward on the gravel road. There was no need for haste now. He turned down the music in the car. The bass became a low, almost silent ebb, but it was still there, calming his brain. A couple of hundred yards into the campgrounds, he saw an area of low brush and a clear spot to the right of it. He drove around the brush and behind it. He stopped the car, turned off the ignition and took a deep breath. From here it was safer to remain hidden rather than to travel on further by foot.

A thorny bush scratched the side of his face as he traveled towards a row of cabins in the distance. Sweat mixed into the cut and stung his face. He pulled a red bandanna from his back pocket and wiped his face. He was close to the cabins now, only fifty yards from them. He was well hidden in the brush. Now was the time for patience, but it was difficult for him. He wanted to get this next kill over with.

Twilight approached to a chorus of birds kissing the day goodbye in song. Poppin stayed crouched in the shadows as lights began to come on in the various cabins. He fixed a set of binoculars back and forth across the lighted windows and could see the movement of small shadows against the glass. He was looking for a large shadow. Jason Vickman was a big man, weight he had gained from years of overeating. Poppin popped a downer and followed it with a slug of water from his water bottle. Ten minutes passed and he began to grow calm again, but he realized he may sit outside these cabins for hours and nothing may happen.

From his research on Vickman, he knew the man was a heavy smoker. He knew the inevitable would come, sooner or later, the man would step out on the porch for a smoke. He just had to remain patient. The time would come.

Poppin knew that if he didn't get some action soon he was going to have to go over and take a piss by another bush. He was just about to rise and do so when the large bulk of a man stepped out onto the front cabin porch. The man stepped forward to the edge of the stairs and quickly lit a cigarette.

Puffing on the cigarette, the man proceeded down the stairs and looked up at the full moon. Poppin cursed himself in his mind. He was a good thirty yards away from the man, what if the man didn't move out any further. It would be a long shot with only a pistol. He chastised himself for not bringing along a rifle. There was no way he could move in and get any closer without Vickman noticing him.

Just as Vickman was finishing his cigarette, the cabin door flew open behind him and a young, blond-haired boy of about twelve years of age stepped out and walked to the top of the steps. Vickman turned and said something to the boy, and the boy lowered his head.

Vickman threw his cigarette down and stamped it out. He motioned for the boy to come forward, and the boy complied. Vickman put his arm on the shoulder of the youngster, and the pair began to walk away from the cabin.

Poppin's eyes followed them intently. Maybe this was the break he needed.

Scout and Scout leader walked to the edge of the asphalt parking lot when Poppin saw that they were going to enter what looked like a foot path. White painted stones lined both sides of a pathway and disappeared up a small knoll into the darkness. The pair of campers walked up the pathway and into the darkness.

He decided to wait a few minutes and follow them up the pathway. Somewhere up there he would run into them and deal with Vickman, but the boy, he didn't want to harm the boy. He would have to figure something out. Poppin rose, pulled a red bandanna from his back pocket, wiped his face, and crossed the clearing quickly to head up the trail.

About a hundred yards up the trail Poppin came to a small knoll. Poppin could hear voices on the other side of the knoll. He proceeded carefully. He looked over the top of the knoll. At the top, the land flattened out into a small plateau and an open circular space about thirty feet in diameter. In the center of the circle there was an eight foot long wooden bench on which sat the leader and his scout.

Poppin watched in silence as the leader talked to the boy. Putting his hands on the boy's shoulder the leader stood up with him. The scout leader positioned the boy a foot in front of him, but the boy stepped back as soon as the leader took his hands off his shoulder. The leader mumbled something. The boy stood silent and still. Vickman's back was to Poppin, but he could see the man's ass clearly in the moonlight when he dropped his pants. From the angle he was at he could also see the look of fear on the young scout's face.

Poppin knew he had to move quickly. In seconds, he slipped across the circular opening to stand behind the scout leader. He put the pistol up to the back of the man's head.

"What, what's this," Vickman stammered.

"It's the cold steel barrel of a pistol, and you're going to die if you don't listen to me," Poppin responded.

Vickman's voice shook in a low pitched squeal. "Okay, okay, I didn't mean nothing here. We were just playing around. I wasn't going to really make the boy do anything, honest."

"It doesn't matter what you were or weren't going to do. Just stay still and facing the way you are right now."

"Can I pull up my pants?"

"No," Poppin answered bluntly. He turned to the young scout. Listen young fellow, everything is going to be all right. I have come here tonight to save the death of your soul. The soul this man would have killed if he were given the chance. You don't have to worry. Come around behind Vickman and stand by me."

The boy was still in somewhat of a daze from looking at Vickman's privates, but he had been brainwashed by the man and was used to complying with authorities. He complied readily. It felt good to walk away from the front of the naked man.

"What's your name young man?" Poppin asked.

"Tommy," the boy said simply.

"Well Tommy, here is what I am going to do. I am going to blindfold you and head you back on down the trail. You can feel your way along the edge by feeling the stones with your feet. Just follow them until they stop. Then, I want you to count to a hundred before you take off your blindfold. Once you take off the blindfold, you can go get another counselor and tell them what happened. Is that clear Tommy?"

"Yes sir, it's clear, and sir, thank you for helping me."

"Okay Tommy, here goes," Poppin said as he turned the boy around and blindfolded him.

Poppin took the boy to the edge of the semicircle and started him down the trail. He turned and looked to see that Vickman hadn't moved. He was still showing the full moon to the full moon. Poppin walked back up behind the man and put the gun barrel to his head. Vickman flinched when he felt the cold steel, but before he could say anything Poppin pulled the trigger and blew his brains out through the front of his forehead. Vickman's large body slumped to the ground. Poppin put another one in his heart.

Poppin began the journey down the trail and was almost to the end when he heard car doors slam. He heard excited adult voices talking, and the voice of Tommy answering. He peered towards the cabins just as he saw Tommy pointing out to Wendtworth and Collins the mouth of the trail where he stood in the shadows. Poppin turned and headed back up the trail. Damn, he thought, how did they find him. He knew he would have to go into the forest in order to get away. A ghetto boy in the wilds.

Poppin raced back up the trail. He pulled up to a slow gait when he was back at the large circle where Vickman's body still lay. The body looked liked a beached whale bathed in the moonlight. Poppin stood over the body and looked at the edges of the circle. He hadn't noticed it before but there where trails with small markers at each ninety-degree intersection of the circle. He headed to the east edge of the circle and saw a sign that said Beaver's Hideout. He didn't know what lay ahead there, but he figured it was as good a direction as any to take. He headed off into the woods and down the winding trail.

Wendtworth and Collins stood at the foot of the pathway. Collins kicked at one of the white stones in anticipation. "Let's get up this trail fast. We can get him easy."

Joan turned Collins shoulders towards her. "No, that trail could be a death trap. He could be waiting on the side of it anywhere. He could take us out before we even know he is there."

Collins breathed in a big huff of the cool night air. "I don't care what you are going to do, but I am going to follow him up that trail."

Collins took off and disappeared around the first bend in the trail. Joan whipped out her cell phone and began dialing. She wanted the roads and highways covered. Poppin would have to surface somewhere on some road.

The path Poppin had chosen was wide and easily traveled; long ago any obstruction had been removed. He could feel sweat on his face even in the cool weather. His head swirled from exertion, and he felt a little dizzy. The downers he had taken had been a bad idea. They worked on his brain and body and demanded that he sit down and rest. Rest was out of the question. He had to get away to live another day.

A thick cloud of smoke hit Poppin's nostrils. What was this, he wondered. The moonlight hit him in the face as he broke through the smoke and into a large clearing filled with pup tents. A large campfire burned in the center area of the tents. A dozen young men and two adult camp leaders sat on wooden benches around the fire. One of the adult men was strumming a guitar and playing some kind of folk song that Poppin couldn't make out. Always the music judge, he wasn't too good, Poppin thought. Poppin stood frozen for a moment, should he go around this group or through it. He knew he had to keep making good time. He had to hit a road and soon.

Fully brazened, he walked up to the circle of people. The man strumming the guitar looked up with a look of dumbstruck awe on his face. He took his left hand off the guitar frets and motioned a what is this sign by lifting his hand slowly in the air. The man had a look of anxious fear in his eyes.

Poppin walked up and stood beside him. "I'm lost, how do I get out of here?"

"Just go back the way you came, when you come to the large open circle, just head south along the trail marked camp."

"I just came from that way, I know, but I want to get to the nearest road. If I keep heading east how far will it be to a road. I think I need to go east, but I'm not sure, I'm all turned around."

The counselor stood up. Poppin saw that he was a tall, large man, who had just looked small sitting down in his scout outfit. "You can go east through the woods to the road, but why would you want to do that. Just go back that way, it's easier," the man gave Poppin a wary look.

"Thanks anyway, I need to get to the road and fast. I'm going through this shit. Is there anything I should know about the conditions out there?" The statement seemed more like an order than a request.

"No, the woods are pretty clear. Campers have been working on it for years," the counselor said quietly.

"All right, continue on campers, sorry for the interruption," and with that, Poppin was off into the woods.

Wendtworth called the Waushara County Sheriff's Department and requested assistance. She asked all available police units in the area to be on the lookout for either a black Mercedes or a golden Taurus with a black man driving. She got in her car and headed out onto the entrance road. Gun on the seat beside her, she surveyed the dark edges of the road as she traveled. He had to come out to a road somewhere.

A pine branch smacked Poppin hard in the face. It hit his right eye and stung him into a temporary blindness. He paused only a few seconds to try and regain his vision and then walked forward. His legs buckled as he hit a felled tree trunk and fell over forwards. The air rushed out of his lungs with a thump. The musty smell of rotten mold blasted his nostrils. He fought to get his breath back. He was glad he was young and worked out. He pulled himself back together and proceeded through the darkness of the grove of pines until he came to their outside and was hit once again by the bright moonlight.

Poppin stepped forward and fell against the opposite side of a ditch. Hands and knees were covered with mud as he rose and tried to brush off. He shinnied up the ditch bank and came to a gravel road. Shale stones glistened like diamonds in the moon-

moonlight. Poppin looked both ways and saw the lane empty. He turned left and headed in the direction he believed to be North and away from the main scout camp.

Joan passed a turnoff to an old, rusty, mobile home on her right. She thought momentarily about turning off and checking out the home to see if Poppin was hiding there, but she figured it would be too soon. She gunned the engine and proceeded more quickly down the road.

Poppin broke into a trot and began to make good time. The open space of the road helped clear his head. His vision cleared and he began to settle into a comfortable runner rhythm. He had traveled only a half mile up the road when he came upon a driveway that had a mobile home at the end of it. Without breaking stride, Poppin turned into the drive and raced to the end of it. His eyes alighted on an old Silver and white Ford F150 off to the left of the mobile home. Getting closer he saw that it was heavily rusted and had bad tires. The front windshield was cracked, but the side window was rolled down. He put his hands on the door and peered in. He had to put his head far inside before he could see the key in the ignition. He failed to notice the light on in the side window of the home.

Poppin turned the key and could have ground a pound of meat, but nothing else happened. The engine remained dead. Poppin took a deep breath, damn he thought, this bitch has got to turn over.

"Come on honey, come on sweetheart, give it up to Poppin."

He turned the key and the starter whined in its metallic twist. The engine popped and began to turn over. It sputtered a moment and then stalled.

Poppin groaned. "There better be gas in this bitch." He turned the key again and when the motor caught he gunned the engine. A black cloud of smoke belched from the back end. Poppin gunned the engine several more times trying to get it to run smoothly, but he soon decided that was not to be. Running

252

rough or not, at least it was running. Poppin backed the truck up into the turnaround.

The front door to the trailer house opened up and a man who looked fragile, rusty, and old as the trailer stepped out onto the rickety, front, top-step platform. Poppin looked at the old man and saw him raise a clenched fist in the air. Poppin reached in his shirt pocket, pulled out a couple of hundred dollar bills and threw them in the air, hoping the old man would see them and not cause him any trouble.

The old truck was surprisingly spry as Poppin gunned the engine and turned right onto the gravel road. He headed down the road with his eyes straight ahead. He relaxed when he saw there was nothing in sight.

Joan had traveled to the end of the gravel road and stopped. She knew she would have to go back for Collins, but she had probably already missed Poppin. She swung the car around and headed back towards the scout camp. Two miles down the road she passed an old Ford pick-up coming towards her. She couldn't make out the driver. She could only see blackness in the front of the truck. She traveled another two hundred yards before she stopped and swung the car around. It had to be Poppin, at least, it was worth a shot.

Poppin got up to county trunk H and took a left. Twenty seconds later, Wendtworth was at the county trunk intersection. There was nothing in sight. Right or left, she thought, she had lost her bearings. The main highway was by the BP gas station and Poppin would be headed there. She was confused. She turned right.

Poppin drove three miles down County H until he saw the yellow BP sign and the bright overhead lights of the station. He pulled the old truck into the parking lot and drove it directly around the building. He took a quick piss back there in the darkness and then headed towards the front of the building.

Sonnentag

Poppin stood by a garbage can by the front door and waited for a dirty-looking old man to come out the door. The man had on a dark-blue, flannel shirt that was ripped in several places. He burped as he looked over at Poppin.

Poppin stepped towards the man. "Hey man, I need your help. My truck broke down out on the road a ways back, and I've got to get into Oshkosh to a motel. I've got an important meeting there in the morning. I will be willing to pay you well."

The man's eyes lit up. "How well?"

"Two hundred bucks man, not bad for an hour or so of your time, and a little wear and tear on the vehicle."

"You must want to get there pretty bad to give me two hundred bucks. Well, it's none of my business. I can always use the money. Let's go."

The old man led Poppin to a rusty 1982 Dodge colt economy car. The car looked ready for death. Poppin climbed in, brushing a bunch of pop cans and potato chip bags on the floor.

"It ain't much, but it will get us there, I just hope it will get me back," the old man grunted.

"Get back, get back, way back," Poppin laughed and then slumped into the front passenger seat. He knew he was safe for now. He closed his eyes and rested, letting the smell of the wilds leave his nostrils to be filled with the surrounding smell of moldy garbage. To the sounds of country music he slipped off to sleep.

Chapter 28

Adam Sampson, the head of United States Home Security took his seat with a nod of his head to the new President. President Lewis Duncan sat quietly with his hands clasped in front of him on top of the shiny desk. He was a strong, athletic looking black man. His hard face could have been chiseled out of granite. Intelligent, leery, black eyes looked out at his advisor. The assassination of U.S. President Justin Millard had made him the first black United States President.

Just six months in office, Duncan had the feeling he was about to solve a big problem, but he had learned already too well that problems at the level of the presidency always created more problems. Spin-offs, there was always a spin-off and a spin to be put on. He expected answers from the man who sat before him, but he knew they would come with a price.

Sampson leaned slightly forward, "Mr. President, I'll get right to the point. We know where there is a copy of the tape of the man who assassinated President Millard."

Duncan smiled broadly. "Where is it, do you have it?"

"No, the man who has it wants to broker a deal, but it's a hell of a deal, it's a decision only you can make, a decision you will have to live with the rest of your life."

Over the next ten minutes Sampson went over the particulars of the case. The President's face was grim as he sat in silence for what seemed an eternity. Pardon one sin to assuage a greater sin, this was his dilemma. He got up and paced the oval office behind the desk.

Finally, he paused, put his hands on the desk, and leaned forward. "Do it, make the deal, and when it is done make sure this Slayer Player is extradited to some other country where we never hear from him again."

Security advisor Sampson quickly left the office. The President sat with his hands over his eyes and against his forehead. A small tear came to his eyes. He knew that the nation must know who had murdered their President, but he also knew that the decision could come back to haunt him. No matter, if things were handled correctly, if the man with the tape was given what he wanted and never reneged, everything would be okay. He could and would live with it. It was a question of the greater justice, but in the chair he sat in, he knew that it always was. He sighed and composed himself to get on with the rest of the day's work.

It would be a busy day like always.

Chapter 29

Poppin had to dress down. It was time to make an escape to a hide-a-way. The streets were hot for him in every which way. Dealing and death were closing in on him. He had to change up, catch his breath; think about what he would do next.

Dressed to the maximum in hundreds of dollars worth of clothes, he did look strange to the Two A.M. customers that were riding the main-street Milwaukee bus. Pretty conspicuous, but he wasn't worried. He would trade a bum for some trashed clothes if he had to.

Poppin looked out the window as the bus crossed Thirty-Fifth Street. Set back a little from the main road behind a large parking lot, he saw a Good-Will charity store. The bus flashed by quickly, but he thought that he saw a couple of boxes in front of the store. His anxiety was proving difficult to control so he pulled the overhead wire to ring the buzzer and got off at the next stop. He backtracked to the store.

Poppin smiled when he opened the top box. It was full of extra-large men's clothing. He even found a tattered pair of jeans that would fit him just fine, and a badly worn pair of tennis shoes that were the perfect size. The only problem was going to be a coat. He opened a second and third box and found none. He figured he might as well get started with the changeover. He could always go in and buy a coat at nine-o'clock when the store opened, but that was unfortunate for the store opening was still many hours away.

Slipping along the side of the building and down an alleyway, Poppin came to a large, green trash dumpster. He stepped behind it and changed his clothes, bundling up his own, new clothes, he threw them in the trash.

"Hey, what the hell you doing there? I'll take that stuff," came the grumble, growl of an old man's voice.

Poppin startled. He looked up and saw an old man sitting not more than five yards away and next to a small recyclable material can against the brick wall of the building. He looked through the dim lighting at the man and saw the hard, white stubble of a dirty beard. A stained and grimy canvas overcoat protected the man from the chill of the night. Poppin stepped up slowly towards the man. The man cowered a little back against the roughness of the brick wall.

For a moment, the two stared at each other in wonder. Neither could figure out who was really the fish out of water in this situation. Without saying a word, Poppin unbuttoned his coat and held it out to the man.

Rotten, blackened teeth managed to somehow still grasp a small twinkle from the overhead light of the building. The old man had trouble rising to his feet. Poppin stepped forward to try and help him.

"Don't touch me. You don't want to touch me. No, you don't want to be doing that," the old man snarled.

"Take it easy old man. I don't want nothin' from you but that old coat."

"On the run huh, I used to be on the run too a long time ago, but then I finally stopped running, sat down, and got lost in the streets."

Poppin was surprised that the man was able to put together such a comprehensive package of thoughts. "The trade, is it all right for you."

An alcoholic mind can still be surprisingly sharp when it comes to finding a way to get more alcohol to dull it. The old man said nothing more. He took off his tattered coat and threw it at Poppin's feet. Poppin handed his coat over to the old man, and the man greeted him with his dirty, semi-toothless grin. The old man put on the coat and walked away proudly. For a few hours that morning he would look pretty good. Later he would sell the coat to a second hand store, get a cheap one from the Good-Will store, and buy some liquor. It was going to be a good day of oblivion for him.

Not for Poppin. It seemed there was no way he was ever going to find the peace of oblivion again. It didn't seem there was any amount of drugs or alcohol that was going to help him forget this time. The only solution that kept coming to him was that he had to find a woman to talk to, and he knew without a shadow of a doubt that the woman he needed to talk with was Latoya. That had been his goal when he had set out at One A.M. and nothing had changed it.

The hell with the bus, he thought. Poppin walked. It was a full twenty-eight blocks down and two blocks over to get to Latoya's building, but he needed to get in the mood and the right frame of mind for a street bum. Changing clothes helped, but the walk through the streets would stretch out his mind to calmness even better.

He was fully in the mode of a street bum when at last he stood before Latoya's apartment. He wondered if she would even recognize him when she opened the door. His vanity knew that she would recognize his smile.

Latoya's voice was groggy from slumber when she answered the door pager and let him in. In spite of the sleep in her eyes, she became wide-eyed when she saw the tattered bum standing in front of her. She did a double take and saw that it was Poppin.

Latoya stepped back and motioned for Poppin to follow her in.

Having just walked the streets at night, Poppin adjusted quickly to the dim lighting in Latoya's apartment.

Latoya stretched, her white extra long T-shirt rising up halfway over her hips. She did not seem at all taken aback by Poppin's appearance. "It sure is early street bum, I don't know about you, but I could sure use some coffee." Latoya sauntered across the room and into the kitchen.

Poppin sat in the burnt-orange armchair opposite the water color painting his father had once done. His legs and back ached from the long walk. He shook his head knowing that he would need some practice if he were ever going to be poor. Yeah, right, he laughed to himself.

The quiet humming of a happy female emanated from the kitchen. He sat and looked at the water color, orange-leafed tree painting that his father had painted so many years ago. For some reason, a reason he could not put his finger on, the painting gave him a sense of peace. Maybe, he thought, it was just the relaxation coming into his body after such a long walk.

Latoya entered with two steaming cups of coffee. Rainbows swirled up the sides of the cups. Poppin smiled. There were just some things that only a woman could add to life.

Taking a sip of the steamy liquid, Poppin jerked his head back. "Wow, this is strong."

"Yes, sorry, but it's early, and I'm quite impatient when it's early, especially this early. I poured the two cups when the pot was only half done. It's quite a jolt but I need one right now."

"That's okay, so do I. It is early, and I'm a little cold. I'm sure this liquid nitro will be just fine," Poppin answered.

Latoya sipped her coffee and looked at Poppin. Poppin didn't seem to want to meet her eyes.

"What's wrong Poppin, why aren't you looking at me?"

Poppin leaned back and slouched in the chair. His voice was melancholy. "I was just thinking about a pet I had once as a kid."

"Tell me about it," Latoya said simply.

"Well, actually, it involves a couple of pets. When I was about five years of age my dad took me to a carnival that came to town. It was a wonderful day, the kind of day I seldom had. I was able to ride a lot of rides, and right before we left, my dad let me throw five ping-pong balls at some small globes that contained goldfish. I thought I had lost when I threw the last ball and it went in. I won a big, bright-orange goldfish."

Poppin finally had a smile on his face when he looked at Latoya.

Latoya took another hard slug of coffee and was coming awake
now. "That's so nice."

Poppin turned towards Latoya. "There's more to the story.
Before we got home my father took me to a store and bought
some goldfish food. Once home my father pulled a large, goldfish bowl out of the closet and gave it to me. He told me to keep
this fish fed and keep the water clean, feed it every day. That
was all he said, and then he left my bedroom. I always wanted
to do exactly what my father said, so the next night I cleaned the
fish bowl. Only problem is, I put hot water in the bowl," Poppin
paused.

"Oh no, was the fish all right?"

"He was at first of course, but then he went sideways. I didn't
know what to do so I kept holding onto the fish and trying to
keep it straight. I would let go, and he would get worse. He was
now floating upside down. I kept trying and trying. Finally I
fell to the floor crying." Poppin shuttered and didn't want to
continue.

"That must have been really traumatic for a boy the age of
five."

"It was, but it gets worse. I finally got frantic, and went to get
my dad. He was drunk and passed out in a chair in the living
room. I shook him and shook him but he wouldn't awaken. Finally, I gave up and went back to the bathroom. I dumped the
fish into a small bowl and cleaned the large one thoroughly, but
by the time I got back to the fish he was dead."

"Poppin, I'm so sorry."

"There's still more to the story. I sat down on my bedroom
floor with the dead fish in my hands and began crying heavily.
My father then came in the room and saw me crying over the
dead fish. He grabbed me by the shoulders, picked me up and,
and,..."

Poppin began crying now. He leaned over towards Latoya and
she held him.

"It's all right, that kind of thing is tragic, but from what you have already told me about your father, what he did next was probably worse, you can tell me about it, it'll be okay."

Poppin breathed deeply. "After he was done shaking me, he hauled me into the kitchen. He had the fish food in his hand. You dumb ass, he called me. He took the fish food, put it in a bowl, put water on it, and made me eat it. Then he told me I was ready for the main course. He took me back to my room, carried the dead fish into the bathroom with me and stuffed it in my mouth."

The silence in the room was as thick as the deepest fog had ever been. Latoya had tears in her eyes.

Poppin's voice was hard now. "I tried to swallow the fish, but I couldn't, I threw up all over myself. My father pushed my head in the toilet bowl, hollered clean yourself up and left."

"Poppin, that is such a sad story, I'm so sorry for you. Is that why you're here tonight, the bad memories."

"No, not really, you see Latoya, the bad memories always seem to be with me. There are so many. After that I made a wild mouse a pet. He just killed that one night in a fit of rage. On and on, I could tell you stories, but the real story I want to tell you tonight is the full truth of what is going on with me lately."

Latoya turned cold. She wasn't sure she loved this man enough. Their relationship was still fairly new, only a couple of months old. She took a deep sip of her coffee and put it down. She took Poppin's hands in her own.

Poppin shook her hands off and stood up. He paced around the room a bit and then stopped to sit in a chair opposite Latoya.

Latoya took this as not a good sign.

Poppin looked down and then up to the ceiling for what seemed an eternity. He sighed. "You know how I told you I had killed a man, well there's more to it..... Latoya raised her right hand to stop him. Poppin complied, but looked puzzled.

"I know who you are Poppin," Latoya said.

"No, I don't think you really do, I think you're too young to really know."

"No, Poppin, I think I know." Latoya gave Poppin a blank smile. "You're the Slayer Player."

Poppin jumped about six inches from the chair, settled back down, and then rose again to pace wildly about the room. After three trips around the room, acting as though he was looking for a way out that wasn't there, he sat back down and collapsed in the chair. He held his head in his hands and leaned down. He was somehow relieved, but he had no idea what his next move should be.

Poppin looked down at the floor. Honesty was still a virtue hard to come by, but he forced himself. "Yes, I am the Slayer Player."

Latoya rose from the couch, went over and knelt before him. "You're secret is safe with me, but I doubt it is safe with a lot of people. I don't know where we stand, but you have to get out of this city and hide somewhere. Maybe in time we can hook up again."

Poppin's mind was swirling with mixed emotions. He didn't know what to do. He didn't know if there would be a future for the two of them. As his mind cleared, he saw only his death in the future. He felt that Latoya saw the same thing.

Poppin rose from his chair and pulled Latoya up to him. He gave her a big hug and she accepted it. Without saying another word, he turned and left.

Back down on the street, he pulled his hat down tight over his forehead just above his eyes. He surveyed the street. He didn't know what direction he was going to go. He felt every direction would be bad no matter what way he turned.

He began to stroll down the street towards the dawn sunlight.

One more kill to go, he thought to himself, just one more kill to go.

Sonnentag

Chapter 30

Jack it up, crank it up, slap'em up, take the last of these fuckin'
abusive assholes down. Harrison dead and five others down,
only one to go, on with the show, put the gun to their head and
give em a blow.

Poppin slugged some whiskey, and popped a couple of pills, he
didn't even look to see what the pills were, and he didn't care.
He was a dirty, rotten, street bum now. Going into the office
building he would appear way out of place. He would have to
ignore everyone and move quickly. He would be on camera
here, but he didn't care, on with the show. The Slayer Player
Grand Finale, game on.

Poppin slipped through the revolving glass doors right behind a
man in a three piece suit. He followed close behind the man as
if to show that he was with him. The man went to the row of
three elevators at the far end of the entrance hall. Poppin veered
left to the stairwell.

By the time Poppin reached his destination at the fifth floor he
was sweaty and winded. He sat down at the top of the stairs to
get his breath. He fingered the handle of the revolver he had
kept hidden in a shoulder harness. The gun had warmed now
from his body heat, but soon he would make it so warm it was
smokin'.

Man, he thought, he was just another killer clown, and now,
sitting in such ridiculous clothing at the top of an empty concrete
and steel stairwell he felt forlorn and forgotten. All this killing
that had already been done. They were closing in on him. He
didn't want this kind of fame because he knew it would replace

the real fame he had gained through the recording industry. He knew the former fame was gone now, gone forever. His chest felt heavy. Was it worth it, he wondered. Fuck it, too late now.

Poppin took a final slug and finished off the 200 milliliter bottle of whiskey. He threw the bottle, and it skidded off the steel railing to smash against the corner turn of the concrete stairwell and disintegrate. The glass shattered into what seemed to be hundreds of little shards. The shards sparkled gaily in the stairwell light and looked remarkably like snowflakes.

Poppin stood, took off the dirty, tan top-coat and threw it over the stair rail. He stood before the door and puffed up his chest. Hocus-pocus another shithead is gonna die. Full of lead, he's goin' to bed forever. Into the lobby, onto the camera, into the office, fire the gun, and it would all be done. Like hell, you never can tell, might be the end of the Slayer Player as well.

There was always the chance that this escape would go all right. There was always the chance to take a ride in a rollin' coffin too. That chance was closer now than it had ever been since the beginning of his vendetta. He could almost feel the breath of the FBI agents on the back of his neck. He even turned and looked to see if they were behind him. He wondered what he would do if they were already in front of him. Too late, who cares, if they were there, then they would have to die too.

Poppin took a deep breath and opened the door to the office lobby. Silence and emptiness greeted him. A young, blonde secretary sat with a headset on and was transcribing notes. She didn't hear him come in. As he brushed past her she sensed he was there. She looked up with a smile that quickly turned upside down when she saw the gun in his hand. She drew back in her chair and was shocked, but Poppin was already flying past her.

He went into the operating area. The smell of antiseptic and blood blasted his nostrils wide. His increased sense of smell made the odors ignite his mind. His nostrils flared wider, his eyebrows raised, his adrenaline pumped. The bright overhead light ignited the face of the patient who was going to live. In the adjoining area, a bright light also shown over the dental hygienist and her patient. They would live too.

Poppin grabbed the drill from the dentist, wrapped the cord quickly around his neck, and threw the man against the wall. The man slumped on the floor in a daze. Frozen in shock, he could not move.

Wendtworth and Collins exited the elevator to see the receptionist frantically crying and trying to dial the phone. The receptionist trembled so badly she was unable to dial the numbers.

Poppin grabbed the chubby dentist by a long, blonde wisp of his hair, jerked his head back, and put his pistol in the dentist's mouth. Pointing the gun towards the ceiling inside the man's mouth, he fired. Brain matter and blood painted the wall. The man in the chair covered his eyes, and he figured he would be next.

Poppin turned and flew towards the office door. He swung the door open and hit Wendtworth who went sailing several feet back to land on top of the receptionist and then bounce to the floor.

Collins raised his gun at the same time Poppin froze and raised his. The two men stood face to face in a showdown.

"Don't move Joan, I've got him," Collins stated firmly.

Joan turned her head around and saw the standoff.

The men held each other's gaze. They should have both fired, but they didn't. Collin's hazel eyes questioned Poppin's coal black eyes.

The guns fired once each.

Both men took a bullet to the side of the head. Collins fell backwards a couple of feet and slammed down hard on the floor. Poppin had tilted his head slightly as he fired. Collins bullet grazed the right side of Poppin's forehead. Poppin shook it off as if it were a drug or alcohol tremor. His eyes never even glazed over. He turned towards Joan and saw that she was trying to get to her feet. He stepped forward and hit her hard on the side of her head with his fist. Joan crashed back into the receptionist, and the two sprawled to the floor.

Poppin's mind raced. It was time to slip and slide the hell out of here. He raced past Collins who tried to get up but couldn't overcome the dizziness in his head. Poppin hit the stairway. The broken glass sparkled in a mysterious intensity. Poppin turned left and raced up the stairs. He knew that Wendtworth would pursue, but she would have to choose which way to go. She chose down as he knew she would. She would be able to cover the lower exit of the building from below.

Poppin grabbed his coat. He turned quickly and traveled up a couple of flights of stairs. He stopped for a few seconds to catch his breath. What was he going to do now, hit the roof and do a Spiderman? Soon there would be a lot of cops. He knew he had to get out of the building quickly.

The building would be sealed in no time. He knew he had to get out and hide somewhere. Latoya's place was out of the question for every reason now. He would have to hit the streets and blend in as a bum again, but now, they would be looking for a bum. I'm fucked, he thought to himself. The only way out down below was going to be violence, and he knew he wouldn't make it, he would be killed.

Up and over was his only hope. If not Spiderman, at least he was going to have to become an aerialist. Poppin picked up his gait on the stairs again and rose to the opening of the roof. He blasted the door lock a couple of times with his gun and was soon standing in the open, clear, fresh air of the sky.

Going to the west edge of the building, he saw there was another building only a few feet away. Problem was it was fifteen to twenty feet lower than the building he was standing on. He paced frantically back and forth. He paced back about ten feet to the left, calmed down, and saw an old mattress on the rooftop.

Sex, somebody had picked a strange place to have a rendez-vous. It didn't matter. Poppin stepped back a few feet and plunged towards the mattress. The bulkiest part of his body hit the mattress on the top corner. He bounced off and slid across the gravel. The side of his face bit into the loose gravel and ripped his skin in a couple of dozen small cuts. The dirt burned into his cheek. His left leg hurt from when he hit the hard surface.

Poppin rose slowly and tested his leg. It wasn't broken, but it hurt like hell. He pushed himself hard. He knew once the police got there in any numbers they would figure quickly that a fleeing suspect would probably jump the buildings if he had no choice.

Poppin got to the door that went below the roof. He tried to pry it open, but it was locked from the inside. He knelt and pried the gun under the metal lip. With all of his might he pulled up on the door. The door gave about a half an inch. He lay on his side and was able to see the latch. He put the gun up against it and fired.

He thought of the report of the gun, and if it could be heard below by anyone on the street. It didn't matter. He was hurting. He had to get inside, take the elevator down and take his chances. The gun had a slight twist in the barrel now. It wouldn't fire straight, but it would still probably fire. When the elevator door opened, he would be ready. He would have to be.

The bell came as the elevator door opened. A woman holding a baby was all that stood before him. Poppin made quickly for the lobby exit door. He rushed out onto the street and looked left. He saw a policeman turning from the other building towards him.

The cop didn't know what to make of the bum who was exiting the building, but he knew it didn't look right.

"Hey you, stop, I want to talk to you," the cop shouted to the bum.

Poppin ignored him and took off running. The cop pulled his weapon and prepared to fire just as Poppin slid left into an alleyway. Sweat burned in the bloody streaks on Poppin's face. His leg throbbed. He pushed the pain from his mind and broke into a run that a track star would be proud of.

By the time the cop who was in pursuit rounded the corner into the alleyway, Poppin was out of sight. He was running north away from the building. He didn't break his stride until he was three blocks away.

Poppin slipped behind some bushes to catch his breath and get his bearings. He was in a small park of some kind. He wiped the sweat from his cheeks and forehead. He almost screamed when the rough material went over the gravel in his cheeks. He proceeded slowly towards the back of the street and found himself in front of a bus stop. He looked down the street and saw a bus approaching.

The city bus stopped to pick him up. The bus driver's eyes grew wide when he saw Poppin's face, but he said nothing. Poppin took the nearest seat right behind the bus driver. He watched the city pass outside of the windows. The surrealism of the left behind pursuit for a man who was no longer there made him chuckle. He couldn't believe he had made it out alive.

*****

Wendtworth stood over Collins who sat quietly in the office chair.

"Are you all right?"

Collins grunted. "Yeah, sort-of, blinding headache, but I think I'm going to be all right."

"What about Poppin, did you get him?"

"I got downstairs and he was no where around. By that time back-up had arrived, and I just turned everything over to the local police. I was in no shape to continue, so I just let them do their job. I don't know if they ever got him or not. We'll find out when we get to the hospital to be checked out I suppose."

Collins shook his head. "Do you think they got him Joan?

Joan frowned. "No, that would be too easy. He's still out there, I can feel it."

The medical personnel escorted the agents to the elevator. The two agents looked at each other and said nothing. They wondered if the chase was over, but in their hearts, each of them knew that it wasn't.

Chapter 31

Poppin slipped the key in the lock to his secret apartment across the river and near the University of Wisconsin Milwaukee. He put the key in the door and turned it slowly. There was a barely audible creak as he let the door open into the hallway. The apartment was dark except for the sixty-watt light that shone beneath the lampshade of a table stand lamp next to the brown, suede recliner. Beneath the light of the lamp sat a middle-aged, blonde woman with her hands resting lightly on her knees.

As Poppin froze, the woman raised her right hand and motioned for him to come forward. Poppin stepped closer and stopped to tensely stand five feet in front of the woman. The woman smiled. Poppin let out a small grin, and took in the sight before him. He recognized the female FBI agent as his eyes grew used to the dim lighting, but he wondered why she didn't have her gun drawn.

The woman smiled again. "You can relax, you're safe here with me."

"Relax, yah right, you must be even crazier than me. You're FBI and you're sitting here in my apartment. But maybe you're right. You don't have your gun out. You could arrest me, or you could even have shot me already."

Poppin took a deep breath and let his shoulders relax. Beads of sweat showed on his face in the glint from the dim light bulb underneath the shade. He slightly lowered the thirty-eight in his right hand and let out a small grin, a smile was just asking too much right now under the circumstances. The woman however did continue to smile at him.

Poppin finally relaxed and dropped his weapon to his side.

Poppin let out a sigh of exasperation. "What are you doing here?"

"You probably remember that my name is Joan Wendtworth from when we met in your office. I'm here to help you in a way you couldn't possibly imagine."

Poppin laughed. "That sounds wonderful, but I doubt it?"

Joan leaned forward in her chair. "No, really, I am here to help you. I'm here to offer you a deal."

Poppin walked over and sat on the faded, green couch. "A deal at this stage of the game? I've killed seven people, and you know it. What kind of a deal could you possibly offer me?"

Joan brushed a troublesome blonde hair off the front of her forehead and spoke sternly.

"Kill no more and you are free to go. That's it. That's all there is to it."

Poppin laughed in a fit of small hysterics. "How can you offer me a deal like that? All the time and man-hours you people have spent on me. I've killed seven people. I know you've wanted to catch me bad. Why such a deal? I don't get it, why?"

Joan smiled briefly. "Someone has intervened on your behalf. Someone has made a deal with us that was too good to pass up. We needed what he had, badly. The deal he made is to give us what we want and we in turn would let you go. We're ready to fulfill our half of the bargain. Kill no more, and you are free to go as long as you leave the country, and we will even help you with that."

"I can agree to that. My job here in this thing is done. I fulfilled all of my promises. You know, it wasn't for me that I did these killings. It was for the innocent others."

"We know why you did it," Joan said in a low voice.

"I had good reason to do it, but that doesn't make me innocent, I still can't see how you can let me go."

Joan sighed. "We made the deal, all I can say is we made a deal with someone. Watch the news tomorrow and you will see that the FBI got a break on a big case, a Presidential case you might say. Watch the news, and you will have your answer.

Keep your half of the bargain and kill no more, and you are free to live out the rest of your life."

"Okay, I agree to this, but how do I know you will hold up your end of the bargain? How do I know that this person who intervened on my behalf has enough goods for you that I will be guaranteed your half of the promise?"

"Your friend kept a video tape of a deed we needed on tape, and he also kept a video and audio tape of our promise to him. If we ever renege on our part of the deal, he will release the tape to the press and some very high heads will roll, the highest really."

Poppin rose, walked over in front of the chair, and knelt down. "This all sounds great, but how do I know that what you're talking about is the truth and not just some trick to take me in."

"I had the drop on you and the element of surprise when you came into your apartment. I could have taken you down. Don't worry; your friend has bought your freedom."

"This friend of mine, who is it that brokered such a great deal?"

Joan relaxed in the recliner. "I can't release his identity directly, but he said to tell you something. He said to tell you he figured out where a single line for a song that he's had for a long time belongs."

"I don't understand, that could be anyone, what did he say to tell me?"

Joan leaned forward in the chair and smiled. "He said to tell you. When you get this message, eat the (W)rapper."

Sonnentag

EPILOGUE

The final number at the most recent BPD concert.

Stayin' high
Life on the fly
Slayer Player's ass is fine
And so is mine.

24/7/365
He's still alive
At the top of his game,
A millennium of fame.

He was abused as a child
Went through life with a hitch.
He's surrounded by women now
So perverts out there,
Go such on that bitch.

Turnin' O.C.
Don't even count the cash.
Cut him short,
He'll hit you back.

Your time has come,
Put you on the run.
Slayer Player's gonna have some fun,
Make you suck on his gun.

And when you're all dead and gone
And it won't be long.
I'll be all finished
Singin' his song.

KEEP IT REAL

www.ingramcontent.com/pod-product-compliance
Lightning Source LLC
Chambersburg PA
CBHW030529030726
47495CB00004B/920